What readers are saying:

'Wow! What a journey this is... a complex weaving of space, engineering, Luna, and most of all, humanity.'
(Top 500 reviewer)

'Edge of the seat stuff pretty well for the whole book.'

'The best scfi book I've read in ages!'

'Amazing. Really enjoyed reading this book as much as I have all of Kilby's books'

'...kicks into overdrive to the point where it is nearly impossible to put down'

'Very well written, fantastically created, and quite believable. Very hard to put down. Can't wait for the next book in the series.'

'This is a clever and fascinating take on Moon survival after a massive solar storm hits Earth. Good solid characters, and fast moving pace........it's a ripper of a yarn.'

'One of those books you can't put down.'

BY GERALD M. KILBY

POWER VACUUM

MOON BASE DELTA
BOOK 3

GERALD M. KILBY

OUTER PLANET
MEDIA

For notifications on upcoming books and access to my FREE starter library
please join my Readers Group at geraldmkilby.com.

CONTENTS

CHAPTER 1
BLOCKADE

In a dimly lit interrogation room, situated deep within the secluded inner recess of Moon Base Delta, a Xilinex mercenary sat firmly chained to a sturdy metal chair bolted to the floor. He radiated an air of stoic indifference, seemingly unperturbed by his current predicament. Across from him, separated by a stark, unadorned metal table, a stick-thin, middle-aged bureaucrat named Selene Mene attentively studied the screen of her compact communications slate. She occasionally glanced up at him, her sharply gaunt features becoming more pronounced in the reflective glare emanating from the illuminated screen. The atmosphere in the room felt notably cold and sterile; shadows, cast by the intermittently flickering wall light, created an eerie dance upon the walls. A continuous, steady hum emanating from the life-support system punctuated the thick, tense silence that hung in the air.

He was hungry. Then again, so was everyone.

"Tell me, Captain," Selene began, her voice maintaining a calm, almost casual demeanor, "what precisely made you decide to become a mercenary for the Xilinex Corporation?"

He responded with something that was a cross between a guttural grunt and a hollow laugh. "What makes anyone do anything?" he sneered derisively, his eyes narrowing into slits as he regarded this seemingly feeble creature with palpable disdain. If this was the best interrogator that these people could muster, then their cause was already doomed. He was accustomed to more intense interrogations, where questions were accompanied by the liberal and persuasive use of a blow torch.

"Would it be because you felt a deep sense of futility about your previous existence on Earth?" A disconcerting, disembodied voice resonated throughout the claustrophobic room, prompting him to glance around in confusion, searching for its source. He was aware they had advanced intelligence tech here, but couldn't be certain whether it was an AI speaking or just another tactic to try and rattle him.

"Who's that?" he demanded sharply, his gaze oscillating between Selene and the hidden origin of the voice.

"That's DOA," she answered, maintaining eye contact. "An AI. An exceptionally powerful one, semi-sentient. They were all banned on Earth because of their uncanny, almost spooky ability to mess with people's heads."

The Captain's previous bravado started to waver. He had heard tales of these AI entities, knew something of the tricks they could do to manipulate the human mind. He shifted somewhat uncomfortably in his seat.

"Now consider your current situation, Captain. Abandoned by the Xilinex Corporation and slowly starving to death," the AI continued in its emotionless tone.

"Go screw yourself," he retorted, attempting to raise a finger in defiance, but found his hands were securely bound by the unyielding chains.

"You know," Selene said, casually jerking a thumb over her shoulder, "there are some among us who aren't too happy about having to provide you with food. They'd much rather shove you out an airlock."

The Captain's facial expression transformed into a scowl.

"But, I say no." Selene shook her head. "They could be useful, share some information that could help us."

He had by now regained some of his detached disinterest. "You're all pathetic."

"Tell me, Captain. Why did your mother abandon you when you were only four years old? Was it because she didn't love you?" DOA asked, its tone laced with compassion.

Renton Hicks sat in the central operations room of Moon Base Delta, his eyes fixed on a small section of the panoramic wall monitor that displayed the ongoing interrogation of the Xilinex Captain. Beside him, Mackenzie sat with her arms crossed, her brow furrowed as she let out a huff of impatience.

"I can't see the point of this crap," she muttered. "It's just wasting time and time's the one thing we don't have."

"Time and food," Matteo added somberly, running a hand

through his hair. "And feeding these scumbags is just making things worse."

Mackenzie clenched her jaw, frustration evident in her voice. "I still say we should throw them out an airlock."

"Or simply starve them to death," offered Chen Jun, one of Mackenzie's fellow rebels from DaVinci Crater.

"Or we could just eat them, if things get really bad," said Okamoto.

All eyes turned to her.

"Don't say that. Don't even think about it," Matteo admonished.

"Just saying," Okamoto replied with a shrug.

"There has to be some way to get to one of those supply capsules," said Alice. "They'll be due in lunar orbit in just a few days."

"We're all out of options," Yuna chimed in. "The Xilinex blockade leaves us with no easy way out of here. If we try and lift-off with the shuttle, we'll be blown out of the sky."

"There might be a way." Renton raised a hand to point at the scene unfolding on screen. "And it lies with these Xilinex guys."

The others in the room glanced up at the monitor to see the Xilinex Captain erupt into a blood rage, trying to break free of the chains that contained him.

"It would appear that DOA is beginning to get under his skin," observed Professor Hendrickson.

"Maybe Selene should get out of there just in case those restraints don't hold and he really does try to strangle her,"

Matteo said, a genuine look of concern on his face. But the Captain's rage passed and he slumped back down in his seat.

"DOA?" Renton asked. "How's the overall phycological evaluation of the captives going?"

"It is mostly complete. I can provide you with some preliminary observations concerning the general state of mind of the Xilinex Corporation mercenaries," the AI replied.

"Please do," said Renton.

"Most of these mercenaries are fiercely loyal to the corporation, and they hold General Wagner in high regard specifically. Their perspectives on the conflict or broader political implications are largely limited to tactical considerations. They are quite convinced that the ongoing blockade will soon be followed up with a full military assault, and that they'll be rescued by Xilinex forces imminently. In their minds, they don't perceive any significant threat to their lives. They believe that the colonists here at Moon Base Delta lack the willingness to inflict serious harm on them. This, they see as a disdainful weakness on the part of the colonists," DOA elaborated.

"We'll see about that," Mackenzie retorted, jabbing an angry finger at the monitor.

"Indeed," DOA continued, unperturbed. "However, within the group, there exists a smaller subgroup of approximately five individuals, including the two shuttle pilots, who are not entirely certain about the mission they've undertaken. They are grappling with regrets concerning their life choices, specifically having chosen to participate in this particular mission. While they remain loyal to Xilinex Corporation, they do harbor doubts about the leadership capabilities of Pompodur Rossen Adarok."

"I still don't see how any of this information benefits us," said Tanaka, skeptically.

"Do you think Xilinex actually wants these mercenaries returned?" Renton inquired.

"The captives seem to think so," DOA confirmed. "They feel that General Wagner places a high value on his contractors and therefore would be quite anxious to secure their release as soon as possible."

"Did we gather any useful intelligence? Have any of them revealed anything that could help us?" Renton asked, a hint of hopefulness in his voice.

"Unfortunately, no one has offered up anything of any great value so far," DOA replied, dampening expectations. "And it's unlikely that they'll divulge any useful information without the application of... more aggressive techniques."

"Then let's employ those techniques," Mackenzie urged, her eyes hungry for action. "Introduce them to the business end of some power tools."

"Absolutely not," Professor Hendrickson countered, his jaw clenched. "I am vehemently opposed to such actions. Resorting to torture would mean abandoning our core principles; we're better than that."

"Yes, I'm with you. It would be a very nasty business," Matteo added, echoing the sentiment.

"Agreed," Alice stated firmly. "Count me out if that's the path you want to go down."

"If Xilinex really wanted their mercenaries back safe and sound, then why are they just... sitting out there, doing absolutely nothing, simply waiting?" said Kimura, frustration evident in her voice.

"Their immediate focus is likely on retrieving the two food supply capsules from Earth first," DOA clarified. "Once they've accomplished that, they'll begin to plan their assault."

"In the meantime, our resources get lower and we grow weaker," Alice observed.

"If the Xilinex command does indeed place a premium on having their captives returned," Renton began, drawing the attention of everyone in the room, "then perhaps we should extend them an offer."

The room fell into a hushed silence for a moment, as all eyes turned to Renton. Professor Hendrickson raised a skeptical eyebrow, breaking the silence. "And what sort of offer do you propose?"

"We could offer to exchange the captives for one of the supply capsules," said Renton, outlining his thinking.

"I can't see them agreeing to that." Mackenzie shook her head skeptically. "In fact, they'd probably be rolling on the floor, doubled over in laughter if we made that offer."

"Maybe so," Renton conceded, "but what do we actually stand to lose by putting the offer on the table? Let's just do it and then gauge their reaction."

Alice chewed pensively on her lower lip. "And what if, by some chance, they actually agree to this?"

"Then it's most likely a trap," Renton answered

straightforwardly. He then turned his attention to the AI. "DOA, what's your analysis of this proposal?"

"The likelihood is high that the Xilinex Corporation would agree to the exchange," DOA responded.

This generated an excited murmur throughout the room.

"However," DOA continued, quickly quelling any optimism, "they would likely agree solely because it would be viewed as an opportunity to execute a Trojan Horse–style attack on Moon Base Delta."

"In that case, there's absolutely no reason to go through with it," declared Chen Jun, shaking his head dismissively. "The risks involved are simply too great."

"Everything we do at this juncture is fraught with danger," said Professor Hendrickson. "However, I believe that we have reached a point where we must make some sort of move. If we don't act decisively now, we'll either starve to death or be mauled in a Xilinex assault on this base."

"Look." Renton sat up more attentively, leaning in over the table. "If we know that they'll be planning something underhand, then we can prepare accordingly. We structure the exchange in such a way that we maintain maximum control throughout the process. We take measures to mitigate the risks involved."

"I still don't like it. The whole thing sounds too risky," Chen Jun persisted in his reservations.

"Sure, it's risky, there's no denying that," Renton acknowledged. "But the professor has a valid point—what alternative do we have? If we know they're planning to trick us, then being forewarned gives us a tactical advantage."

Mackenzie let out a snort, her eyes narrowing skeptically. "And what's our plan B if they reject the offer? What then?"

"In that event," Matteo quipped with a grin, "we eat the captives. And you can even have the first pick, Mackenzie."

CHAPTER 2
COSMOS

Renton jolted awake from the depths of a troubled dream, his eyes snapping open in the dimly lit bedroom. Almost instinctively, he rolled over to place a hand on the space where Alice usually lay, only to encounter cold, vacant sheets. This wasn't entirely unexpected; Alice was a person who seemed perpetually at odds with the very notion of a good night's sleep. Her slumber was light and easy to disrupt, making nocturnal wanderings a fairly common event.

He entertained the thought of activating his comms unit to ask DOA about her current location. But he had a pretty good idea where she would be: the operations room. Yet, she would not be there out of some immediate need to get an update on the status of the base; her reasons were entirely different. With its expansive panoramic display screen, the operations room served as her preferred nocturnal sanctuary, a unique space where she could fully immerse herself in the tranquil activity of star gazing.

Realizing that he would not get back to sleep for a while, Renton rolled out of bed and, with measured steps, ambled toward the galley kitchen.

He immersed an herbal tea bag into a mug of hot water. Leaning casually against the counter, he momentarily closed his eyes, letting the warmth of the mug and the calming scent of the tea briefly soothe his tightly wound nerves. The vivid remnants of his unsettling dream started to fade. After taking a few more sips of the tea, he decided to go and find Alice.

When he arrived in the operations room, the panoramic screen—that made up over a third the room's circumference—was resplendent with a galaxy of stars, making him feel as though he was floating in space. Alice was nestled in a low chair, a blanket drawn around her as she studied the stellar tableau. Spotting him, she lifted a hand, waving. He moved toward her, and as he did, she shifted to create space for him and patted the empty spot. He took a seat. She snuggled into him, pointing toward the vast cosmic expanse.

"It never fails to impress," she mused, her voice a soft whisper. "The sheer vastness of it all."

"Yeah," Renton agreed, his gaze fixed on the cosmos. "It makes everything else seem... inconsequential." He sighed.

They lapsed into a comfortable silence, just taking in the spectacle.

Then, with a sudden surge of energy, Alice rose from her seat and moved toward the holo-table. "Hey," she began, a note of excitement in her voice, "I've got something to show you."

She gestured at the control interface, and a stylized view of the solar system with its orbital pathways neatly etched blossomed out from its surface. Alice zoomed in on the image, centering on a region not too far from the Moon, a few million kilometers out. An illuminated marker flashed periodically along a thin vector line.

"What is it?" Renton asked, his gaze locked onto the blinking marker.

"That's the Mars evacuation ship," said Alice, lifting her arm to point at the enigmatic dot on the screen. "It's on a trajectory that should bring it into lunar orbit in about two to three weeks' time."

Renton studied the marker more intensely now. "I hadn't realized they were so close."

"Yes, approximately nineteen days away, give or take," Alice confirmed.

A flurry of thoughts ran through Renton's mind, primarily concerning on the approximately one-hundred and fifty colonists who had made a hasty evacuation from Mars. With the Carrington Event plunging their own lunar settlement into a state of turmoil, coupled with the chaos of the evacuation, they had had little time to give any thought to those further out in the solar system—the Mars colony and the far-flung survey ships located near the moons of Europa and Titan. Without a doubt, those people must have watched the systematic disintegration of the communication constellation networks orbiting Earth with a sense of impending doom, fully aware of the looming catastrophe.

But unlike those living here on the Moon, these distant colonies had not had the chance to return to the home planet before the window of opportunity irrevocably slammed shut. And yet, staying put was also unfeasible. While they had attained a certain level of self-sufficiency, especially regarding resources like water, oxygen, rocket fuel, and energy, they remained critically reliant on the periodic supplies from Earth to sustain a community of one-hundred and fifty souls. So they found themselves with no choice but to abandon the outposts, gather everyone onto an interplanetary vessel, and evacuate. And since returning to Earth was no longer possible, their last remaining hope of survival was now Luna.

"I wonder if they have any idea of the colossal mess they're about to arrive into?" Renton mused aloud.

"Somehow, I doubt it," Alice countered, shaking her head. "I imagine that Earth, or possibly Xilinex, would have spun them an optimistic narrative and nothing about the internal strife or the grim status of our food supply."

Renton considered his lack of knowledge about these colonists. "I have to admit, I don't know much about these guys, or the colony on Mars."

"Apparently, it was a public–private venture, with several corporations having their fingers in the pie. I vaguely remember that genetic engineering was a key area."

"Genetics?" Renton gave her a surprised look. "That's

interesting. What could they possibly be doing out there, so far from Earth?"

Alice shrugged. "Who can say? Possible they were doing things that are legally forbidden on Earth." Then her gaze shifted back to Renton. "But the thing is, it's very likely that the ship has a bunch of genetic scientists on board, which I imagine would be of interest to Xilinex."

They were silent for a beat as Renton mulled over the implications of the arrival of this ship and its crew. He wanted to know more, find out what the history of the colony was, what they were working on. He was about to ask DOA, but the AI spoke first.

"Apologies for the intrusion," the AI's rich, resounding voice resonated within the operations room, "but just to inform you that the Xilinex Corporation has successfully commandeered the two food capsules dispatched from Earth, approximately seventeen minutes ago."

"Thank you, DOA," Renton acknowledged, casting a worried glance at Alice. "Now that they have the capsules, they'll soon start redirecting their attention back to us. I think it won't be long before they start turning the screws."

Alice sighed. "I don't suppose they would just leave us alone?"

"Yeah, that would be nice." Renton grinned, then gave a long slow sigh and jerked his head in the direction of their accommodation module. "I'm heading back to bed." He felt a deep fatigue wash over him.

Alice gave an understanding nod, then her eyes drifted back

onto the cosmic panorama displayed on the screen. "I won't be long. I just want to savor the peace and quiet of the universe for a little bit longer."

"Sure. And who knows, it might be a while before you get another chance," Renton replied.

CHAPTER 3
WEAPONS

In one of the numerous expansive workshops within Moon Base Delta, a fervent cacophony of activity reverberated throughout the cavernous area. Originally designed as a hub for repairing rovers, industrial robots, and various machines, the space had now undergone a transformation into a weapons manufacturing facility. With Xilinex having successfully secured the two vital supply capsules in lunar orbit, a reinvigorated sense of commitment and urgency pervaded the base's inhabitants. The prospect of an impending military assault sharpened everyone's mind, directing their collective energies toward reinforcing the base and bracing for the inevitable confrontation.

Despite the considerable size and abundant resources that Moon Base Delta had at its disposal, it was critically deficient in weaponry. Mackenzie had managed to bring a modest arsenal with her from the DaVinci Crater, during her escape across the

Sea of Tranquility. They also possessed weapons seized from the Xilinex captives, which were high-grade plasma firearms. However, the issue with these armaments was that a significant number had been damaged by the EMP device. Nevertheless, they were pretty sure that these could be repaired and rendered combat-ready. In addition to all this, they also had a reasonable contingent of industrial robots and maintenance drones, which were to be refurbished and weaponized.

Renton, Matteo, and Alice were the nucleus of this weapons manufacturing initiative. They also gathered together a team from those who had been evacuated from the Axial Luxor Hotel, and some members of Mackenzie's crew, individuals who possessed the necessary technical expertise to repair and refurbish the critical equipment. Tanaka and Kimura ran another crew who were a scavenging unit. Their task involved scouring the vast depths of Moon Base Delta to locate any machinery that could be disassembled for valuable components.

Nevertheless, simply restoring the existing gear to operational status would not be enough. They needed to fabricate new types of weapons, with the primary focus on railguns, EMP devices, and even some forms of conventional explosives. While Renton and his team had the know-how to both construct and repair these complex devices, it fell upon Mackenzie and Chen Jun, in coordination with DOA, to craft the overarching defensive strategy for the base.

·   ·   ·

At first glance, Moon Base Delta would appear to be an impregnable fortress, mostly located underground with a central core spanning an extensive ten levels. These levels were connected by a labyrinthine network of tunnels stretching for several kilometers. Each of these intricate tunnels led to multiple access points dispersed over a broad area. Yet, each of these points represented a potential vulnerability if the right tools and strategic mindset were employed. And judging by the continuous assembly of Xilinex forces and equipment outside the base on the lunar surface, it was clear that the mercenaries possessed both of these vital elements in spades.

It was almost an impossibility for such a small defense team as that of Moon Base Delta to safeguard all these potential entry points against a determined and resourceful foe. So they developed a strategy built on a series of successive fallback positions. At each of these strategic locales, the enemy would be engaged and, in an ideal scenario, significantly weakened. The implementation of this plan would involve a carefully orchestrated sequence of traps. As many EMP devices as they could manufacture in the available time would be deployed, along with conventional explosives and even the use of good old-fashioned fire.

However, there was the ambition to create something new, something the enemy would not anticipate—a weapon with the potential to be a real game-changer. For Renton and the team, this materialized in the form of a heavy-duty, rapid-fire railgun. The underlying technology was straightforward, essentially the same as in some of the smaller handheld weapons they already had at their disposal. The challenge lay in scaling it up to its maximum potential. Matteo took the lead on this ambitious project, assembling a team, gathering up the necessary components, and ultimately overseeing the construction phase. Yet, there was still a long way to go before the weapon would be ready for its initial testing.

Each evening, after working all day in the maintenance workshop, everyone would make their way to the canteen for a meager meal. Following this, Renton and a few others would proceed to the operations room to evaluate progress.

"Any word from Xilinex about the proposed exchange?" Renton inquired, directing his question to Selene, who had recently assumed the role of monitoring communications.

"Nothing as of yet," she responded, speaking between mouthfuls of rehydrated vegetable soup.

"It's a pointless endeavor," Mackenzie said with a sense of finality. "I knew they'd never go for it."

"Perhaps," Renton conceded.

"It was still worth an attempt," Professor Hendrickson chimed in optimistically. "And now that they've successfully secured the capsules, they might be more inclined to reconsider our offer."

"Maybe so," Renton acknowledged.

"We've been closely studying the buildup of Xilinex forces just outside our perimeter," Yuna announced as she set aside her empty plate and began interacting with control interface for the holo-table. Almost immediately, a stylized 3D topographic visual of the lunar surface surrounding the base flickered to life above its surface. This was overlaid with satellite imagery revealing a cluster of Xilinex forces gathered around an assortment of rovers and recently established mobile habitats.

"The main concentration of their forces seems to be assembling near the northern gate," Yuna pointed out, indicating a specific area on the display. "We believe that this is serving as their command center. However, as we are all aware, there are also smaller groups dispersed around other potential entry points," she elaborated as the visual switched from one group to another. "But what's interesting is that we've begun to discern certain patterns, especially concerning the shuttle flights. These shuttles don't stay for very long; just long enough to offload fresh supplies or additional forces. DOA has been tracking their flight patterns. Can you give us an update, DOA?" she asked.

There was a brief moment when the holo-table display zoomed way out, giving an intricate topographic rendering of the terrain surrounding Moon Base Delta. This covered an area within a two-hundred-and-fifty-kilometer radius of the base, and various significant outposts were highlighted with glowing markers.

"The Xilinex supply ships typically land in close proximity to Moon Base Delta for a brief few hours just to unload essential supplies," said DOA, its voice echoing throughout the room. "Then, they make their way back to their respective bases of operation. On average, the time span between these supply drops is approximately fourteen hours."

"That potentially opens up a window for us to undertake a scavenging mission," Mackenzie mused, contemplating the options. "If we can create an effective distraction, engage the Xilinex forces enough to keep their attention diverted, then we might be able to get our shuttle away from the base and out of range."

"Wouldn't they see that coming?" Selene chimed in, her finger hovering over one of the highlighted Xilinex bases. "How long would it take them to intercept us?"

"Intercept time from the nearest base would be approximately two hours," DOA informed.

"Two hours?" Alice considered. "That seems like an extremely narrow window of time. Given that much of this area we've already scavenged, how far would we need to go? Are there still places out there that might contain supplies?"

"There's an abandoned Hamamatsu Corporation mining outpost located approximately one-hundred-and-ten kilometers northwest of our base," Saito Yuta pointed out, highlighting the spot on the map. "It's been deserted for around a year, and it not been searched by us yet. It's possible that some viable supplies might still be stored there."

Kato Tsubasa chimed in, "Also, there's an emergency shelter operated by JAXQ-KARI situated about one-hundred-and-seventy-five kilometers due west. But I imagine that's the furthest distance we could manage within the time constraints."

Renton took a moment to contemplate these options. It was clearly a high-risk operation, but if Xilinex were unwilling to engage in the proposed exchange of captives for supply capsules, they might have no other choice but to entertain this plan. Ultimately, it could be a risk worth taking.

"We'd have to keep the Xilinex forces thoroughly occupied to have any chance of getting a shuttle to lift off without being detected," Renton finally said. He then turned toward Mackenzie, who had become their de facto military strategist. "Any thoughts on how we could do that?"

"What about that new railgun you've been working on, Matteo? Could that keep their main force pinned down for a time?" Mackenzie inquired.

"Possibly, but it's still not operational," Matteo replied, shaking his head somewhat ruefully. "And even when it is finished, we're not sure about its actual performance capabilities."

"Then this might be a good opportunity for us to test it, see what it's really capable of," Mackenzie optimistically suggested.

"How long until it's completed?" Selene asked.

Matteo exhaled deeply. "It's difficult to say. Could be a day or two, possibly more. There's a tricky synchronization issue with the feeder mechanism that we still need to sort out."

"It seems we're at a standstill, since the mission is heavily contingent on the completion of the railgun," said Professor Hendrickson, echoing the collective sentiment. "I propose that we reconvene tomorrow evening and get an update from Matteo on the railgun's status. We can determine our next move based on that." He scanned the faces of the others, gauging their reactions, but the consensus was clear. They had all spent a long day in the maintenance workshop and were visibly weary. There was nothing more to be accomplished this evening.

Gradually, each of them exited the operations room in search of some much-needed rest. Yet, sleep would be uneasy for everyone. No one could predict when the impending assault might commence, and with the capsules now secured, that moment could happen at any given time—even this very night.

CHAPTER 4
BIOMASS

As accustomed as Chancellor Adarok had grown to the opulent surroundings of the new Xilinex administrative facility, formerly the luxury Axial Luxor Hotel, he had a compelling reason to leave its extravagant comfort and venture to the more utilitarian military headquarters overseen by General Wagner, previously the Xilinex Lunar Corporation's HQ Orbital. It was not a journey that Pompodur relished. It meant putting on an EVA suit and embarking on a military transport—experiences he found both unpleasant and somewhat claustrophobic. Nonetheless, the unfolding events in lunar orbit had rendered this particular trip an imperative.

The supply capsules from Earth, which had been successfully secured, were currently in the process of being meticulously disassembled and inspected in one of the expansive storage bays on board the old Xilinex HQ orbital. A select group of botanists and horticulturalists, who were left stranded following the chaotic evacuation, had been assembled to lend their expertise to this endeavor. These technicians had previously been employed at one of the last food manufacturing plants still functioning, itself a merger of several original facilities that couldn't all be maintained due to the sharply diminished workforce. With the lunar population having been culled to around a tenth of its original size, a single, large food processing facility was now sufficient, provided they had access to the indispensable seed stock and biomass. It was the hope that this vital resource was now safely ensconced within the cargo bay of the newly designated military headquarters.

When he arrived at the orbital station, Pompodur was greeted by General Wagner, who presented the initial reports with his usual blunt, succinct manner. However, Pompodur was more preoccupied with the task of freeing himself from the uncomfortable constraints of his EVA suit, so mostly ignored the General. Once he had finally extricated himself, he let out a substantial sigh of relief and could now turn his full attention to the task of inspecting the newly retrieved capsules.

The storage bay was situated in one sector of the immense, rotating torus that provided an artificial gravity roughly half that of Earth's. The two food supply capsules were laid out on two expansive metal tables, in varying degrees of disassembly, their individual components neatly organized on several additional tables and workbenches around the bay. A dedicated team of technicians were diligently carrying out an array of scientific tests designed to assess the viability of the biological cargo. While the physical capsules had clearly survived the trip through space, one question remained: Had the fragile life forms housed within them also survived the journey?

The techs all paused in their tasks as Chancellor Adarok and his entourage entered the bay. "Carry on," the General commanded, making a sweeping gesture with his hand. The techs all returned their attention to their work.

Pompodur walked over to examine one of the partially disassembled capsules more closely. The object was a squat, blunt-nosed cylinder, roughly the same height as an average adult male. Its exterior hull displayed numerous signs of its hazardous journey through a debris cloud surrounding Earth. Multiple impact sites were clearly visible; some were just superficial scratches, while others were deep gouges in the outer hull. Particularly striking were several regions that showed evidence of high-impact, high-velocity collisions, where the capsule's outer shell had been ripped open, exposing the inner strata of its layered protective shielding.

A portion of this capsule had been carefully disassembled to reveal the interior storage compartment. It was evident how much of the capsule's overall diameter was taken up by a complicated arrangement of Whipple Shields. Each of these shields was meticulously designed to absorb and deflect high-velocity impacts from space debris. This extensive shielding arrangement left relatively little room for actual storage. The cargo itself was housed in a variety of sealed stainless steel containers that were aligned along the capsule's central core, giving the whole assembly the appearance of a mechanical worm.

One of these internal steel containers had been carefully

extracted, and its contents systematically laid out across a nearby workbench. A diligent lab technician was presently subjecting samples from this container to a battery of analytical tests. The aim was to determine if it had been exposed to potentially harmful radiation levels—a real concern if the capsule's outer shields had at some point failed to perform their protective function.

Accompanying Pompodur on this inspection tour was Anton Levrosky, another senior director within the Xilinex organization. Levrosky was currently over at a separate workbench, engaging in conversation with one of the lab technicians. The technician was making explanatory gestures toward a collection of samples neatly organized along the bench's surface. Levrosky appeared to grasp the information being conveyed, nodding his understanding. Subsequently, he moved away from the workbench to join Pompodur and General Wagner, who were continuing their inspection of the external damage sustained by one of the retrieved capsules.

"All initial tests conducted so far look quite positive," Levrosky reported, his expression displaying a blend of relief and satisfaction. "The contents appear to be viable biomatter. The team tells me that the next procedural step will be to carefully catalog and securely store everything. The stored biomatter will be put into production as the need arises— which, I suspect, will be sooner rather than later." He exhaled a deep sigh and looked around the room once again, his face radiating palpable relief.

This collective sense of relief was reciprocated by all those present within the confines of the storage bay, Pompodur included. At the very least, with these newly secured food supplies in hand, they could look forward to some measure of respite from the relentless grind of daily rationing. Easing such restrictions had the potential to reduce mounting tensions within the already anxious populace. However, it was one facet of the overall agreement. The counterpart to this arrangement involved restoring the steady supply of Helium-3 back to Earth —a project that, thus far, had seen only limited progress.

"What about the status of the return mission?" Pompodur directed his question toward Clara Dixon, arguably the most competent project manager who still remained with the Xilinex Lunar Corporation. The majority of the other managers had chosen to evacuate in the wake of the devastating solar storm. "How's that progressing?"

"They've already sent us the engineering designs to construct new capsules." She gestured toward the disassembled containers arrayed on the table. "Which are remarkably similar to these. Given that we now have tangible, physical examples to work from, the overall fabrication process should be appreciably more streamlined and quicker."

"And what's the projected timescale for this?" Pompodur probed.

"Based on our most reliable estimates, we're looking at approximately six to eight weeks for the initial testing phase," she replied.

"Let's not forget, failure isn't an option in this," General Wagner interjected, issuing her a stern reminder. "Our earthly superiors have made it abundantly clear that there won't be any additional food supply capsules coming our way until the first shipments of Helium-3 have begun their journey back to Earth."

"It's downright extortion," Levrosky said, his expression turning into a scowl.

"Quite so," mused Pompodur. He then paused for a brief moment before raising a finger to refocus their collective attention. "However, there have been some recent... developments... that could potentially offer us a way to loosen the grip that Earth currently maintains over us."

This immediately sparked ripples of raised eyebrows among the assembled group. However, before anyone could ask for the specifics of these developments, Pompodur preemptively raised a hand to silence them. "I can't go into details at the moment, except to say that we're actively working avenues to extricate ourselves from Earth's grip." Those who were acquainted with Pompodur's modus operandi understood that pressing him further would be pointless. Casting one final, comprehensive glance over the storage bay, he said, "Alright, I've seen what I needed to see. Let's reconvene in the war room. We have a lot of matters requiring our collective attention."

What was once a spartan, minimalist boardroom in the orbital HQ had undergone a transformation into a full-fledged war room, now that it was under the stewardship of the Xilinex mercenary command. Where the room previously exuded a sleek, unadorned aesthetic, it now teemed with complex workstations, each operated by technicians vigilantly monitoring satellite imagery, communication feeds, and an array of other critical systems.

Pompodur, along with multiple members from his administrative cadre, took their places around the room's central holo-table, joining General Wagner and his aides. The General kicked things off by delivering a comprehensive situational report. The first point of discussion was the evolving status of the blockade around Moon Base Delta, a scenario still in its developmental stages and characterized by a methodical accumulation of troops and essential resources. So far, they had been very effective in curtailing any attempts at unauthorized departure from the lunar outpost.

The second topic on the report's agenda concerned the ongoing blockade of the last remaining SINO outpost situated in the Sea of Crises, Mare Crisium. This particular blockade presented a different sort of challenge, owing largely to the outpost's expansive surface area, which resulted in a considerably larger perimeter ring that demanded significant numbers to be deployed. SINO were also better armed and resourced than the ragtag group at Moon Base Delta, enabling them to hold out for an extended period. As a consequence, to undermine their resistance and sustain a secure blockade, the General had directed the majority of his resources toward this mission.

The final point of the report was the surge in protests among the general population. This was largely fueled by frustration and anger over the imposition of rationing, further inflaming opposition sentiment toward the Xilinex

Corporation, and also requiring considerable resources to police.

Once General Wagner had wrapped up his briefing, all eyes in the room pivoted toward Pompodur. Leaning forward, he clasped his hands together purposefully and rested them on the holo-table in front of him.

"With the successful acquisition of these crucial supply capsules, we are now in a position to transmit a lunar-wide announcement declaring an end to the food rationing. Scarcity will soon cease to be a concern," he emphatically stated. "This move should have a calming effect on the ongoing protests at Shackleton and other troubled regions. However, the incessant propaganda broadcasts being disseminated from Moon Base Delta continue to pose a threat. These broadcasts must be terminated forthwith; otherwise, even a surplus of food provisions will not be sufficient to mollify a rebellious populace." His gaze locked intently onto the General as he continued, "I can't help but notice that you're exercising a level of caution that seems excessive when it comes to dealing with these... agitators. What's stopping us from preparing for a full-scale assault on the base?"

The General shook his head, clearly unmoved. "The issue largely boils down to allocation of resources, a significant chunk of which are currently committed to the SINO blockade. Also... Moon Base Delta still holds eighteen of our mercenaries captive." Meeting Pompodur's unyielding stare, he added, "I'm keen on getting them back. They're assets we could do with. Given our closed ecosystem up here, we simply have no way to replace these fighters." Pausing for emphasis, he continued,

"That's precisely why I would recommend accepting their offer for an exchange." He let the implications of that statement hang in the air.

"A supply capsule as ransom for captives?" Pompodur nearly spat out the words. "You can't be serious. Going along with such an exchange would set an extremely dangerous precedent. Caving in to even one demand effectively opens the floodgates to an endless series of further ultimatums. Not only that, it would signal weakness to SINO, and also embolden those elements within our own population who are already itching to foment descent. While the loss of skilled fighter is regrettable, they sealed their own fate by failing to secure the base when they had the chance."

"Be that as it may," the General responded, seemingly unfazed by Pompodur's heated response. "I also see this situation as a golden opportunity to set a trap that could effectively neutralize their leadership in a swift stroke." He clicked his fingers. "It would give us the edge we need to gain complete control over the base."

Pompodur leaned back, taking a moment to contemplate the General's proposal. He had to concede, his curiosity was definitely piqued. Any creative solution that could break the longstanding deadlock surrounding Moon Base Delta was worth at least some exploration. "Okay," he said, somewhat hesitantly. "I'm listening."

"If they're asking for a food capsule," the General began, outlining his plan, "let's go ahead and give them one. However, what they won't know is that in addition to some seed stock, we'll include an explosive device—something powerful enough to eliminate anyone standing within a reasonable radius on detonation. We can remove the majority of the actual food supplies, leaving only enough behind for them to inspect. They'll no doubt be suspicious initially, but once they gather around the capsule to examine it more closely... boom. That should spell the end for Moon Base Delta's leadership."

Pompodur reclined slightly, nodding his head in recognition of the simplicity of the plan. He found himself wondering why such a straightforward yet effective strategy hadn't occurred to him earlier. Then again, he had been largely preoccupied by other pressing developments, chiefly the tantalizing possibility of finally shaking off Earth's blackmail.

Levrosky, appearing skeptical, chimed in with a question. "Do you really think we could successfully execute this? Wouldn't they be on high alert for some sort of trap? If our plan fails, we stand to lose some of our valuable food supplies."

Raising a hand to interject, Pompodur responded, "If we follow the General's recommendation and only risk a minimal quantity of the supplies, then the potential rewards may very well outweigh the risks. Eliminating the leadership at Moon Base Delta and assuming control of the facility—especially that AI that governs its operations—could be a pivotal move. It could be the operation that changes our fortunes.

"So, are we agreed," the General questioned, casting his eyes around the room at his colleagues, "that we move forward with this exchange operation?"

One-by one, all of them signified their agreement with a nod.

CHAPTER 5
ATTACK

D r. Han Sundar was roused from his slumber by what he thought to be the booming sound of a thunderstorm rolling across the Strawstack Mountain Astronomical Facility. However, this was not the crack and rumble of a weather event; it was the sound of explosions, likely the handiwork of the same local warlord who had previously tried to breach their fortifications only three weeks prior.

"What was that?" Sheneese sat bolt upright in the bed beside him.

"I think we're under attack," he responded in a hushed tone, his ears straining to identify the far-off symphony of explosions.

An abrupt chime from his comms slate sent a jolt through his already fraught nerves. Extending a hand, he picked it from the bedside table, his eyes quickly skimming the critical alert that had been broadcast to all inhabitants of the facility.

Please remain calm. An incident has occurred that is swiftly being contained. Stay in your current location and await further instructions.

"I can't believe that we're going through this again," Sheneese murmured, her face a mask of concern. "This is the second time this month."

"They say that they have things under control." He showed her the terse message on the slate.

Sheneese looked somewhat appeased by his words, lapsing into silence. Han followed suit, their ears now straining to make out any discernible sounds in the night. He thought that he detected the faint chatter of gunfire, but he couldn't be sure, entombed as they were in their subterranean accommodations with the action unfurling aboveground. They remained motionless, the minutes stretching into a what seemed like an eternity, until Han sensed the disconcerting symphony of explosions and gunfire had ceased. The slate chirped again.

"All clear!" he said, reading the alert update.

A wave of relief washed over them. Yet, in spite of the "all clear" that had been given, both of them had trouble getting back to sleep, each hyperalert to any sound emanating from beyond their bedroom walls.

By the time Han reached the canteen the next morning for breakfast, it was evident that he was not the only one suffering from a sleepless night. A somber mood permeated the space, now that everyone was confronted with the stark realization that their fortified base of operations might not be as impervious to danger as the military authorities had led them to believe. They shuffled from the buffet to the tables, engaging in hushed, subdued conversations.

Under normal circumstances, the mood would have been much more upbeat, considering that the supply capsules had been successfully retrieved from lunar orbit. This crucial success meant that all their efforts at the facility over the past months had not been in vain. Not only could the stranded lunar population now envision a future free from the specter of starvation, but Earth could also continue to receive the invaluable elements that fueled their fusion-based civilization. Their collective effort had, in effect, saved humanity from further descent into chaos. Under different circumstances, it would have been a day of celebration. Yet, the previous night's attack only served to underscore the fragile balance of their attempts to stave off the rolling chaos that was threatening to engulf the planet.

Carrying a tray laden with coffee and toast, he approached the table where Noah Harris, one of his top analysts, and some of the other people on his team usually sat. They acknowledged him with a nod, and Han could tell that they, too, had barely slept.

"Busy night," he ventured as a greeting.

"You can say that again," Harris responded. "Kept me awake all night. I'm not worth much today."

"That warlord guy must be getting desperate out there. He's probably running out of resources," another of the team speculated. "Apparently, he's joined forces with a neighboring group from the East. They say that they combined to try and take this base."

"What does the military brass have to say about it?" Han inquired.

"I don't know," replied Harris, "I presume we'll find out at the morning briefing. But, if you ask me, this facility is no longer viable. It's just not safe here. Even if they can defend it, it's impossible to work under these conditions. We'll have to move, I think."

"Move? From this facility? But where would we go?" The others at the table began asking the obvious questions.

"Vandenberg, maybe, or somewhere else," Harris informed. "This whole area is becoming bandit country. We've had two attacks in the last month, and that's not including the attempts on taking down the supply transport when it was coming in to land."

As Han sipped his coffee and took a bite of toast, he began to wonder where all this food had come from. Were they consuming dwindling supplies, or were there still active coffee plantations and wheat fields being protected by the state's armed forces, desperate to ensure the traumatized population wouldn't go hungry?

"At least the capsules got through," he stated, waving his slice of toast.

"Yes, they were successfully retrieved yesterday," Decker, another of the team, confirmed. "It's been reported that the entire manifest has since been tested and shown to be viable. We should all be proud. A few months ago, no one thought this would be possible. At least it gives us some hope."

Harris leaned in after quickly scanning his surroundings. The others picked up on his body language and also leaned in.

"Apparently," he said, quickly glancing around to insure that he was not being overheard, "the people up at Moon Base Delta knew that the capsules were coming, found out about them somehow. Rumor has it that they've offered the Xilinex Corporation to exchange their captives for some of the food supplies." He looked from one to another, letting the news sink in, then sat back.

"Seriously? How could they possibly have known that?" whispered Decker.

"It could be any number of ways. People talk. Someone might have said something they shouldn't have," Harris responded.

"Of course, don't forget, they do have a powerful general AI," Decker observed. "It probably tracked the capsules' journey from Earth to the Moon. Who knows what it's capable of?"

"Yeah, you're probably right, but our military friends," Harris pointed a finger at the ceiling, indicating the top brass running the operation, "seem to think we may have an information leak—someone feeding intel to Moon Base Delta."

"No way, that's impossible. Who would do that?" Decker retorted emphatically.

A bolt of fear coursed through Han's body when he heard this rumor. Did they suspect him?

"What do you think?" Harris asked him directly.

"Huh?" Han was a little spooked by the question.

"Yeah, doesn't your wife, Sheneese, work over at comms? Has she heard anything?" Decker added.

"I... I don't think so," Han stammered. All eyes were on him.

"Anyway, I don't think it's possible from here," he finally said, regaining some composure.

"Yeah," Decker agreed, "My guess is that their AI just figured it out from intercepting comms traffic and seeing these new objects in lunar orbit. The top brass are just being paranoid, if you ask me."

Han quickly finished his coffee, and signaled his desire to get to the morning briefing early. He rose from his seat and headed for the boardroom. The conversation around the breakfast table had left his mind spinning like a tumbleweed. He was acutely aware of the dangers he courted by funneling insider information to the ragtag band up at Moon Base Delta. If it ever came to light that he was the source of these confidential information drops, his days at this facility might be numbered. He couldn't take that risk anymore, especially not when it could endanger Sheneese. Nevertheless, it still bothered him that the people up on Moon Base Delta were being abandoned, traded like property, and sacrificed for a so-called greater good. But were they worth him taking these risks? He was conflicted.

The early morning briefing in the spartan boardroom went some way to calm his anxiety. Notably absent from the discussions was any mention of how Moon Base Delta seemed to know so much about the capsule mission. Han reckoned that the rumors were just baseless chatter after all.

For the most part, the mood was jubilant. Now that the capsules had been successfully delivered, the pressure was off, and the staff at Strawstack could pat themselves on the back and relax for a while. Yet, last night's attack on the base had taken some of the gloss of this celebration and the discussions soon turned to options for vacating the facility entirely. This, apparently, had been in the pipeline for quite a while, but now seemed like the best time to implement it. Everybody would be moved to a new, as yet unnamed, safer location. Preparations would begin immediately.

When Han finally arrived back at his modest quarters much later that day, he revealed his fears to Sheneese.

"Do you think they know?" she asked.

Han pressed a finger to his lips and beckoned her toward the shower enclosure. Sheneese understood his meaning and followed him to the cramped cubicle that served as their bathing facilities. Han reached in and flipped the shower on. The cascade of water created a racket, sufficient to obscure a hushed conversation.

"Now we can talk," he said, his voice low. "At the moment, I don't think they suspect anyone. Some are saying it's the AI at Moon Base Delta that figured it out. But for now, this could just be gossip and rumor."

"Do you realize what it would mean if they uncovered the truth?" Sheneese locked eyes with him.

"Of course. Which is why we must take the utmost care."

Sheneese's face stiffened. "No. We need to cease entirely," she said, pausing before adding, "Period."

Han nodded gravely. "I know, I know." He hesitated before continuing, "It's just…"

Sheneese sliced the air decisively with her hand. "Han, we can't jeopardize all this." She gestured around their meager quarters. "You heard the commotion last night. All day today, I've received nothing but reports about the anarchy out there. We wouldn't survive half an hour."

They stood in solemn silence for a moment before Han spoke again. "You're right, the risk is too great."

Sheneese nodded, relieved. She leaned in to embrace him. They stood entwined, clinging to each other as if they were all that mattered in the world.

Finally, she whispered, "I know it's hard to abandon Professor Hendrickson and the others. But we have no choice; we have to look after ourselves now."

Han nodded gravely. "Agreed. We've done all we can for them."

CHAPTER 6
PLOTS WITHIN PLOTS

Renton was not particularly surprised when the news came through that Xilinex had formally accepted their proposal for the exchange. He had had a feeling they might go for it, especially considering the ripe opportunity it provided for some kind of double-dealing on their part. Indeed, no one at Moon Base Delta was under any illusions about the inherent risks attached to accepting this offer from Xilinex. It was almost certainly a calculated trap. It was universally understood among them that Xilinex would unquestionably use this occasion to try and inflict harm, breach their security measures, and attempt to seize a tactical advantage. Consequently, whatever logistical arrangements they made for this exchange, they had to be absolutely certain they'd accounted for all conceivable risks.

Given this rather complex set of circumstances, Renton couldn't help but wonder if it was actually worth the potential risk. Yet, the uncomfortable reality was that they had scant other choices. The only alternative strategy involved an equally high-risk scavenger mission that would necessitate direct confrontation with the Xilinex forces currently blockading their base. Even assuming that Yuna could successfully maneuver a shuttle out of the hangar without incident and achieve liftoff, there were zero guarantees that the mission would uncover sufficient resources at the outlying outposts to effect any significant change to their dire situation. Therefore, when weighed against this reality, the alluring possibility of a supply capsule teeming with seed stock and biomass freshly shipped from Earth was simply too enticing to dismiss. With these supplies, they could not only jumpstart the dormant food production facilities within the base, but they'd also acquire the requisite biomass needed to immediately bootup the food synthesizers. With one bold move, they could theoretically solve their food supply problems for the foreseeable future. But achieving that would entail more than merely handing over the sixteen and two deceased captives they currently held; they would have to find a way to outwit Xilinex, which was no easy task.

A large portion of the current population of Moon Base Delta, had convened in the operations room to discuss Xilinex's recently received response, and come up with a plan. A tangible sense of anticipation and excitement pervaded the room, vibrating through the crowd that had assembled.

"There's enormous potential here for us to get seriously

screwed over," Mackenzie remarked, comfortably seated at one end of the central holo-table.

"We're well aware of that," Matteo replied, "And we also know that they probably know that we know. So, the whole thing's a plot within a plot within a plot."

"My head's spinning just thinking about it," said Yuna, with a half-smile.

"Their proposed offer is to deposit the supply capsule a few hundred meters away from one of our smaller cargo hangars situated on the western side. The stipulation is that the hangar doors must be wide open so they can visually confirm the presence of all the captives, including the bodies of those who died in the recent battle," Selene recited from her comms slate. "On the face of it, it seems like a reasonable request to me," she added thoughtfully.

"The problem I have with that specific arrangement," said Matteo, "is that opening those hangar doors leaves us exposed to the vacuum of space. This would necessitate putting the captives back into their EVA suits, and I had been hoping we could keep those suits; they're exceptionally well-armored and incredibly durable."

"And given that they were all damaged during the EMP explosion, we'll have to invest time in repairing them," Alice added.

"What's the estimated timeframe for those repairs?" Mackenzie asked, visibly concerned.

Matteo replied with a discernible sigh of exasperation. "It's difficult to say exactly. A couple of days, minimum."

"If I can make a suggestion," Tanaka chimed in, "What

about using IVA suits instead? They're designed only for internal flight applications, but they should suffice to keep a person alive for an hour or maybe two on the lunar surface. That might be good enough for our purposes, and we have plenty of them lying around."

"Good idea," said Renton.

There were a few other affirmative nods of approval from around the table. This would at least allow them to preserve some of the valuable, military-grade EVA suits for the battles ahead.

Selene picked up the slate once again and continued reviewing the instructions that they planned to send back to Xilinex. "So, we instruct them to position the capsule approximately two-hundred meters from the entrance to Hangar B12," she began. "As soon as they comply with that, we then proceed to open the hangar doors and present them with visual confirmation of their guys, all of whom are alive and well... eh, with the exception of the two that aren't."

"I keep getting this uneasy feeling that by opening those doors, we're essentially inviting an attack on the hangar," Alice voiced her concern.

"I think we should be safe enough. With the Xilinex mercenaries all neatly lined up and clearly exposed in front of us, they're less likely to attempt anything stupid. Also, because we're situated inside the confines of the hangar, we're effectively shielded on all sides, which is far better than being exposed out in the open," Mackenzie countered. "And let's not overlook the fact that we'll have a substantial amount of firepower aimed squarely in their direction."

"Moving on," Selene continued, after a brief moment to let Mackenzie's words sink in, "we then retrieve the capsule and subsequently release the captives." She paused momentarily, glancing around the table to gauge the others' thoughts on this part of the plan.

"I think we need to exercise a far greater degree of control over the entire situation," Renton suggested. "First and foremost, we should ensure that the capsule's contents are viable and not some lethal device like a bomb or a gas canister, or poisoned in some way. We absolutely need to know that what we're getting hasn't been compromised or tampered with."

"So, are you saying that we retrieve a sample, bring it back inside the hangar, run tests on it, and then if everything checks out, release the hostages?" Kimura clarified.

"Do we actually have the necessary equipment to comprehensively test the supplies for viability?" Professor Henriksen asked.

"Yes, in fact we do," confirmed Dr. Maria Jensen, one of the individuals who had arrived from the Axial Luxor along with Selene's group. "The bio-lab is equipped with chemical analyzers capable of establishing both the viability and the potential presence of any foreign contaminants, like, for instance... anthrax."

"We can't feasibly bring the entire capsule into the hangar," Renton interjected cautiously. "I think that's too much of a risk. We need to open it up outside on the lunar surface and carefully extract one of the sealed canisters for analysis. We can then bring that back into the lab for testing."

"What if we use a robot to extract a canister?" Alice offered.

"That could work," said Renton. "But let's assume for a moment that's precisely what they'd expect us to do. They know we can't open an actual canister out on the surface, as that would expose the contents to the vacuum of space. So, we have to bring it inside to test. Plenty of opportunity there for Xilinex to plant a surprise of some kind."

"We could open it inside a rover," Yuna suggested. "The robot brings it inside, opens the canister within a pressurized environment, and then, assuming everything doesn't explode, reassembles it and brings it to us for testing."

No one could find fault with this option, so Selene continued. "Okay, what about the captives? Do we release them all at once or in batches?"

"Batches," Alice answered. "We release, say, five or six when the capsule arrives. Another five or so when the sample proves viable. The remainder when we have acquired the full capsule, and nothing has exploded."

"DOA, can you take control of the robot and the rover, and operate them remotely during this entire operation?" Renton asked.

"Yes, I can certainly do that," DOA confirmed.

There was a brief moment when everyone in the room considered this proposal, searching for potential pitfalls or oversights. No one seemed to find anything fundamentally wrong with the strategy.

"So, we send this back to them and see what they say?" Selene queried.

"If they actually agree to this, there's probably something

we're missing, something we haven't factored into the equation," Renton stated.

"You sound like you're having second thoughts? After all, this was your idea," said Mackenzie.

"It's an act of desperation; we all know that. And the thing is, Xilinex now knows that too," Renton countered. "They're counting on us being so desperate that we'll overlook some fundamental issue, something we've taken for granted."

The room fell silent as everyone mentally wrestled with what this overlooked detail might be.

"So, are we going ahead with this or not?" Selene finally prompted.

"Renton is right; we don't have a choice," Professor Hendrickson chimed in. "To do nothing is to die a slow death. Faced with that option, I think it's better to risk it all on the roll of the dice."

One by one, everyone around the table began to nod in agreement.

CHAPTER 7
EXCHANGE

A visceral tension filled Hangar B12 as Renton and the others waited for the signal from DOA. This would indicate that the supply capsule had been deposited on the lunar surface just outside the hangar doors and that the Xilinex military personnel had retreated to a safe distance. Xilinex had agreed to most of their preconditions but had added a few stipulations of their own. This was to be expected, and nothing in the new terms would prevent the exchange from proceeding. The only additional requirement from Xilinex, which Renton found somewhat unnerving, was that he, Selene, Mackenzie, and Professor Hendrickson must all be present at the exchange. It had always been the plan for Mackenzie to be there, but the inclusion of him, Selene, and Hendrickson was unexpected. Renton struggled to find a convincing reason for it. Perhaps Xilinex just wanted to reassure themselves that these people were actually inside Moon Base Delta. But then again, why include someone like Professor Hendrickson? This baffled everyone, especially the professor himself. Nevertheless, desperation won out, and they agreed to proceed with the exchange without further deliberation.

Now, here they all were, fully encased in EVA suits standing on either side of Renton. Around fifteen other well-armed colonists from various groups that called this base home were also present. Between Renton and the outer doors of Hangar B12 stood sixteen anxious Xilinex captives, who had been persuaded into submission by an array of weapons aimed at their backs. They were tethered together in two groups of five and one of six, their deceased comrades lying in body bags on a pushcart nearby.

The mercenaries wore lightweight IVA suits, typically worn only by shuttle crews. These suits were pressurized and had a small air supply but were intended for emergency use only. In theory, a person could survive in the vacuum of space for about an hour in these, but they offered little in terms of radiation shielding. As such, the captives standing before them wouldn't want to linger on the lunar surface any longer than necessary. This suited Renton perfectly; once those doors opened, the clock would start ticking, and the captives would want to conclude this handover as quickly as possible.

"Rover approaching the drop-off point," DOA's voice echoed through Renton's helmet. The tension within the hangar increased another notch as everyone received the same message. "An object is being deposited on the surface; its dimensions indicate that it is most likely one of the supply capsules from Earth," DOA continued.

"Get ready," Mackenzie ordered. "Those doors are going to open soon. Everybody stay sharp."

Renton, like everyone else, snapped his visor closed and pressurized his suit, anticipating the hangar's decompression as a klaxon began sounding a warning. The Xilinex captives shifted uneasily, no doubt hoping their light IVA suits would hold up. When the hangar finally depressurized, the massive doors slid open, revealing a ghostly, monochromatic lunar landscape.

"Okay, DOA, send the rover with the robot and go check it out," Mackenzie's voice came through Renton's helmet comm.

Resisting the urge to step past the line of captives—the human shield between them and the Xilinex forces—Renton stayed put, eager yet anxious to see the robot retrieve a sample canister from the supply capsule. He had to be content with DOA's staccato updates over his comms, which indicated that the retrieval process was progressing at a painfully slow pace, further heightening the tension.

Eventually, a canister was retrieved from the capsule and opened within the pressurized confines of the rover. It contained seed stock and biomass. The rover returned to the base, and the samples were taken to a bio-lab for rigorous analytical tests assessing their biological viability. Anxiously, everyone waited for Dr. Jensen to report back.

"Good news," she finally announced over the comms, after what felt like an eternity. "Initial tests confirm eighty-three percent viability of the bio-stock, with no indications of any toxins or foreign agents."

Renton looked over to see Mackenzie and Chen Jun, one of

her lieutenants, nudging the first group of five captives forward with well-placed jabs from their gun muzzles. The captives moved slowly toward the open doors to exit the hangar. Like animals held in captivity too long, they glanced apprehensively at the lunar landscape, scanning their surroundings and exchanging glances. However, with persistent prodding, they began to exit. Their steps quickened as they crossed the hangar's threshold and moved onto the lunar surface, heading for the Xilinex transport waiting four-hundred meters away.

Renton immediately felt vulnerable. Even though only the first batch of five captives had left, and more than twice that number remained, the thinning of their human shield was disconcerting. The rest of the team felt it too; they all began clustering behind the remaining captives. By this time, the rover had returned to the capsule's location on the surface. The robot disembarked again, approached the capsule, and began extracting the remaining canisters. This phase was the riskiest part of the operation; once the rest of the canisters were stored in the rover, another five captives would be released.

When the last canister was loaded into the rover and given the all-clear, Mackenzie's team began prodding the next set of five captives forward. This group needed little persuasion; they had seen their predecessors safely cross the lunar landscape back to the Xilinex forces. They didn't waste any time exiting through the hangar door and crossing the dusty no-man's land.

Now, Renton and the others started to crowd behind the final group of six captives, waiting anxiously for the rover to return to the base. Once they received the all-clear from the DOA, they would start closing the hangar doors while simultaneously releasing the remaining captives, aiming to minimize exposure. At least, that was the plan.

"I'm detecting two rover-mounted plasma cannons powering up," DOA's voice broke in over their helmet comms. "Target acquisition established on the hangar bay."

Confusion swept through the assembled group. *They're not seriously going to fire?* Renton thought, panic setting in. *If they do, they'll kill their own people.* That's when he realized the fatal flaw in their plan: they had all assumed that Xilinex actually gave a crap about their own. They were wrong.

Before Renton could react, an incandescent orb of blue light erupted from the darkness along the horizon, heading straight for him. Like a rabbit in the headlights, he was frozen. The plasma ball expanded as it raced toward the hangar. All Renton could do was stare. In that moment, he became acutely aware of his impending demise—and there was absolutely nothing he could do to prevent it. He braced for impact.

Out of nowhere, the rover that DOA had been controlling raced back into view, plowing up a trail of dust in its wake. It came to a skidding halt directly in the path of the oncoming plasma ball and disintegrated as it absorbed the full force of the blast. A cloud of shrapnel erupted from the impact site, flickering and flashing with the dissipating energy of the plasma blast.

"Close the doors! Close the damn doors!" Renton heard someone shout. It might have been Mackenzie, but he wasn't sure. The cry snapped Renton out of his stupor and thrust him into the chaos engulfing the hangar bay.

"Get out! We need to get out!" another voice yelled. Turning, he saw Mackenzie, Chen Jun, and Saito gesturing urgently toward the exit. The remaining captives seemed paralyzed by indecision. Freedom was just beyond those doors, but now their own people were firing on them.

Renton glanced around and saw that Selene was also rooted to the spot. He grabbed her arm, pulling her along—anything to get her moving toward cover. He looked up to see the hangar bay doors closing, but agonizingly slowly. That's when another bolt of plasma tore through the gap between the closing doors and slammed into the rear of the hangar with a blinding flash. Renton's EVA suit sparked and glitched, blaring alerts at him as it began to fail. The hangar area turned into a chaotic maelstrom, lit by arcs of high-energy plasma that sparked and crackled as it dissipated.

Seconds later, his suit finally gave out. All he had left to breathe now was the limited volume of trapped air; he had only minutes before the CO_2 buildup would become lethal. He glanced at the hangar doors, now fully closed, just as a third plasma blast struck them from the outside. Energy crackled and arced across the interior surface, but the doors held. Renton quickly checked on his aunt Selene, whom he'd lost his grip on while dragging her to the side when the second blast hit. She was on the floor nearby, sitting up and clawing at her visor. Her EVA suit must have also failed. He knelt beside her and grabbed her hands to prevent her from opening the visor, gesturing to communicate that doing so would be lethal due to the lack of pressure. She seemed to understand, although it was hard for Renton to tell from her panicked expression.

Overhead, the air vents in the hangar opened, beginning to

repressurize the space. From experience, Renton knew it would take a minute or two for the pressure to stabilize at one atmosphere. He needed to slow his breathing, to conserve any remaining oxygen in his suit. Gesturing at the ceiling, he tried to convey to Selene that the hangar was being repressurized. He then signaled for her to stay calm and slow her breathing, reassuring her that everything would be okay. He wanted to find Mackenzie and the others but was reluctant to leave his aunt. He feared she might panic and open her visor prematurely. So, he held her hand and waited.

Renton's suit, now entirely nonfunctional, provided neither comms nor any indication of the hangar's interior pressure. Since all electrical systems near the blast site were offline, there were no external visual or audible alerts to indicate that normal pressure had been restored. He could only rely on a rough time estimate. As the hangar pressurized, rushing air stirred up gray clouds of dust and smoke. Additional oxygen ignited fires, fanning flames that began to consume equipment and producing more smoke, which obscured visibility.

Ultimately, he took a leap of faith and unsealed his helmet visor. He felt a tingling sensation on his face; the atmospheric pressure was not yet fully restored but was close enough to be safe. Coughing, he choked on the smoke and then removed his helmet altogether. Selene followed his lead.

Now he could hear shouts, cries, and screams from the center of the hangar. He stood and peered through the clearing smoke. The air filters had activated and were recycling the hangar's air, gradually reducing the smoke and dust. As visibility improved, he began to see scattered bodies—colonists and captives alike. It was the one thing none of them had considered: that Xilinex would willingly kill their own. They had all been naively optimistic, especially Renton. He simply couldn't fathom the mindset of someone willing to commit such an act. He had anticipated a trap; but in reality, this could have turned into an unmitigated disaster.

CHAPTER 8
CARNAGE

Renton quickly surveyed the chaos in the hangar bay. Around half of its occupants were splayed across the floor, incapacitated, while the other half were busily tending to the wounded. He wanted to locate Mackenzie, hoping to find her still among the living. This sudden, unexpected attack on the hangar could very well serve as a prelude to a full-scale Xilinex assault. They urgently needed to organize a defense.

He cast a concerned glance down at Selene, who was seated on the cold floor, her back leaning against a packing crate. Her breathing appeared labored, and her face was noticeably pale and bathed with sweat.

"Are you okay?" he asked, crouching down beside her.

"Yeah, yeah, I'm fine. Just... you know—" her sentence abruptly trailed off.

"Stay here," Renton advised as he stood back up. "I have to go find Mackenzie, and find out what's really going on."

He spotted her in amongst a pile of unmoving bodies, where she was being helped to her feet by Chen Jun. Thankfully, she appeared to be largely unharmed, albeit extremely angry.

"You okay?" he shouted out as he drew closer.

"Those damn bastards. We should've known they'd pull some crap like this." She dusted herself off and straightened her posture. She picked up her plasma weapon, checked it, then flung it on the ground again. "Dead," she announced. "That plasma blast fried all the electronics."

"Same here, comms are completely dead," Renton confirmed, tapping his earpiece for emphasis.

"Me too," chimed in Chen Jun, "everything's basically fried."

Just then, the internal doors to the hangar were flung open. Dr. Jensen and a handful of colonists surged in, carrying an array of emergency medical equipment. Matteo was among them. Catching his eye, Renton signaled and hastily made his way over.

"My god, what an absolute mess," Matteo murmured, his gaze sweeping over the chaotic scene of the dead and the wounded.

"Is it a full-blown attack?" Renton asked urgently. "What are they doing out there? Are they advancing?"

"I don't think so. Alice and Yuna managed to launch two kamikaze drones at them," Matteo explained, still visibly in shock, still attempting to process the extent of the carnage around him. "One hit the target and neutralized one of their plasma cannons. They shot the other one down. But so far, no sign of them advancing." He shook his head. Reaching into his shoulder bag, he pulled out a spare comms unit and tossed it in Renton's direction.

Renton deftly caught it, clipped the unit to his ear, and immediately tapped to activate it. "DOA, talk to me, what's the situation? Are we under attack?"

"The Xilinex forces have pulled back to their original positions," said DOA. "It may very well have been their intention to initiate a full-scale assault on the base. However, their attack on the B12 hangar didn't produce the results they were likely expecting. And I strongly suspect they were not anticipating a retaliatory drone strike."

Matteo, in the meantime, was busily handing out spare comms units to both Mackenzie and Chen Jun, ensuring everyone was looped into the comms network.

"What's DOA saying?" Mackenzie inquired as she fitted the comm unit into her ear.

"They've pulled back. Alice and Yuna launched a drone strike on them," Renton filled her in.

"Damn it," Mackenzie swore, her eyes scanning the devastation. "I knew this was too risky. We've essentially lost everything," she added, giving Renton a hard stare.

"We knew the risks," he responded, unfazed. "We knew we had to attempt something, anything, otherwise we'd be staring down the barrel of starvation."

"Well, with that rover destroyed with a direct hit, all the supplies are lost. So in the end, it was all for nothing," Mackenzie's frustration seemed to be reaching a peak levels.

"We haven't lost absolutely everything," Matteo interjected. "We still have the contents of the first canister that we took inside for testing. There are seeds from various plant species, and sufficient biomass to activate several of our bioreactors."

"Then at least this wasn't entirely in vain," said Chen Jun, looking somewhat relieved.

For a moment, Mackenzie was silent.

More colonists had begun to arrive, bringing additional medical supplies. Some of the injured were receiving immediate treatment on the spot, while those sustaining minor injuries were being transported on gurneys to the med bay. Unfortunately, others weren't as fortunate; body bags were being requisitioned for them.

"Renton?" Alice's concerned voice came through newly acquired comms unit.

"I'm okay, I'm fine," he assured her.

"And what about the others?" she asked.

"Selene's okay, so is Mackenzie and Chen Jun. As for everyone else, I can't really say at the moment. It's pure chaos down here; still attempting to process the whole situation. Nice work on those drones, by the way," he added.

"We had them primed and ready to go. I've got two more drones on standby, just in case they decide to try another stunt. But for now, they appear to be holding their positions," Alice reported.

"Good to hear. I'll need to check on Selene, see how she's coping. We'll talk more later." With that, he ended the communication.

Now that Mackenzie had a functioning comms unit, she got busy checking on the defensive group back in the main base, keeping them alert and focused as they took up positions.

Renton scanned the area for Selene and found her crouched over a body. As he approached, he realized it was one of their own, its abdomen gruesomely impaled by a large fragment of metal. Getting a closer look, he recognized the lifeless gaze of Professor Hendrickson staring up at him.

"Oh shit," he muttered as he identified the body. "Not the professor."

Selene held Hendrickson's limp hand, clenching it in both of hers as she stared at his lifeless face.

"Why him?" she asked, still looking at his face. "He was a decent human being, not a single bad bone in his body. Why do the good ones have to pay the price?"

Renton reached down and placed a hand on Selene's shoulder. That was all he could do, not knowing what to say.

"He wasn't built for this," she continued, looking around and surveying the hangar, "this... war. He understood the complexities of orbital mechanics, the movement of the planets, but he could never comprehend how human nature could be so violent."

"None of us were built for this," Renton replied. "We were all shaped by a different world, one where all this would seem like a bad dream."

"It is a nightmare," Selene agreed, "and for what? We have nothing to show for all this carnage today."

"That's not true," Renton countered. "We still have the first supply canister. It will get things going, provide us with the food supply going forward. It wasn't for nothing."

Selene looked up at him, her face reflecting her pain. "For how long? And at what cost? The outcome is still inevitable.

There will come a time when we run out of food again, with no way to resupply. What we have now is still just... temporary."

Renton shook his head. "You can't look at it that way, Selene. To do so is to abandon all hope."

She was silent for a moment, her head lowered, her hands still gripping Hendrickson's. Then, she seemed to wipe a tear from her face, let go of the dead man's hand, and rose. "We need to inform his friends back at the Strawstack facility. They'll want to know what's happened here. They need to understand the reality of what Space Division and FISA's abandonment of their people truly means."

Later that day, when the bodies had been counted and the injured taken to the med bay, a deep despondency began to settle over the colonists at Moon Base Delta. Yes, they could technically call the exchange a partial success, in that they now had the largest food supply that had been in the base for more than two decades. Enough to last many months. But all this came at a high cost, the professor was dead and so too was Saito Yuuta, he had asphyxiated in his EVA suit, along with two others from Mackenzie's crew. Several more were in the med bay, some critical. Of the six remaining Xilinex captives, four were dead, the other two were now tied down to gurneys in the med bay. And they too would have been dead, if Mackenzie had had her way. She was prevented from slitting their throats on the spot by various interventions not least persuading her that they could still be useful in the future.

In the end, it was Selene's words that kept resonating in

Renton's mind. *We're just not built for war.* It was true, they lacked the mindset necessary to do whatever it takes to win. So maybe Mackenzie was right, just kill these people now, show no mercy.

But even if they all turned into bloodthirsty killers, how could they possibly overcome a determined Xilinex Corporation with all their resources. There was simply no route forward that Renton could see. It was clear from the events today that Pompodur Adarok wanted the leadership of Moon Base Delta decapitated, and with the death of Professor Hendrickson, he at least partially succeeded. Yet, each of them in their own way had chosen this confrontation with Xilinex, and to a lesser extent with SINO. So they were in many ways responsible for the situation they now found themselves in, isolated, and threatened from all sides. Where was the solution? Where was their way out? These were the questions that tormented Renton's mind that evening. In the end, he realized that what they really needed was a miracle.

CHAPTER 9
STARK REALITIES

B efore the solar storm hit, whenever Han would embark on a new research project, the process was pretty streamlined. He would simply prompt his personal AI on the specific topic of interest and set it to work. The AI would then diligently search through all relevant information repositories —both public and private, general and academic—sifting through terabytes upon terabytes of data. It would filter, select, and compile relevant information, ultimately presenting Han with a concise, well-written, and meticulously structured report; complete with a comprehensive summary, appendices, source material links, and even suggested areas for further study.

Now, however, the situation had dramatically changed. The once-vast global datasphere had been reduced to little more than a cloud of orbital debris, making any connection to an external data repository extremely challenging, if not near-impossible. Han suspected that many of these once widely used information repositories still existed in some form, but were now offline and inaccessible. They had turned into isolated islands of information, accessible only to those fortunate enough to have a direct, physical connection to them. Moreover, these data centers required a considerable amount of energy to remain operational. Given that most were commercial enterprises, a pressing question arose: Who would pay to keep them running now that their customer base was essentially cut off? If they weren't already powered by renewable resources and instead relied solely on the grid for energy, their situation was indeed dire. Han, along with those few lucky enough to still have some level of access to global information, was painfully aware that an energy crisis was looming on the horizon. Any Helium-3 harvested from the Moon for energy production would be allocated based on a strict hierarchy of national security priorities. As a result, many of these valuable data centers would likely remain offline, their treasure troves of information withheld from the world, until energy production and connectivity could improve sufficiently to bring them back into service. And judging by the ongoing, rapid deterioration of society at large, Han understood that this restoration was unlikely to occur for a very long time. These repositories of knowledge could ultimately become nothing more than archaeological curiosities for a future society, perhaps many centuries from now.

So even if Han still had a powerful personal AI at his disposal, the fact remained that there was very little information available for it to search through. He did have some access to localized information stored on servers here within the confines of the Strawstack Mountain facility. Additionally, through a painfully slow and often unreliable broadband connection, he could connect to a central FISA database and sift through some declassified information provided by the Space Division. However, leveraging this limited connection now required explicit board approval. And even as a sitting board member himself, Han would need to justify why he was allocating this scarce resource for something other than his primary responsibility of tracking orbital debris. This was particularly true if he was devoting it to an unrelated personal project, such as his newfound interest in the history of Mars exploration.

Han's curiosity had been piqued when he discovered that a Mars evacuation ship was currently en route to the lunar colonies. Like many, they had seen the grim writing on the wall in the aftermath of the devastating solar storm and had come to the sobering realization that their colony on the Red Planet was simply unsustainable. So they had no other choice but to pack up their belongings and seek sanctuary on the Moon. At least there, they stood some semblance of a chance for survival.

With the recent successful completion of supply capsule mission and the strategic decision to relocate much of the workforce away from Strawstack Mountain, Han found himself with considerably more free time than he had grown accustomed to. But he had another, more personal reason for diving into a new project; he had given a solemn promise to

Sheneese to cease sending unauthorized data dumps to Professor Hendrickson at Moon Base Delta—a commitment he was fully intent on honoring. To occupy his mind and divert his attention away from all the complex conflicts that were raging both on the lunar surface and here on Earth, he needed an interesting project to get his teeth into.

In many ways, the fractured and incomplete nature of the available information on Mars colonization resonated deeply with Han's analytical mind. It made him feel like he was diligently piecing together a complex jigsaw puzzle with only fragmented scraps of the complete picture available to him. This challenge drove him to sift meticulously through a diverse array of old reports, archived news feeds, scientific papers, detailed ship designs, intricate engineering drawings, topographical maps, and a multitude of other fragmented data sources.

The initial human expeditions had set foot on Mars shortly after the second phase of lunar colonization was already well underway. However, unlike the Moon, Mars had not experienced the same level of rapid, accelerated development. This was primarily attributable to the daunting logistical challenges presented by the planet's vast distance from Earth, as well as the enormous financial costs of supplying and sustaining a crew for nearly two years at a stretch. As a result, most of the early exploratory missions to Mars were government-funded endeavors spearheaded by national space agencies.

Nevertheless, the involvement of private enterprise soon fundamentally changed the equation. The development of innovative, reusable, fusion-powered ships had a dramatic impact, significantly reducing both transit times and the overall financial burden. Recognizing these benefits, government agencies, eager to mitigate their own burgeoning expenditures, began to appreciate the untapped potential of leveraging the resources they had already accumulated on Mars through strategic private sector collaborations. The first corporations to make this pioneering move were typically those that had existing associations with national agencies, especially those involved in supplying essential resources. Santomon was among these trailblazers, establishing a dedicated genetic research facility designed to develop crops better adapted to Martian conditions. This facility would later expand its scope through joint ventures with other like-minded biotech firms. The exact details of their work, however, remained shrouded in confidentiality, ostensibly to protect valuable intellectual property rights.

Tech entrepreneurs also began to show increasing interest, lured not just by the promise of the ultimate adventure tailored for the ultra-wealthy, but for other reasons as well. According to an insightful article that Han had stumbled upon, this influx of tech mogul enthusiasm was actually driven more by the largely unregulated genetic engineering research that was now being conducted on Mars than by anything else. Many saw this as a unique, albeit somewhat controversial, investment opportunity in groundbreaking, life-extending biotechnologies.

However, one particular name caught Han's attention and made him sit back in his chair: the enigmatic and eccentric trillionaire, Jack Stark. A well-known public figure, Stark was also a somewhat controversial personality who had a knack for fascinating the general public. His notoriety reached peak elevation when he made a bombshell public announcement about his sudden and unexpected retirement from the world of business. He vowed to devote the remainder of his life, along with his vast accumulated wealth, exclusively to the betterment of humanity.

This startling revelation purportedly occurred while Stark was under the influence of a unique concoction of hallucinogenic frog venom. He was participating in a private, spiritual retreat located in a secluded, untouched zone in what still remained of the Amazon rainforest. The story of this transformative experience was widely known and disseminated; Han didn't need to dig particularly deep to find multiple accounts of it. Stark had appeared on numerous news broadcasts and interviews, where he vividly recounted this pivotal, life-altering moment. According to his own narrative, while in the midst of this chemically induced, out-of-body experience and traversing some distant, esoteric astral plane, a powerful and enigmatic alien being materialized before him. This being proceeded to solemnly inform him that Earth was teetering on the brink of a major, catastrophic extinction event. The specific details—such as how and precisely when this event would unfold—remained tantalizingly vague. However, this mystical revelation shocked Stark so profoundly that, upon his return from this mind-altering, transcendental journey, he pledged to use all his available resources and the remaining years of his life to preserve as much of Earth's biodiversity as humanly possible.

He ambitiously named this noble endeavor the Ark Project, envisioning it as a massive, comprehensive biological doomsday vault, a bio-bank.

As you would imagine, public opinions on Jack Stark were sharply divided—although, in hindsight, he might have actually been on to something with his ominous warnings about a looming extinction event. Some skeptics simply considered him insane, suspecting that his brain had been irreversibly fried by an overdose of powerful hallucinogens. Others viewed him as divinely inspired, and were quite eager to learn more concrete specifics about the predicted, imminent apocalypse. Then there was also a group of people who argued that, ultimately, it was his hard-earned money and he had every right to do whatever he pleased with it. This laissez-faire viewpoint was often countered by impassioned advocates who believed that, given the world's numerous, pressing challenges —such as rampant food insecurity and crippling poverty— Stark's enormous wealth could and should be better spent addressing these more immediate, tangible problems.

The concept of a doomsday vault was certainly not new or unprecedented, however. In fact, similar structures had been constructed well over a century and a half ago. These expansive physical vaults were strategically situated in either extremely arid or intensely cold locations on Earth. They were designed to house a vast array of seed samples from a multitude of species, mainly those of food crops. In addition to these physical repositories, there were also extensive, comprehensive digital databases that contained a significant percentage of the DNA sequences representing all life on Earth. These sequences were, of course, meticulously stored in digital form for future use.

But what Stark was proposing was something on a vastly grander and exponentially more complex scale. The storage of seeds and plant samples was relatively straightforward; they could, in technical terms, be preserved indefinitely under the right conditions. However, with our current scientific understanding, it was not yet feasible to create a multicellular, complex life form solely from a raw DNA sequence. Up to this date, only single-celled organisms like bacteria had been successfully reproduced from their basic DNA sequences, and even those intricate processes invariably required a donor cell to be effective. What Stark ambitiously envisioned was the creation of a far-reaching database that would contain biologically viable samples of as much life on Earth as it was humanly possible to collect and preserve.

Therefore, it didn't come as a major surprise to Han when he discovered that Stark's name was closely linked with a consortium of cutting-edge, state-of-the-art genetic engineering corporations. These companies had collaboratively established an advanced research facility on Mars. Most people viewed the research operations taking place there with a fair amount of suspicion, largely assuming that whatever experimental work they were doing was probably illegal or, at the very least, highly questionable under Earth's existing laws. However, this kind of secluded research facility would be exactly the type that Stark could utilize to further advance his ambitious Ark Project. And there was little doubt that these corporations would be more than willing to accept his generous financial backing.

Yet, lingering questions remained: Had Stark ever made any substantial progress with his grand, visionary concept? And where could he possibly be now? Han could find only limited and somewhat dated information to shed light on these questions. While Stark was always more than willing to discuss his grand vision and ideals with anyone receptive enough to listen, he was notoriously tight-lipped when it came to divulging any specific details, including even the probable location of the project. Some people speculated that it could be situated at the South Pole, while others guessed it might be located in the arid Atacama Desert. A select few even ventured to suspect that he might be constructing this doomsday vault on Mars itself, especially given his heavy investment in the Martian research facility and the significant amount of time he had already spent on the Red Planet. However, all of these theories remained mere speculation that Han had managed to unearth in some very dated and fragmented news archives.

Leaning back in his chair, Han took a moment to stretch out his shoulders and neck muscles. He had been tirelessly combing through the labyrinthine archive files at the Strawstack Mountain Facility for the past four hours. It was already getting late into the evening, and he knew that Sheneese would be wrapping up her own shift in the communications center shortly. Mindful of this, he reached out and grabbed a half-empty bottle of water that was resting on the corner of his cluttered desk. Taking a sip, he took a moment to reflect on the swath of information he had unearthed thus far in his deep dive into Mars research.

While he was certainly getting a clearer, more defined picture of the history and development of the Mars colony, the pieces of fragmented information that were bouncing around in his head were not yet sufficient to formulate any solid insights regarding what the impending arrival of this Mars ship might mean for the lunar colonists. All he had was an unsettling gut feeling that the larger implications could be much more significant than most people were anticipating.

"I thought I'd find you in here."

Han swiveled his chair around to find Sheneese stepping into the secluded library area where he had been engrossed in his work. He glanced quickly at his watch. "Is it that time already? My apologies, I got completely engrossed in something." Offering an apologetic smile, he then motioned toward an old archive photograph of Jack Stark displayed prominently on his screen. "Hey, do you remember this guy?"

Sheneese seemed reluctant to engage, possibly due to exhaustion from her own workday, she gave the photo a cursory glance. "Is that the mad, rich guy who wanted to build an ark because some extraterrestrial being told him to?"

"The very same," Han confirmed. "It turns out he's been extensively involved in the genetic research program being conducted on Mars."

"I see," Sheneese replied, sounding uninterested in this intriguing tidbit of information.

Sensing her distraction, Han pressed a little further. "What's the matter? Are you worried about the upcoming move or something?"

"No, it's not that," she clarified, contorting her mouth into an awkward expression. "I have some rather bad news. Your friend, Professor Hendrickson, has been tragically killed in an explosion at Moon Base Delta. The report came in about half an hour ago."

"Lars is dead?" Han was shocked to his core.

Sheneese responded with a sympathetic nod of her head.

"Wh... what exactly happened? Are there any details?"

"We don't have the complete picture, but it seems that there was some sort of accident when... uh... the Xilinex Corporation was in the process of transferring supplies to the base. Initial reports are saying it was an explosion of some kind; several individuals are confirmed dead and numerous others are injured."

"That hardly seems possible," Han shook his head in disbelief. "There's no way that Xilinex should have been supplying Moon Base Delta; they've been conducting a blockade."

"I know, it doesn't make any sense," Sheneese agreed. "However, the fact remains that the professor ended up being an unfortunate casualty of whatever happened there."

"Those bastards, they killed him," Han seethed with anger. "Lars was simply a physics professor; he was no threat to anyone."

Sheneese gently placed her hand on Hans tense shoulder; he clasped it in his own.

"He's unlikely to be the last, I'm afraid. More people are going to lose their lives before this craziness ends."

CHAPTER 10
TREAD CAREFULLY

Han poured himself a cup of steaming-hot coffee from one of the communal pots in the canteen of the Strawstack Mountain Astronomical Facility. He had come down early for breakfast for a couple of reasons: primarily because he had gotten very little sleep the previous night, and also because he was in absolutely no mood for idle chatter before the scheduled morning's board meeting. He wanted to have his breakfast alone, well before the other members of his research team showed up.

Choosing a table situated in a quieter corner of the canteen, he sat down with his back deliberately turned to the kitchen. He had a vague, somewhat tentative plan to review some of the detailed documentation he had downloaded on the enigmatic Jack Stark, but he found that he just couldn't focus his attention on it. His thoughts kept drifting back to the fate of his friend, Professor Lars Hendrickson. It felt so unjust that a person endowed with a mind as extraordinarily brilliant as Hendrickson's should be abruptly snuffed out in such a manner. The enormity of his loss would be acutely felt, not just by Han personally, but also by the broader scientific community at the facility, since everyone who worked here held Hendrickson in high regard and had enormous respect for him.

The unmistakable clatter of the coffee pot emanating from the kitchen alerted him that someone else had just made their way into the canteen and was pouring themselves a mug. This was followed by the sound of footsteps drawing steadily closer to him.

"Han, don't normally see you down here this early."

Glancing up, Han found Alan E. Dyson, the former head of FIFA, standing beside him, coffee mug in hand.

"Yeah, I... well, I couldn't get much sleep last night," Han replied, momentarily averting his gaze from Dyson to concentrate once again on his own coffee.

"I just wanted to extend my condolences and say how deeply sorry I am to hear of Professor Hendrickson's untimely death. It's an absolute tragedy," Dyson solemnly stated, placing a compassionate hand on Han's shoulder for emphasis.

Raising his eyes to meet Dyson's, Han asked, "Do you know what happened up there?"

Dyson's mouth tightened, and he glanced over toward the kitchen to check who else had entered the canteen. Then he sat down across from Han, clearly troubled by the news of the professor's death. "There was an incident," he began.

"An incident?" Han asked, his voice edged with both curiosity and skepticism.

"I don't know the full story," Dyson continued, his voice weighed down by the solemnity of the situation. "All I know is that Moon Base Delta somehow discovered that two supply capsules sent from Earth had successfully arrived in lunar orbit. How they found this out, I'm not sure, but the top brass have a few theories. Anyway, Moon Base Delta offered to exchange the captives held from the failed attempt by Xilinex to take over the base for one of these capsules. Xilinex agreed, but something went wrong during the handover. There was an explosion of some sort. Hendrickson died, along with several other colonists and some of the Xilinex captives they were exchanging. Many more were injured."

Han leaned back in his chair, shaking his head in disbelief. "My God, that's insane."

"Yeah," Dyson agreed, nodding solemnly.

"And what do our military overlords think of all this?" Han gestured toward the ceiling as if the powers that be were right above them.

"They're being tight-lipped about it. Their main concern seems to be how Moon Base Delta knew about the capsules in the first place."

Han felt a momentary jolt of panic rise up inside him. He tightened his grip on his coffee mug. "You said they had some, eh... theories?" he asked tentatively, uncertain if he really wanted to hear the answer.

"Oh, there are several, but the general consensus is that the AI they have at the base figured it out."

Han breathed a sigh of relief. For now, it looked like he had gotten away with it. They weren't even considering that someone from Strawstack might have been sending the information.

"Are they going to help them now? Will there be a change in policy?" Han asked, more to change the subject than anything else, since he already knew what the answer would be.

"I don't see that happening anytime soon." Dyson shook his head.

"It's not right," said Han, locking eyes with Dyson. "These are our people—FISA, JAXA-KARI, INDOCON. And we just abandon them at Moon Base Delta and Shackleton, enclaves that are being taken over by that megalomaniac Adarok." His tone rising in frustrated anger.

Dyson raised a hand, as if to ward off Han's outburst. "Look, I'm not saying I disagree with you; it's bad business, for sure. But you need to understand that there are far greater issues at stake here. It's not just about the fate of a handful of colonists. The future of human civilization here on Earth is on the line."

Han sighed, his head lowered, slumping over his coffee. He understood the larger argument; there was a lot at stake. But he was beginning to see potential downsides in the strategy of extorting Xilinex to ensure exclusive supplies of Helium-3.

"I know," Han finally said, his voice tinged with frustration. "I get it. It's just that it all seems so... Machiavellian."

"Hey," Dyson said, raising his hands in a gesture of resignation, "ours is not to reason why, and all that."

They fell silent for a moment, and Han sensed that Dyson was about to get up and leave. But he preempted him with a question.

"Tell me, do you remember a guy named Jack Stark?"

Dyson seemed a little perplexed by the question, unsure of its relevance. He furrowed his brow as he searched his memory. "Wasn't he that mega-rich guy who went mad from licking too many mind-altering frogs?"

Han nodded, taking another sip of his now lukewarm coffee. "That's him. Although, it's debatable whether he went completely mad. 'Eccentric' might be a better term."

"What about him? Don't tell me you're dabbling in magic mushrooms," Dyson joked.

Han gestured at the screen of his slate to bring up an old archive article entitled *Stark's Ark: One Man's Mind-Bending Mission to Save the Planet.* He slid the slate across the table.

Dyson glanced at the photograph, which showed a cheerful-looking Stark in hiking gear, out on an expedition in some remote corner of the world. "Yeah, that's him." Dyson began to skim the text.

"Don't bother," Han said, taking the tablet back. "I'll give you the executive summary." He then began to outline what he had learned about Jack Stark.

"So, he offloads most of his business interests and puts everything into this doomsday vault project. However, there's very little I could find about him or the progress of the project after that, except..." Han paused for dramatic effect. "Guess who pops up as one of the major investors in the biotech research facility on Mars? Our good friend, Jack Stark."

Dyson sat back, arms folded, with a fascinated look on his face. He had been enjoying the story up until the mention of

Mars, and now Han could see the wheels in his brain starting to spin.

"Mars?" he asked, his expression shifting to one of confusion.

Han leaned in, lowering his voice to a near-whisper. "Think about it for a moment. Imagine you're Stark, and you want to build this... doomsday vault. But you don't want just a seed bank buried at the North Pole or a simple DNA database. You're looking for something at the cutting edge of bio-engineering. You also want complete secrecy, and you need this vault to be safe from any Earth-shattering events, like an asteroid strike. Luckily for you, there's a group of genetic scientists working off-planet, on Mars, who are also looking for funding."

Dyson's eyebrows rose sharply, yet he still hadn't fully grasped the implications of this revelation.

"And guess what's scheduled to arrive in lunar orbit in a few weeks?" Han prompted.

Understanding washed over Dyson's face, but he was so stunned he couldn't finish his thought. "You... think..."

Han completed the sentence for him. "Do I think Stark's Ark is on that ship? I don't know. Maybe it is, or maybe it was beyond even the capabilities of the scientists on Mars, or maybe the project never reached completion. But whatever was developed up there is very likely on board that ship now, especially since Mars has been abandoned. And it's probably in the hands of some very knowledgeable geneticists, the type who could potentially reverse-engineer Santomon crops."

Dyson's eyes widened, his mouth falling open in astonishment. "Damn," he finally managed to utter.

"Now consider the implications if that maniac Adarok gets his hands on this. He wouldn't need supply capsules from Earth anymore, would he?" Han sat back, watching as the gears in Dyson's mind shifted into overdrive.

"Who else knows about this?" Dyson finally asked, his voice tinged with apprehension.

"I imagine the top brass over at Vandenberg Space Port are likely piecing it all together, especially now that the Mars evacuation is a hot topic and the ship's arrival in lunar orbit is only weeks away," Han replied.

"Yes, of course, of course. They must already be in the loop," Dyson answered, a touch of alarm in his voice. "I know they've been using our X Band dish here to communicate with Mars, but the specifics of those conversations are classified." Dyson paused for a moment, then ran his hand through his hair before glancing at his watch. "We have a meeting in a few minutes. General Grant's back from Vandenberg; he'll likely update us on the logistics of the relocation."

Han's curiosity got the better of him. "Do you think it's worth mentioning to the General and the others what could possibly be on that incoming Mars ship?"

Dyson's tone was tinged with caution. "To what end? It'd be mostly speculative on our part. Besides, as you said, our military overlords probably have a lot more information than we do."

"But wouldn't you want to know where they stand on this?" Han persisted, still not entirely convinced.

Dyson looked at him sternly. "Tread carefully, Han. The atmosphere is already fraught with paranoia, what with the recent incidents at Moon Base Delta and Professor Hendrickson's death. They've tightened communications, restricted who can communicate with the lunar base. They're also building their own X Band system over at Vandenberg. Once that's operational, this facility will be shut down and relocated. It's their way of centralizing control, of narrowing the circle of people in the know."

Han leaned back and assessed Dyson. His friend had a point, and the last thing Han wanted was to draw unwanted scrutiny.

"You're probably right," he reluctantly agreed, his tone laced with a hint of defeat. "Still, it could be enlightening to gauge their reaction."

Dyson raised his hands in a gesture of resignation. "It's your call, Han."

CHAPTER 11
PREPARATIONS

Arriving for the meeting, they found that General Grant was already there, flanked by two "intelligence" officers who had accompanied him back from his recent trip to the headquarters at Vandenberg Space Port. Han immediately sensed that Grant appeared to be somewhat uneasy, almost disquieted, in the company of these two officers. They were briefly introduced as Officers Harvey and Lewinsky, both of whom were ostensibly present to oversee the implementation of the evacuation procedure at Strawstack Mountain.

However, the mood of the meeting noticeably shifted, becoming more guarded and awkward, when Grant made the unexpected announcement that these two officers would also be participating in the board meeting. Technically, this was a violation of established protocol, but no one in the room challenged this unusual arrangement. It was implicitly understood that if General Grant declared they were to be part of the meeting, then his word was final.

Dyson, who was presiding as the chair of the meeting, opened the proceedings by offering some thoughtful, carefully chosen words about the unfortunate and tragically untimely death of Professor Lars Hendrickson. His heartfelt remarks created a brief but intensely poignant moment for collective reflection on a colleague who had commanded all their respect. The room descended into a contemplative silence, a pause that was abruptly interrupted by Noah Harris, who could no longer contain his simmering curiosity. Speaking out of turn, he asked the question that had been troubling everyone in the room.

"What the hell happened up there?" He directed this squarely at General Grant.

General Grant looked visibly uncomfortable, taking a moment to glance momentarily at his two accompanying officers before giving a response. "We're still not entirely sure," he said cautiously.

Harris, clearly dissatisfied with this vague response, pressed further. "There are rumors circulating that they were engaged in a prisoner exchange, in return for one of the supply capsules."

"That's what we heard too, but at this point, it still remains speculation," Grant cautioned. "The truth of the matter is, we don't have a confirmed explanation for what occurred. There is nothing more I can add that isn't already known." He opened both hands in a disarming gesture.

Before Harris could continue his line of questioning, Dyson raised his own hand, attempting to restore a semblance of order to the meeting. "I understand that we are all deeply affected by this tragedy and are seeking some logical explanation for such a senseless loss. However, we have a lot to get through so can we please proceed with the meeting's agenda." He surveyed the faces around the table, seeking a consensus.

Harris shook his head in slight disagreement but chose to remain silent.

Dyson nodded, signaling that the discussion could proceed to the next topic. "Let's now move on to the evacuation plans for this facility," he said, gesturing to Grant to take the lead.

Grant began to outline the comprehensive plans for the impending relocation of personnel from the Strawstack Mountain facility. The formal evacuation process would officially kick off once the newly expanded communication system—currently under active construction at Vandenberg Space Port—became fully operational. When that milestone was reached, all communication responsibilities would be transitioned from Strawstack to Vandenberg, and the evacuation procedures would truly begin in earnest.

Taking a mental note, Han quickly calculated that they likely had a time frame of less than seven days before the communication system at their present location would be permanently decommissioned. This realization meant that if he wanted to send any message, whether clandestine or official, to Moon Base Delta, he had an increasingly narrow window of opportunity in which to do it. Even though he had previously made a solemn promise to Sheneese, and a personal commitment to himself, to refrain from engaging in any more high-risk communications, the looming deadline still continued to weigh heavily on his mind.

The evacuation plans also included the strategic deployment of additional military units, designated to oversee various critical aspects of operational security as well as logistics. This component was considered absolutely crucial for guaranteeing the safety of all individuals during the take-off and departure of the VTOL (vertical take-off and landing) aircraft specifically designated for executing the mass evacuation. Once the civilian staff had been securely evacuated to safety, the military was slated to assume full control of the Strawstack Mountain facility, effectively transforming it into a purely military base.

For Han and his dedicated team, Vandenberg was shaping up to be a much more secure and fortified environment in which to conduct their work. The teams already stationed there had been industriously assembling and calibrating a broad range of new equipment that was essential for the accurate tracking of orbital debris. Most remarkably, they had even managed to successfully relocate the supercomputer that had previously served as the nerve center of the now-defunct MASTERM campus. This substantial upgrade would significantly bolster their capabilities in the area of predictive modeling. What's more, the move would be bringing them into more collaborative engagement with the aerospace design team, which had been based at Vandenberg right from the inception of the project.

As soon as Grant had finished his briefing on the evacuation procedure, a subtle ripple of low-level murmured conversations began to spread around the boardroom table. A few minor questions were posed, touching upon specific logistical details, but on the whole, everyone appeared to be relatively content with the plans. There was a palpable sense of relief in the air of finally leaving Strawstack Mountain, given its security vulnerabilities.

"I guess we've got plenty of time now to focus on cataloging and packing up," Decker mused aloud. "Given that the recent capsule launch was successful, and we're not planning on doing any more until we see the return of Helium-3 supplies."

"Not quite," said Dyson. "Actually, it's the next item on the agenda. We've just received a fresh request directly from Vandenberg urgently asking for the most current data sets we have in our possession. Apparently, they are in the early stages of planning a brand-new series of launches."

This unexpected revelation was immediately met with startled expressions of surprise from almost everyone.

"Why would they be doing that?" questioned Harris. "We've already dispatched two capsules into lunar orbit. Where's the need for additional launches?"

Dyson glanced over at General Grant, who then began to elaborate. "The exact nature of this new mission is highly classified, so I'm afraid I cannot disclose specific details at this juncture. However, what I can definitively tell you is that fulfilling this urgent data request as efficiently as possible is absolutely critical."

"Classified? What the heck does that mean?" Decker chimed in, clearly bewildered.

"It means precisely what it means," the General responded,

his tone edged with authority, effectively silencing any further queries.

"Could this possibly have any connection to the Mars evacuation ship that's currently approaching lunar orbit?" Han cautiously ventured to ask.

At this, there was a noticeable shift in the body language exhibited by the two intelligence officers, accompanied by a lot of side-eye. Grant seemed to notice this subtle change as well. But he spread his hands in a disarming gesture. "To be entirely honest, Han, I couldn't possibly say. My briefings are strictly on a need-to-know basis, they don't tell me everything. All I can say is that our colleagues stationed at Vandenberg Space Port are in urgent need of this data."

At this point, Dyson shot Han a stern look, silently reminding him of his prior warning against delving into such topics. It had the intended effect: Han chose to rein in his curiosity for the moment. Although he strongly suspected that General Grant was bullshitting him, he also realized that pressing for answers would only spotlight him as a potential troublemaker. With a resigned sigh, he waved a dismissive hand. "Alright then," he said, glancing at the General. "We'll start working on the orbital cloud data right away."

After that, the meeting segued into more routine matters. The participants worked through the remaining agenda items with the practiced efficiency of professionals eager to wrap things up. Just as the meeting was drawing to a close, reaching the "Any Other Business" section—an often-unspoken cue to prepare for departure—Han raised his hand.

Dyson, betraying a hint of exasperation, responded, "Yes, what is it?"

"I was thinking that it might be a fitting gesture for us to send a message of condolence to Moon Base Delta on the tragic death of Professor Hendrickson, and his colleagues. Many of us here at Strawstack had personal connections with him," Han suggested. Given that communications with Moon Base Delta were officially restricted to military personnel, he figured that the high-ranking officials at the table could hardly deny such a humane request without looking insensitive.

Grant exchanged a quick glance with officers Harvey and Lewinsky, and Han detected an almost imperceptible nod in response.

"Yes, that seems appropriate," Grant agreed.

"Thank you," Han said. "We'll record the message later today and forward it to the communications department."

"Very well," Dyson said, his tone shifting to brisk efficiency. "If there's nothing more to discuss, then I'll declare this meeting adjourned."

With that, everyone rose from their seats, gathered their belongings, and filed out of the boardroom.

CHAPTER 12
NEW LIFE

Professor Lars Hendrickson was dead, as were Saito Yuuta and three others from Moon Base Delta. Two had been part of Mackenzie's group that had fought their way out of DaVinci Crater. The other had come down from the Axial. Selene was taking it badly; she had become very subdued, spending most of her time alone. Kimura was also taking Saito's death hard. Renton was never sure what the relationship between these two was, but there was obviously some history there. At least Kimura had Tanaka to talk to. As for Selene, Renton wondered how to comfort her. She needed to grieve, but events were moving fast; they would need her to engage again sooner rather than later.

His opportunity came when, for the first time in almost two decades, a batch of viable plants began to germinate within

Moon Base Delta. It was an oddly euphoric moment for all its inhabitants. A special announcement from the DOA was broadcast over the communications network, informing everyone that a tray of seeds had just cracked open their protective shells and that delicate, fragile green shoots of new life had burst forth. Practically everyone in the base felt an irresistible urge to witness this minor yet deeply symbolic miracle of nature firsthand. Before long, a steady stream of people were making their way down to the mid-levels to where the agri-sector was located, all eager to see for themselves this awe-inspiring phenomenon. To many of the colonists, this felt almost akin to a pilgrimage, a journey to witness what could be considered a sacred artifact. This pilgrimage had, in essence, begun the moment each of them had first set foot inside this lifeless base. No one felt this more keenly than Renton, who was especially eager to witness this momentous occasion for himself, and he persuaded Selene to join him along with Alice.

They stepped out from the elevator that had transported them to the sprawling agricultural level. Stretching out before them was an enormous chamber, its distant edges fading away into ambient darkness. It was nearly impossible not to feel utterly dwarfed by the scale of the space they found themselves in. They followed a gently curving pathway, lit by soft overhead lamps, passing row after empty row of dusty, derelict hydroponic beds—abandoned relics from a time nearly two decades past. But now, at long last, signs of life were returning to this previously sterile and forsaken place.

Up ahead, they could see the first of the newly installed hydroponic systems, humming with activity. A sea of dazzling overhead lights bathed the area, and several industrial robots were diligently at work, meticulously cleaning and preparing the beds for future growth. Situated on the far side of this hive of activity were the bio-labs.

As Renton and Alice approached, they saw that around half of Moon Base Delta's population had already gathered, looking in amazement at the long, brilliantly illuminated tables that housed the newly sprouted seedlings. An almost tangible sense of awe and wonder hung in the air.

"Wow," Alice exclaimed as she leaned in to get a closer look at the rows of delicate green filaments emerging from their seed pods. "I never thought I'd be this excited just to see a plant grow."

Renton nodded, equally moved by the simple beauty of it. "I know what you mean," he replied. "It's been so long since I've seen a plant, I've almost forgotten what they look like."

After months of surviving on limited rations and protein cubes synthesized from some long-dormant bio-matter of dubious provenance, the sight of fresh produce kindled a renewed sense of hope and purpose among the colonists. Even the tremendous costs they had incurred and the grave risks they had undertaken to acquire these precious seed stocks seemed to fade into the background now that the first tender buds were rising up, spreading their leaves in a miraculous display of new life.

"It must be the first time in all of human history that a bunch of sprouting alfalfa seeds has drawn a crowd," said Matteo, a broad grin spreading across his face.

"Ha, yes, you're probably right about that," Renton replied

with a short laugh, glancing around at the others, who were in a jubilant mood. They were beginning to put the horrors of the disastrous prisoner exchange behind them. Even Selene seemed to be responding to this promise of the future.

Matteo put a friendly hand on Renton's shoulder and pointed across the cavernous expanse toward the newly revitalized hydroponics. "Before long, all of these beds will be overflowing with lush greenery," he said, gesturing expansively.

"How soon do you think we'll start to see more of these seeds sprouting?" Selene asked eagerly, sweeping her gaze across table after table of seed trays.

"Oh, other varieties will start sprouting in just a few more days, like these here," Matteo explained, indicating several trays of green beans. "Others will take longer. But this place will be utterly transformed in a few more weeks."

"Renton?" DOA's voice broke in over his comms. He lifted a hand to cup his ear, straining to hear the AI more clearly.

"Yes, what is it?"

"We've received a communication from the scientific team at Strawstack Mountain. It is a message of condolence for Professor Hendrickson and the others who were lost in the assault on Hangar B12. However, there's also a second, encrypted message from Dr. Han Sundar, concealed within the signal."

"What does it say?"

"I think it's best if you come to the operations room to see for yourself."

"Okay, I'll be there shortly." He ended the call and noticed that both Alice, Matteo, and Selene had also received the same message from DOA, judging by their reactions.

The message of condolence came in the form of a video, featuring a small group of people who had gathered around a stationary camera for this occasion. Dr. Han Sundar stood prominently at the center of the group, reading aloud from a carefully prepared script. This initial reading was followed by individual messages from some of the other assembled team members, each of whom wanted to personally express their thoughts and emotions. Alongside mentioning their colleague, they also included references to the additional lives tragically lost during the catastrophic attack on Hangar B12. However, Sundar seemed to avoid directly referring to the incident in explicit terms; instead, he spoke of it more as a deeply unfortunate event that had transpired. As Renton listened, he found himself wondering if Sundar and his team were even fully aware of the specific circumstances that surrounded Professor Hendrickson's death.

The atmosphere within the room shifted to one of more somber introspection as each person reflected on the tenuousness of their existence here at Moon Base Delta. Hendrickson, Saito, and two others from Mackenzie's group had died in the attack on the hangar, along with four Xilinex people. But that was just one battle; no doubt, more were to come. Who would be next?

Once everyone had been given sufficient time to reflect, DOA proceeded to outline the substance of the encrypted message embedded within. As Alice had suspected, the approaching Mars evacuation ship did indeed carry a number of individuals involved in experimental biotechnology, including the eccentric trillionaire philanthropist, Jack Stark. This revelation immediately captured everyone's attention. Sundar also revealed the possibility that the ship might be transporting a version of the doomsday bio-bank that Stark had been trying to develop—Stark's Ark. However, he was not certain of this; it was merely speculation on his part based on some minimal research he had conducted. Yet, the implications were not lost on Renton and the others. If such a bio-bank did exist, it could potentially free the lunar population from its dependence on Earth. This meant that whoever controlled this so-called vault could essentially control the Moon and, by extension, would wield considerable leverage over national governments back on Earth, all of whom were competing for limited supplies of Helium-3.

But there was more: the message went on to mention that a new supply capsule launch was being planned by Space Division. However, no information was provided as to why this was happening, its purpose, or even what these new supply capsules might contain.

CHAPTER 13
CONTACT

"DOA, what do you know about this Jack Stark guy?" Selene asked, after the encrypted message had been fully transcribed by the AI.

DOA then proceeded to offer a condensed history of this enigmatic figure, describing his life-changing epiphany deep within the remnants of the Amazon forest and his subsequent ambition to use his immense wealth for the betterment of humanity. As for the existence of this mysterious doomsday vault, DOA had little information available, other than to mention that many in the scientific community questioned the plausibility of such an ambitious project.

"I really can't see how any of this is going to help us," Mackenzie announced finally. "Even if this bio-bank thing actually exists and it's aboard that Mars ship, there's not much we can do about it. It will be offloaded by the Xilinex Corporation at the first opportunity, and no doubt the scientists will all be assigned to work in the bio-labs at Shackleton Crater."

"DOA, do you have any technical information on that ship?" Renton inquired, trying to gather as much information as possible.

"The vessel is known as a Mars Cycler," DOA responded. "It has been operational for over a decade, serving as a transport vessel for both people and goods between Earth and Mars. It features a rotating torus of over one hundred meters in diameter, which creates an artificial gravity that is approximately half that of Earth's gravitational pull. The ship has the capacity to accommodate approximately one hundred and fifty people. Its propulsion system utilizes fusion plasma technology, which gives it a transit time of approximately one hundred days when Earth and Mars are at their closest point. It's worth noting that the ship does not take a direct route; rather, it's engineered to make use of gravity assists, enabling it to orbit both Earth and Mars over a set period of time. The ship is designed specifically for interplanetary travel and is therefore not capable of landing on any celestial bodies within our solar system. However, it is equipped with two ascent/descent vehicles that facilitate the transfer of passengers and cargo to and from the Martian surface. Theoretically, these shuttles could be capable of landing on the Moon, although they are not designed to land on Earth, even if that were still possible."

"Is it possible for us to establish contact with the ship?" Alice asked.

"Yes, this is possible," DOA replied.

"For what purpose?" Selene interjected skeptically. "I mean, what exactly would we say to them?"

"Well, we could find out what their plans are," Alice proposed. "If they have the ability to land on the lunar surface, then they may simply intend to put the ship into lunar orbit and use it as their primary base of operations. Given that the ship has reasonable artificial gravity, it would provide a comfortable living environment, unless, of course, it's absolutely jammed full of people."

"I imagine they won't want to get involved in the power struggles happening here on the Moon," said Yuna.

"That's assuming they even know anything about it," Selene replied. "They might be completely unaware of what's going on or, if they have been in contact with Earth or even Xilinex, they may have a completely warped view of what's happening here."

"Their primary objective is to simply survive, same as any of us. So as long as someone can provide them with the supplies they are lacking, that will be their number one priority," Matteo reasoned.

"We should get straight to the point and ask them if this bio-bank exists and if they have it with them," Mackenzie suggested. "Because if they do have it, there's going to be a scramble to try and take control of it, and it won't really matter what the Martians want or don't want."

"If they do have it, we should invite them down here to Moon Base Delta. We have ample space, numerous bio-labs, and massive agricultural areas. They could do worse than decamp here," Kimura offered optimistically.

"Good luck with that," Chen Jun scoffed. "There's no way

they would agree to it and even if they did want to come here for whatever reason, there's no way Xilinex would allow that to happen."

"I wonder what Earth thinks about all this?" Renton mused. "Assuming they have some idea that this bio-bank might exist on that ship, then their plan to blackmail Xilinex for Helium-3 by withholding food supplies seems doomed."

"So why are they sending more supply capsules then? Why would they do that if they think their blackmail plan won't work?" Matteo asked, confused.

"Maybe it's to compensate for the loss of the last capsule Xilinex tried to exchange with us," Tanaka hypothesized.

"Alternatively, they might be shipping them weapons or some means to help Xilinex take control of this base and the last SINO enclave," Mackenzie speculated.

Selene released a long, slow sigh. "Let's face it; we're just going around in circles here, trying to navigate through the unknown here. The only thing that we know for certain is that soon, everyone's attention will pivot toward this Mars ship. And our options are very limited. Our only course of action seems to be attempting to establish communication with them. We should try to develop some sort of rapport, let them know who we are, tell them about our circumstances, and perhaps even forewarn them about the chaos they are soon entering into."

"DOA, what's your take on this?" Renton queried, seeking some wisdom from the AI in what was turning out to be a complex situation.

"There are numerous imponderables, the majority of which orbit around the existence or nonexistence of this archive of biomaterial, and the assumption that what it contains is not genetically modified to have a constrained lifespan," the AI began. "Should such a bio-archive actually exist, it could fundamentally alter the trajectory of future actions by the various entities operating both here on the Moon and also on Earth. It would appear then that the first course of action would be to verify the veracity of this research by Dr. Han Sundar. And it seems that the occupants of this ship are the only people who know the answer to this fundamental question. Therefore, it would be logical to initiate contact with them, strive to forge a degree of trust between our personnel here at Moon Base Delta and the crew of the Mars ship, and verify if this bio-bank truly exists."

"I presume we have the capability to communicate with the ship?" Matteo inquired.

"Yes," affirmed DOA, "I have detailed information concerning the ship's specifications stored in my archive, which includes the protocols necessary for communication."

"Okay then," Alice chimed in, her tone pragmatic. "So, we craft a message, and simply start by saying hello."

Her proposition elicited several nods and assorted grunts signifying agreement from the assembled group.

CHAPTER 14
MARS CYCLER

Mission Commander Michael Phillips took a leisurely sip from a bottle of recycled water, his gaze methodically scanning the multitude of monitors adorning the flight deck of the Mars Cycler spaceship. He scrutinized various readouts, assuring himself that all was well with his ship and its contingent of one-hundred-and-twenty-seven Martian evacuees. An aura of calm enveloped him, as he listened to the gentle hum of the "well oiled" vessel traversing the solar system.

Soon though, they would be navigating through the most intricate section of the journey, a phase where they would need to commence the meticulous process of decelerating the ship and maneuvering it into a stable lunar orbit. This would be challenging undertaking, as it necessitated extracting the ship from the Earth/Mars orbital cycle in which it had been continuously traveling for well over a decade. Every crew member needed to bring their A-game: all systems required thorough checking and rechecking, simulations had to be executed and scrutinized, and Commander Michael Phillips needed to ensure that everyone on board knew what to do and when to do it. There would be no room for errors.

They had been progressively slowing the ship down to a velocity conducive for a lunar injection burn. If everything went according to plan, they would loop around the Moon in a broad elliptical orbit, dissipating momentum with each pass to gradually draw them closer and align them into an optimal, near-rectilinear orbit. This approach would utilize the minimal amount of energy to maintain stability while at the same time trying to avoid collision with any of the numerous objects currently in lunar orbit.

However, Phillips was not alone in this task. Several other crew members were also stationed on the spacious flight deck, each immersed in analyzing data, ensuring that the ship was performing as anticipated. Occupying the entire expanse of the far wall of the flight deck, a colossal panoramic monitor provided them with an ultra-high-resolution, real-time feed of the space into which they were traveling—given that, relative to the engines, the ship was currently moving backward, burning hard to shed momentum.

There was no doubt, it was a magnificent ship, a shining example of exceptional engineering, and Phillips held immense pride in being its Commander. However, his singular regret was that he'd never had the opportunity to set foot on Mars, and the reality was, he probably never would.

He had departed Earth accompanied by twenty-eight

others, embarking on the four-month journey to Mars. However, just two months into their journey, the solar event occurred, creating an apocalyptic wasteland in Earth's orbit and preventing all space travel to and from the home planet. The stark realities of this catastrophe began to sink in over the following month, especially when all communications with Earth ceased, only to stutter back to life several weeks later via the ancient deep-space network.

With no more supplies possible from Earth, the colony on Mars became unsustainable. So one month before Commander Michael Phillips entered Martian space, the decision had been made to evacuate the entire planet. Yet, returning to Earth was not a viable option either. Yes, they could get back to Earth space, but they would not be able to ferry passengers from the ship back down onto the planet's surface. Their only alternative was to head for the Moon, where the infrastructure was significantly more developed and better resourced than the fledgling human settlement on Mars. Even with the vast majority of the Moon's former population now evacuated, it was still theoretically self-sustaining—at least, that was their hope. Now, the evacuees were approaching the end of their journey. In less than a week, they would settle into a lunar orbit, and then, a new and perhaps a more challenging chapter would begin: navigating through the seemingly fractious lunar political games that had erupted following their own chaotic evacuation. This was a situation that would need to be managed with utmost care and precision.

"Sir, we're receiving a request for direct communication

from the lunar surface," a bright, young communications technician announced.

"From the Xilinex Corporation again?" Phillips inquired

"No, sir. This is coming from a location in the Sea of Tranquility, known as Moon Base Delta," the tech responded.

Phillips sat bolt upright. *Could it be, he wondered.* "Are you certain?"

"Yes, sir. That's the call sign and origin," the tech confirmed.

"Route it to my station," Phillips commanded. *This could be interesting,* he thought.

An alert now flashed on his monitor, indicating a request for two-way comms. This was unusual in and of itself as they were still seven days out, and a two-way conversation would have a noticeable delay in response time. But that's not what piqued the Commander's interest; it was the fact that this request emanated from what he believed to be a defunct, and possibly derelict, moon base. He gestured at the screen to initiate the connection.

After a brief second or two of scrolling text while the two communication systems established a stable connection, a live video materialized, revealing the head and shoulders of a middle-aged woman. She began to speak.

"Hello, this is Selene Mene of Moon Base Delta, requesting a dialogue with your commander." She articulated this with an air of urgency.

Phillips did a double-take, a flicker of recognition in his eyes. *It couldn't be?* he thought, then gestured at the screen to enable a return video feed. Steadying his voice, he spoke. "This is Commander Michael Phillips." He paused for a beat, eyes locked onto the screen. "You probably don't remember me?"

There was a brief, tense pause, a few seconds of delay before his words registered with Selene. But once they did, he could see that she was desperately sifting through her memory, trying to figure out who he was, and how she knew him? Then, a glimmer of realization seemed to dawn on her, although she still wasn't quite certain. "Would you be the same Michael Phillips that interned for me back at the FISA training center in Johnson?" she responded with a hesitant inflection.

"The very same," he replied with a broad grin. "So tell me, what is a FISA director doing holed up in an old derelict Moon base?"

She seemed to visibly deflate, holding her forehead with one hand, before straightening up to give him with an answer. "It's a long story, but the quick version is, I drew the short straw. I was up on the Axial Luxor, on the FISA negotiating team for the new lunar accord, when everything went to hell. Then, our glorious leaders back on Earth decided that FISA didn't matter, and whatever future the survivors had down here on the Moon was best served by the Xilinex Corporation. I'm sure you've heard of them?" The last sentence was delivered with a distinctly sarcastic tone.

"Yes," Phillips replied with a measured cadence, "we've been introduced. We received a full, albeit potted history of the Moon since the solar storm. But I'm suspecting they may have omitted a few details."

"I don't know what you've been hearing from Earth, or what Xilinex has been feeding you, but suffice it to say, the situation here is… complex," Selene confessed, her eyes revealing a tapestry of weariness and resolve.

She then began to outline a comprehensive sociopolitical overview of the present lunar landscape, including the current situation with the genetically modified food supplies from Earth.

Under ordinary circumstances, Phillips might have harbored doubts regarding the veracity of this snapshot of the situation on the Moon, but he knew Selene Mene personally and by reputation, and they were both cut from the same cloth. This was, after all, a FISA ship in essence. It originated from the same program that constructed Moon Base Delta, representing the last triumphant project of FISA at the zenith of its power and influence. And now, it seemed, if Selene Mene was to be believed, the agency had turned on its own.

"That's quite a story, Selene," he finally said, his voice carrying a mixture of admiration and disbelief. "Food for thought, if you'll pardon the pun."

Undeterred, Selene continued, "We've heard… a rumor. One that says you might be carrying with you a kind of doomsday vault, a bio-bank, one developed by an eccentric trillionaire know as Jack Stark."

Phillips let out a laugh, his shoulders bobbing gently. "You know, you're the third person who's asked me about Jack Stark and his so-called Ark. First, it was Space Division down in Vandenberg, and then this Chancellor Adarok guy, and now you. But to answer your question, yes, we do have this bio-bank, as you call it. Having said that, nobody knows for certain what actually in it, only Stark himself, and he's been notoriously tight-lipped about its contents."

Selene paused for a moment, before asking the obvious question, "And where's this Jack Stark guy now?"

"He's a passenger on the ship," Phillips replied, with a hint of frustration, "but we've not been able to talk with him for the last two months as he has locked himself away to meditate, apparently. No one knows when he plans to reemerge." Phillips gave a resigned shrug. "I presume you know about his eccentric tendencies?"

Selene nodded. "Yes, we've heard. Regardless, it's still a relief to learn of the existence of this bio-bank. As I explained, our food situation here is all genetically modified to have a limited lifespan, so we're all reliant on Earth to get supplies. If this bio-bank is anything like they say it is, then it could be a real game changer."

"I understand. Although Earth seems to be very proactive regarding supply capsules. They even offered to send one to us, to rendezvous with our ship."

Selene seemed to freeze at the mention of this, so-much-so that he began to wonder if the connection had been lost.

"Did you communicate to them that you were short of supplies?" she finally asked.

"No, they just offered. We're okay here for the moment, but we're not going to refuse any help that's sent to us."

Selene leaned slightly forward, her gaze firm, her voice slow and measured "Listen to me, Michael. You need to tread very, very carefully. Remember the Xilinex Corporation will want control over this bio-bank, regardless of Stark's protests. If they do, then Earth has no hold over them. Forgive me for sounding paranoid, but are you really sure what Earth is sending you is a supply capsule?"

"Of course it is. I mean, what else could it be?"

"Remember what we used to say back at the training center in Johnson?" she countered. "No one ever died from an overabundance of caution. If I were you, I would treat that capsule with extreme caution until you are absolutely satisfied that it's safe."

He considered this for a moment. He didn't know Selene Mene that well, but enough to value her judgment, no matter how outlandish it seemed. He shifted in his seat, he was beginning to feel uncomfortable.

He nodded, "Appreciate the warning. I will take it under advisement."

CHAPTER 15
LIKE A WHISPER

R enton lay flat on his back, hands interlaced behind his head, peering directly upward through the transparent, domed roof located on the uppermost level of Moon Base Delta. High above him, the immense, boundless expanse of the universe unfolded in all its starry majesty.

After agreeing to establish contact with the Mars ship, it was decided that Selene would be the most suitable individual to instigate this crucial dialogue. After all, she was a seasoned diplomat with a wealth of extensive negotiation skills, particularly adept in employing a softly-softly approach rather than aggressively going in hard and issuing demands. She had retreated to a quiet, secluded corner to do some essential preparatory work before establishing a communications link. Also, she wanted to handle this alone, without the added weight or pressure of an attentive audience. Nobody disagreed with this strategy; in fact, it appeared to be an ultimately logical and highly pragmatic course of action.

Yet, this situation did get Renton thinking about just how nonconfrontational all their collective decisions seemed to be. He vividly recalled his time back on the FISA maintenance ship, the Aurora, where even in that environment, amongst a highly trained and specialized engineering team, the decision-making process was far more confrontational. It was often fraught with heated arguments—generally instigated by Captain Mackenzie. But now, here in the confines of Moon Base Delta, even she appeared to show a certain level of respect for the broader consensus.

However, he was beginning to formulate some ideas as to what might be causing this unusually harmonious phenomenon.

He cast a glance around the expansive observation area. When he first arrived here, the place was an absolute mess, having languished in a state of disuse and abandonment for over two decades. Back then, he had entertained the thought that it would be an overwhelmingly positive step for everyone involved if this dilapidated place could somehow be cleaned up and made functional again, especially given its awe-inspiring views. And somehow, over the ensuing period, this transformation miraculously happened. Yet he couldn't quite remember who took the initiative to instigate this massive job, or having discussed it with anyone in any meaningful sense, or even having suggested that a team should be organized to get it done. It had simply, yet remarkably, just happened.

"Do you know who cleaned up this place?" he asked Alice, who was lying alongside him.

"Jeff Bodega, I think," said Alice. "He organized a bunch of people a while back. Why do you ask?"

"I don't know. It just seems like things happen around here. Things that need to be done seem to get done without any kind of direction or central authority planning out what we need to do."

"It's just people being people. Everybody has to chip in, keep busy, do whatever they can."

"Yeah, but I can't help but get the feeling that the AI here is nudging people in directions it thinks would benefit us."

"Are you saying DOA is manipulating us?" She did not hide her sarcasm in saying this.

Renton thought about this for a moment. "Yeah," he finally said, "in a way, it is. Not overtly. It doesn't come straight out and make a demand like 'you should do this' or 'you should do that.' It's more subtle—more like a whisper."

Alice laughed. "Oh, Renton, you're letting your imagination run away with you. DOA wasn't the one who instigated a weapons development program, or decided how the defense of the base should be organized, or even that we should go ahead with the exchange with Xilinex."

Again, Renton considered this. The disastrous exchange at the hangar had been a traumatic event for all concerned. Yet, now that the food production facilities were coming online and the threat of an imminent Xilinex assault on the base had partly receded, there was a palpable air of calm among the colonists. Everywhere he looked, people seemed to be busy, all embarking on some work that needed to be done. Yet somehow, nobody had made any broad plan or was giving direction in this. This troubled him, not simply because he sensed the AI's hand in it, but that it may have a plan for him too. And if so, what was it?

All conversations he'd had with DOA concerning this all pointed in the direction of using his talents in strategic planning—not something that Renton had ever considered himself very good at. Yet as his conversations with the AI deepened, it became evident that in many ways, he had been training himself for this very task from a young age. Back then, he loved nothing more than to spend his time in his aunt's garage, building something useful, even beautiful, from the scraps that lay around. It taught him to dispose of nothing and instead to see every item as a useful component in some greater future project.

As he looked around now at the sociopolitical landscape of Luna, with its multitude of complex and interrelated components, his mind was always focused on how he could reassemble them into something that would secure their collective future. Yet every time he asked the AI for a way forward, a path to achieve this goal, it simply replied that there was insufficient data to evaluate an optimal route forward.

He heard the sound of footsteps, accompanied by familiar voices. He looked around to see Matteo and Yuna approaching, both with excited faces. *Maybe there's some good news from the Mars ship*, he thought.

"Hey, there you are!" Matteo exclaimed as he sat down on the bench opposite him. He was carrying a large bag that seemed heavy, judging by the way he placed it on the ground between them.

"We've been looking for you everywhere," said Yuna. "DOA said you would be up here, looking at the stars."

"Yeah, we've been coming up here a lot since they cleaned the place up," Alice replied, now sitting with her legs crossed on the bench.

Matteo reached into the bag and pulled out two stainless steel flasks, slightly larger than mugs. He handed one to Renton and one to Alice. "Here, try this. Tell me what you think," he said, his face expectant.

Renton hefted the flask; it felt heavy, full of liquid.

"Go on, try it," Yuna encouraged.

He unscrewed the lid and heard a familiar hiss of gas escaping. Peering in, he saw a frothy amber liquid that smelled familiar. He took a sip and instantly recognized it. He looked over at Matteo, the shock clearly registering on his face.

"Yes, it's exactly what you think it is," said Matteo, a huge grin on his face.

Renton lifted the flask to his lips again and took another sip. It was beer, no question about it, and probably the nicest he'd ever tasted. He took another sip, followed by a few gulps, which culminated in a satisfied belch.

Matteo and Yuna were laughing hysterically, waving their hands around like two excited kids who had just played an epic trick on their parents.

"Can you believe it?" said Matteo. "I managed to manufacture some beer from one of the bioreactors."

"This is incredible," Alice exclaimed, wiping her mouth with her sleeve. "How did you do this?"

Matteo gave a dismissive gesture. "Ah, it seems all that time I spent obsessing about the bioreactor has finally paid off. It's amazing what you can do with a fresh stock of biomatter to feed it. It also helps that DOA significantly updated its knowledge base once it was connected with the LunaSat constellation. It now knows everything about bioreactors. Anyway, I was chatting with it, asking about things that could be made or manufactured with the right ingredients. Turns out, our old friend beer is just one of those products. Who would have thought?"

"Well, this is great," Renton said, taking another swig. "I thought it would be a very long time before I could sit and have a beer with some friends." He raised his flask and smiled.

By now, Matteo and Yuna had also cracked open a few flasks and raised theirs in salute. "Here's to the future," said Matteo.

"The future," they all chorused and took a sip.

"How much of this did you produce?" Alice asked, examining the flask.

"Oh, just a small batch, enough to test," said Matteo. "But we do have some fast-growing grains, so it's possible we could produce quite a lot." He glanced over at Yuna in a manner that suggested they were sharing a secret known only to them.

"Eh, we're thinking of having a party," Matteo finally announced. "I reckon we can brew up enough in the next couple of days to have a bit of a shindig."

"Yeah, it would be good," added Yuna. "A way for everybody to shake off the doom and gloom of the past few months."

"That's a great idea," agreed Alice, taking another swig of her beer.

"Actually, it was partly DOA's idea," said Matteo. "Or at least the AI suggested it."

"Interesting," said Renton, raising an eyebrow. "It's nice of DOA to always be thinking about our well-being."

"What do you mean?" asked Yuna, confused by his response.

"Oh, don't mind him," Alice laughed. "He's convinced that the AI is inside everybody's head, manipulating us to do its bidding."

"That's not what I said, Alice." Renton shook his head, sounding a bit exasperated. "It's just that it seems to know what we should be doing and when we should be doing it. And before you know it, someone or some group starts getting it done."

"Maybe it's in the water," teased Yuna, who was beginning to show signs of inebriation, judging by the amount of hand-waving she was doing.

"I don't know," Matteo shrugged. "Considering all the different groups of people we have here, we all seem to get along pretty well. And now that we have a secure food source, things are getting better."

"Yeah, I agree," said Renton. "And don't get me wrong, I'm not saying it's a bad thing. Clearly, the base is functioning well at the moment, so we can't really complain. It's just that everyone seems to accept it."

Alice leaned over and put a hand on his shoulder, giving him a gentle shake. "Hey, you need to lighten up. A party will be good, even better now that we all know the AI will be helping to organize it." She laughed.

Renton smiled, realizing the joke was on him. He hefted the flask again in salute to the upcoming party and took another swig.

CHAPTER 16
NEXT STEPS

Preparations for the upcoming party were well underway. Absolutely everyone in the lunar base appeared to be embracing this communal celebration with enthusiasm, all except for Renton, who found it exceedingly difficult to share in the pervading atmosphere of optimism. Yes, they had successfully secured vital seed-stock and biomass from the recently acquired capsule—which had come at considerable cost. However, Renton was all too keenly aware that this brief reprieve wouldn't last. It was really only a matter of time before the harsh reality of their long-term situation began to overshadow this fleeting, ephemeral moment of optimism.

Then there was the earlier conversation between Selene and the commander of the Mars ship, Phillips, which, as luck would have it, revealed a shared history. This gave Moon Base Delta an unexpected but welcome ally on board the spacecraft.

Better yet, it was also confirmed that the enigmatic Jack Stark was also on board, and in possession of the mysterious bio-bank.

Many people in the base were now firmly convinced that Stark and the crew of the Mars ship would inevitably come to their aid, that salvation was practically at hand—further fueling the optimism that was surrounding the upcoming party. Renton, however, cautioned that the most likely outcome was that the Mars ship would end up being commandeered by Xilinex forces and that they'd all be back to square one. Added to this complex situation was the rather strange decision by Earth to send up another supply capsule, not for Xilinex to pick up, but specifically for the crew of the Mars ship. This development had spooked Selene, and very possibly even the Commander of the vessel as well.

Yet, the more he thought about all these various interconnected parts, the clearer the overarching dilemma became in his mind: there simply would be no sustainable future for them as long as the Xilinex Corporation maintained its oppressive stranglehold on the majority of the Moon's vital resources. The corporation was exceedingly powerful, extraordinarily well-resourced, and utterly committed to establishing complete and total control over the entire lunar environment.

While most of the base was occupied with party preparations, Renton found himself in the main workshop, inspecting the ongoing progress of their weapons development program. His focus was particularly on the new railgun, a substantial piece of engineering that Matteo and another colleague from Mackenzie's team were developing. Designed to rapidly disassemble anyone or anything that came within its range, the railgun could obliterate a ground-based rover or a shuttle transport in mere seconds. Although they had a limited stock of the short metal spikes used as ammunition, three more sets were now in production. As a fire-once weapon, careful consideration would be needed before deploying it.

As Matteo enthusiastically explained the capabilities of the railgun to Renton, they were interrupted by a message from DOA: it had just received a new, urgent communication alert originating from the Mars evacuation ship. They dropped everything and immediately headed to the operations room.

Selene and Mackenzie were already there, with many others arriving along with Renton and Matteo. This time, Selene wouldn't be communicating alone; most of the base's leadership would be in attendance.

"If you are all ready, I will initiate communications with the Mars ship," DOA announced.

A rectangular portion of the wall-mounted monitor flickered to life, unveiling the head and shoulders of Commander Michael Phillips. He looked uneasy, frequently adjusting his position in his chair.

"We, eh... decided to take your advice, Selene, and

approached the Earth supply capsule with extreme caution. We kept ourselves at a respectable distance and dispatched a surveillance drone for a closer inspection. However, as the drone approached within close proximity of the capsule, a detonation occurred, obliterating both the capsule and our drone. This led to a widespread debris cloud, necessitating that we reposition our ship onto a safer vector. Needless to say, this incident has deeply shaken everyone on board, forcing us to reevaluate our existing safety protocols," Phillips elaborated.

There was stunned silence in the operations room as everyone digested this sudden turn of events.

"It's as I feared," said Selene. "Their likely intention was to destroy the bio-bank, ensuring that it does not fall into the hands of the Xilinex Corporation. If that meant obliterating the ship and all its passengers, well... collateral damage."

"I just can't believe it," Phillips replied, clearly shaken by the event. "There must be some other explanation. Space Division or FISA could not possibly contemplate such a heinous crime."

"The world has changed," Selene responded, her voice filled with matter-of-fact gravitas. "People are now in a desperate fight for survival, compelled to take whatever measures are necessary. The bio-bank you're transporting poses a very real existential threat to Earth. If it truly is a repository of biologically unmodified food stock, then Earth could lose its grip over Xilinex and their megalomaniac leader, Pompodur Adarok. Should that come to pass, Adarok would gain unchallenged control over Earth's primary energy source. There's little reason to believe that he would hesitate to cut off all Helium-3 supplies and simply revel in the ensuing global chaos. Some people just want to sit back and watch the world burn, and Adarok is potentially one of them."

The camera lens abruptly zoomed out, revealing a broader perspective of the ship's impressive flight deck. Sitting next to the commander was a fit, middle-aged individual sporting a shaved head and striking blue eyes. Gathered around behind them were several other high-ranking officers and crew members.

"This is Mr. Stark," Commander Phillips announced, extending his arm to indicate the enigmatic figure seated beside him.

"They never wanted me to embark on this project," Stark began, gesticulating wildly as he spoke. "Those short-sighted, greedy fools back on Earth viewed my work as a challenge to their stranglehold over the global food supply. I resisted their attempts to thwart me back then, and I won't bow down to their intimidation now. In their willful ignorance, they fail to recognize that this is the most crucial endeavor ever undertaken by humanity—surpassing even our advancements in fusion technology, our colonization of the solar system, and even our efforts to digitize all human knowledge," he continued, hardly able to stay in his seat as he vented his pent-up anger and frustration. "This project stands for the preservation of our biological heritage. These myopic individuals don't seem to grasp that Earth may very well be the sole planet in the universe that harbors life. My singular mission is to ensure its preservation. I won't let them dismantle my life's work." Having expended his energy on his impassioned rant, he slumped back into his seat, appearing visibly drained.

"That's an admirable and, dare I say, noble commitment, Mr. Stark," Selene responded, her voice steady and composed. Renton admired how she could maintain such a calm tone of voice while subtly praising this guy's ego at the same time. He could see why she had been chosen to lead the FISA negotiating team. He wondered if she'd ever tried playing poker.

"I once contemplated acquiring Moon Base Delta," Stark resumed, leaning toward the camera, his voice tinged with a nostalgic undertone as if he were momentarily lost in recollection. "That was in the early days when I first launched this project."

Selene remained unflappable, as usual. "Oh? That's something I wasn't previously aware of."

"To my mind, it was the optimal location, especially since it was home to one of the most sophisticated AI systems in the known universe," Stark said, suddenly leaning further forward to lock eyes with the camera, his eyes widening in urgency. "Does that AI still exist? Was it brought back online when you took possession of the base?"

"Yes, and we did reactivate it. The running of this base is highly dependent on that AI; without it, the entire facility would be virtually inoperable," Selene confirmed.

A flash of excitement lit up Stark's eyes. "Excellent, truly excellent!" He cast a brief, meaningful glance at Commander Phillips before refocusing intently on the camera. "Given Earth's evident betrayal and Xilinex Corporation's plans to weaponize my life's work for their own gain, I've resolved to relocate to Moon Base Delta. With the aid of your advanced AI, I could potentially achieve groundbreaking discoveries that have long eluded both myself and my research team."

Stark's abrupt announcement sent a ripple of murmured shock throughout the operations room. Selene, however, swiftly raised her hand to restore order and silence the room.

"That's certainly fantastic news, Mr. Stark. However, there are some significant obstacles you ought to be cognizant of. As it stands, we're currently under a blockade enforced by Xilinex. They're preventing any access to the base. Penetrating their blockade would be virtually impossible. And even if you were somehow able to do so, rest assured that Xilinex would mobilize all of their resources to assault this base and confiscate your life's work," Selene warned him cautiously.

"Let's be clear," Commander Phillips interjected before Stark had a chance to reply. "The safety and security of our crew and passengers are our primary concern. We will not be taking any reckless decisions that could endanger lives." This was obviously a pointed message to Stark to cool it. He sat slumped in his seat, fuming.

"Anyway," Phillips continued, "it would seem that decisions are being made for us. We've just received word that Xilinex is dispatching a group of high-ranking officials to dock with our ship. They are expected within the next few hours. While their stated purpose is to act as a welcoming committee, we are acutely aware of their ultimate intentions. However, we must base our next steps on ensuring the safety and security of our crew and passengers." He paused for a moment. "That being said, Mr. Stark is the legal owner of this bio-bank, so it's only right he has a say in its future use."

This seemed to buoy Stark's spirits a bit, as he nodded appreciatively.

"Much as we appreciate the vote of confidence you've expressed in our community here at Moon Base Delta, Mr. Stark," Selene responded, "our hands are tied, especially now that Xilinex is en route. There's simply no way that we can secure safe passage for you or your team, even though we desperately want to."

Renton raised his hand to chime in. "Uh, there may be a way to achieve your goal, Mr. Stark."

All eyes turned to Renton.

Stark became instantly animated again, his eyes darting between the camera and Commander Phillips, and then to the ship's crew behind him, with a mix of frantic energy and hope. "Finally, someone with a backbone!" he shouted, jabbing a finger at the camera. He turned to Phillips. "Someone who won't simply surrender!" He then refocused his attention on the camera. "So, what's the plan?"

"Did you say a Xilinex shuttle is due in a few hours?" Renton inquired.

"Yes," Phillips confirmed, a little reluctantly.

Renton was now beginning to feel the weight of the stares from others in the operations room. "Uh, we'll need some time to discuss it here and work out the details," Renton said cautiously. "We'll contact you again as soon as possible."

"Very well," Commander Phillips responded. "But regardless of Mr. Stark's personal wishes, my primary responsibility is the safety and security of our crew and passengers. All our decisions will be based on that." He cast another pointed look at Stark.

"Understood," Renton acknowledged.

The connection terminated.

CHAPTER 17
WHAT IF

"You're free to go," Renton declared, jerking a finger toward two EVA suits that were in the process of being carried into the communal canteen and meticulously laid out on a table.

The two Xilinex mercenaries, both shuttle pilots, and both survivors of a brutal attack on the hangar, momentarily paused their eating. They looked up from their food, took in the sight of the EVA suits, and then shifted their gaze back to Renton. Their faces wore an unmistakable look of suspicion.

"Just like that?" inquired Parker, the more outspoken of the two mercenaries.

"Just like that," confirmed Mackenzie, who was seated next to Renton. She was joined by Matteo and Selene. "You're free to walk out of the airlock and join your comrades blockading the base."

The mercenaries hesitated, exchanging glances.

GERALD M. KILBY

"Unless, of course, you'd like to stay," Renton continued, his voice imbued with a hint of intrigue. "You could live and work here with us."

"And you'd still have the freedom to leave whenever you desire," Selene interjected, adding another layer to the offer.

Both men were silent, but the contemplative expressions on their faces didn't escape Renton. Of all the Xilinex captives they had interrogated, their in-house system, DOA, had marked these two as harboring clear doubts—which was probably what saved them in the hanger attack. They had been hanging back, clearly not relishing their imminent return to Xilinex. According to DOA's comprehensive psychological evaluation, both men were questioning whether their decision to fight for Xilinex as lunar mercenaries had been among the wisest life choices they had ever made.

Now that their own faction had deemed their lives expendable and attempted to kill them, they were particularly susceptible to a change of allegiance. For Renton's audacious plan to commandeer the bio-bank located on the Mars-bound ship, the willing cooperation of these two men would be absolutely critical.

"Why would we want to do that?" asked Parker, a little unconvincingly.

"Look," Mackenzie leaned in. "We know you guys are a little pissed-off with your former bosses not valuing your contributions to their quest for lunar domination. Remember, big brother here has been reading your minds," she jerked a thumb at the ceiling, "so we know you might be open to a change of scenery. You're mercenaries, after all; you're in this for what you can get."

Parker pushed his plate aside and took a breath. "Maybe. So what's in it for us?"

But before anyone could answer, his buddy Ash spoke up. "I'm not going back to them, no way."

This surprised Parker, who gave him a hard look as if to say to keep his mouth shut, but there was no stopping him.

"Those bastards lied to us, said we'd be here for two years, knowing it was a one-way ticket to Palookaville. Then they try to kill us. No, I'm not going back. I'll stay here, thank you very much." Ash sat back, folding his arms.

Parker looked at him, then back at Renton and the others, and threw his hands up in the air. "Okay, screw them. I only ever signed up for the money, and a fat lot of good that is now."

Renton smiled, reached a hand across the table, "Welcome to the neighborhood."

It was in the midst of the dialogue with the Mars evacuation vessel that a grand, encompassing scheme began to coalesce in Renton's mind. He had glimpsed elements of it before, but they were like fragmented shards, scattered and disconnected. However, as he listened to Stark articulate his own plans, Renton came to the startling realization that he had been thinking on a far too limited scale all this time. He had been framing their challenges as daily, mundane obstacles rather than viewing them as stepping stones leading toward something vastly more significant.

Stark's brilliance lay in his ability to see the overarching narrative, the big picture. Each move he made was meticulously calibrated to advance this grand strategy. While many had dismissed him as unstable, volatile, and even chaotic, nobody was laughing anymore—especially not when the future well-being of the lunar population was now so intricately tied to his bio-bank. Stark was on the cusp of realizing one aspect of his grand vision that he probably never dreamed would actually come to fruition: the pivotal moment when the fruits of his years-long planning would become indispensable.

After the communications link with the Mars evacuation ship was terminated, Renton laid out his revised strategy to the rest of the crew. They would resurrect Yuna and Mackenzie's earlier plan of scavenging, but with a critical modification. Instead of aimlessly scouring antiquated, abandoned outposts for mere scraps, they would set a course for an intercept point with the Mars vessel.

They would employ the Xilinex shuttle they had commandeered during the initial battle for the base, don the Xilinex EVA suits they had collected, and, with the assistance of the two former Xilinex mercenaries on their side, attempt to masquerade as a bona fide Xilinex crew as they neared the Mars ship. DOA would employ its capabilities to scramble Xilinex communications, as best it could, using the LunaSat constellation. This maneuver, Renton hoped, should effectively conceal their location from the centralized Xilinex command structure. It was an audacious plan, one that some might even label as reckless.

"So what's our move once we get there?" Mackenzie

inquired, her voice tinged with skepticism. Renton sensed that even she was hesitant, if not somewhat unnerved, by the sheer audacity of the venture he was outlining.

"Straightforward: we neutralize any Xilinex personnel aboard that ship. Then we transport Stark and his bio-bank back to Moon Base Delta—and anyone else who wants to join us. And all this needs to be executed before Xilinex HQ begins populating the skies with intercept shuttles aimed directly at us," he explained.

"That's an exceedingly narrow window of opportunity," Chan Jun observed.

"True, it is a tight timeframe," Renton conceded, "but I think we still possess some degree of flexibility. I'm not convinced that Xilinex would jeopardize the bio-bank. I don't think they'll try and destroy us. If they do that, they'll find themselves back at square one, grappling with the same challenges they face with Earth." Renton's eyes scanned the faces of those gathered around the holo-table in the operations room. All were silent, each pondering the individual components of this crazy plan. Yet, he sensed that they were still struggling to see the grand strategy in its entirety.

"How can we be certain that these Xilinex mercenaries won't betray us at a crucial moment?" Matteo asked, clearly not convinced at their sudden desire to switch sides.

"They had the option to walk away before any of this plan was laid before them," said Renton. "Had they wanted to leave, they could have done so freely, but they decided to stay and align themselves with our cause. Granted, there's always the remote possibility that they might seize an unexpected opportunity for glory by sabotaging our mission to gain favor with Wagner and Adarok. However, it's a calculated risk that I believe is worth taking."

"And what if Stark has a change of heart?" cautioned Kimura.

"What if! What if!" Renton exclaimed, throwing his hands up in the air in a gesture of exasperation. "What if we sit idly by and do nothing? The answer is clear: we'll all eventually starve to death." Renton inhaled deeply, taking a brief moment to regain his composure. "Look, the way I see it, a wildcard has suddenly emerged on the astro-political chessboard. Nobody anticipated this because they were all preoccupied with screwing each other over. This bio-bank, however, is the linchpin to the future of this little lunar world we're all confined to, and whoever controls it wields immense power. Stark has expressed a desire to bring it here; he's presenting us with an invaluable opportunity, not only to secure our own future but also to tip the balance of power decidedly in our favor. Should we get there and he reverses his decision, then too bad—we simply take the bio-bank by force." He paused momentarily, allowing the gravity of his words to sink in. "Look, we've been living hand-to-mouth, surviving by scavenging for scraps. We all recognize that this is unsustainable in the long run. So if we harbor any hopes of surviving beyond the immediate future—say, the next six months—then we must seize this chance now. Otherwise, we're as good as dead."

"Fine words, Renton," said Mackenzie. "But let's not forget that the last grand plan you orchestrated resulted in four of our team in the morgue and another seven with injuries."

"Yet here we are," Renton emphasized, gesturing toward Matteo and Yuna, "actively organizing a celebration to commemorate our recently acquired windfall." He rose to his feet and leaned purposefully over the holo-table, using both hands on its edge for support. "The harsh reality is, people are going to die. That's an inescapable fact in our situation. If we choose to do nothing, then it's highly probable that we'll all die from starvation. Personally, I'd much prefer to go down swinging than to wither away in some desolate corner during my last days." He scanned the faces of the assembled group. They were beginning to understand, starting to grasp not just what needed to be done, but also how it could be accomplished.

Yet what remained conspicuously absent from their discussions was the contingency for what would transpire if they actually succeeded in pulling this off. Sure, they'd celebrate like crazy, throwing a wild party, but Xilinex would not let this affront go unanswered. They'd marshal every resource at their disposal, and then some, and unleash it in a full-scale assault on Moon Base Delta. It would be a hell of a fight, and Renton had to admit that he wasn't entirely confident in their odds of emerging victorious. However, a tentative strategy was slowly crystallizing in the back of his mind for that specific scenario. He would not divulge it at this point, he was pretty sure that the team would not endorse it under the current circumstances. Instead, he would bide his time, waiting for the opportune moment to spring it on them.

CHAPTER 18
ASHES OF THE OLD

Pompodur Rossen Adarok sat at the head of the holo-table in the cluttered war room, situated on board the Xilinex HQ orbital. He had just finished admonishing General Wagner for his unmitigated failure to effectively neutralize the leadership of Moon Base Delta during the exchange. Informing him, in no uncertain terms, that what should have been a significant tactical advantage turned out to be yet another bungled effort. True, they had successfully reclaimed some of their captured personnel and had not suffered significant losses in bio-stock—the destroyed canisters had, fortunately, been empty—but the bottom line was that they had been tactically outmaneuvered and humiliated once again.

This state of affairs simply could not stand; a substantial corrective action would need to be undertaken. However, for the time being, General Wagner advocated for a more patient strategy, contending that their current resources were insufficient for a full-scale, successful assault on Moon Base Delta, or indeed, the last remaining SINO stronghold. He suggested that they should continue to maintain their focus on enforcing both blockades, which he believed would, in due course, produce the desired outcomes.

It was true that even with the additional supplies that Moon Base Delta had succeeded in procuring, they couldn't sustain them indefinitely. The base would eventually succumb, much like the various smaller groups who had been making a last stand at both Shackleton and Amundsen Craters. To underscore the validity of his approach, the General cited the recent surrender of a small band of agricultural workers. This group had sought refuge in a facility located in the northwest quadrant of Shackleton Crater, naively hoping their food stockpile would sustain them. It had not, and they had all capitulated to the General's forces a mere two days prior. Needless to say, these rebellious individuals were swiftly eliminated, serving as a cautionary example to any who dared defy the authority of Xilinex.

In the final analysis, Chancellor Adarok found himself reluctantly agreeing that the pragmatic approach advocated by the General held merit. Given that their forces were already thinly spread, tasked with maintaining order and enforcing blockades across multiple lunar population centers, amassing an adequate strike force posed a significant challenge. And yes, if the blockades remained effective over time, there could be only one outcome: victory for Xilinex. Ultimately, Pompodur decided not to dwell on this particular point of disagreement with the General, even though he would have personally favored a more rapid resolution.

A far more pressing issue had unexpectedly emerged—the imminent arrival of a Mars evacuation ship into lunar orbit. They had been aware for some time that this ship was en route, and it was soon speculated by the Xilinex Corporation on Earth that the vessel would most likely be transporting some very knowledgeable genetic scientists. This gave rise to the possibility of reverse-engineering the current genetically modified stock being supplied by Earth—a prospect that excited Pompadour no end. However, they further speculated on the existence of a 'doomsday vault', created by the eccentric tech trillionaire, Jack Stark. Yet, it wasn't until they had established direct communication with the vessel that they verified it was, in fact, carrying this fabled doomsday vault—a so-called bio-bank of non-GM, biologically viable food stock.

This was a game-changing revelation for Adarok. In one fell swoop, he now had a solution to the seeming intractable problem of Earth-bound dependency. Xilinex had already invested a considerable amount of time, resources, and effort into establishing a bioengineering division within Shackleton Crater. This specialized unit was assigned the mission of reverse-engineering the genetically modified food crops that had arrived in recent supply capsules. Achieving this would position him in an extraordinarily powerful strategic stance. However, progress had been frustratingly slow; the main obstacle was that they lacked the personnel who possessed the essential skills and expertise required for this complex undertaking. And then, as if guided by fate, a solution just flew into his lap.

Already, a high-ranking Xilinex team had successfully rendezvoused with the Mars ship and was presently engaged in negotiating the transfer of this resource to Shackleton Crater. Wagner had advocated sending a mercenary force with the mission to completely take over the ship. However, Pompadour overruled him, believing this could be achieved through simple diplomacy and negotiation; there was no need to send in the troops. He had been proven right, as arrangements were already in progress.

As for Pompodur himself, he was already preparing to depart from the HQ orbital and board a shuttle destined for the bio-labs in Shackleton. His intent was to personally ensure that the team stationed below was fully prepared to spring into action once the bio-bank arrived.

Yet, even with all this seeming good fortune now coming his way, what had truly unsettled him, however, was Earth's audacious attempt to destroy the Mars ship. They had evidently realized the monumental threat that the presence of this bio-bank posed for their grand plan and, rather than negotiating in good faith, had opted to annihilate it. This was an unforeseen development, another variable he had not anticipated. Certainly, Earth had a strangle hold on both him and the Xilinex corporation, but he had never expected them to resort to such drastic, aggressive tactics. How had he been so blindsided? How had he failed to anticipate this move, despite his longstanding belief in his ability to foresee the maneuvers of his adversaries? What other unforeseen actions might be lurking on the long grass, waiting to catch him off guard?

He shook off these fears and instead focused on the fact that soon, perhaps less than a few months, he would occupy the position he had always coveted: unassailable control over all lunar resources, which would in turn grant him near godlike power over the Earth itself. He would make them rue their recklessness in trying to obliterate the Mars ship. He would tighten the noose, deny them access to Helium-3—the essential fuel that powered their fusion energy society—and make it abundantly clear that their plight was entirely of their own making. Had they cooperated, they would have found themselves in a far more favorable situation. But when their energy infrastructure began to crumble, they would have no one to blame but themselves. He would ruin Earth and take immense satisfaction from watching the slow, inexorable decline of human civilization. Meanwhile, a new, grander, and far superior society would arise on the Moon. And who's to say that this fledgling civilization wouldn't eventually expand out further? Now that he possessed an interplanetary vessel, the Mars Cycler that would soon be here. He envisioned a magnificent, high-tech civilization that would sprawl across the solar system, built upon the ashes of the old world.

CHAPTER 19

OPTIONS

"Why do I have to be the one to go?" asked Selene, shaking her head in disbelief.

"Because your reputation precedes you," Renton answered firmly. "They already know who you are, and the Commander trusts you. They don't know me, nor any of the rest of us for that matter. Once we get up there, we'll be on a very tight schedule. We can't afford to squander precious minutes trying to establish trust. That's why it has to be you."

Selene emitted an exasperated sigh, finally relenting. "Alright, but you'd better be absolutely right about this crazy plan of yours," she said, eyeing the bulky Xilinex EVA suit with a large measure of suspicion.

They had all convened in the expansive hangar where the commandeered Xilinex shuttle was undergoing final checks in preparation for its impending launch. Yuna was in the cockpit accompanied by the two former captives—they had grown to trust them a little more, as both seemed hell bent on exacting some form of retribution from their former employers. Being ex-pilots of this specific craft, it meant they had an intimate understanding of the machine's operation.

Yuna was tasked with piloting the shuttle out of the hangar and, if all went according to plan, safely away from the base and into lunar space. From that point on, the ex-captives, Parker and Ash, would assume control for the approach to the Mars ship. Mackenzie, Chen Jun, and two other members of her crew would provide the necessary muscle. Renton would also contribute in this aspect, albeit in a more limited capacity.

Then there was Selene, whose presence on this mission was crucial for confirming their identity. Given that they would be arriving unannounced and posing as a Xilinex force, it was imperative that once they did gain access to the Mars ship, and their true identities revealed, there would be no doubt that they were indeed from Moon Base Delta and not Xilinex. The most efficient route to achieving this would be to bring Selene. Her presence could also prove invaluable in any negotiations with Jack Stark. If their earlier communications over the comms system were any indication, Stark could very well turn out to be a challenging personality to deal with.

Mackenzie, of course, had wanted more fighters, but the shuttle had its limitations—it could only accommodate approximately twenty people, and the precise mass of the bio-bank they needed to transport remained unclear. Also, Commander Phillips had provided information indicating that the Xilinex group arriving on the ship was intended as a diplomatic delegation, not a military show of force. So they were not expecting too much resistance.

As Renton boarded the shuttle, he began running through in his mind all the various actions that needed to come together to make it possible for them to embark on this mission. First, and foremost, was creating a distraction. This involved direct military action against the cohort of blockading forces located closest to the hanger entrance. Hopefully, this would draw in the mercenaries stationed along this sector. Once these were engaged, the hangar doors would open, allowing Yuna to maneuver the craft onto the lunar surface and then lift-off into lunar space.

The most recent Xilinex supply shuttle had departed and was scheduled to land at its home base around now, providing them with this window of opportunity to lift-off and not be chased down—at least, not for a while. The third crucial element was avoiding detection by the Xilinex HQ orbital. They were counting on a short communications gap when Xilinex's primary data satellite moved behind the lunar horizon, effectively preventing the orbital from accurately tracking their flight trajectory. All these moving pieces were now falling neatly into place. It was time to put the plan into action.

A maintenance airlock on the eastern side of Moon Base Delta opened, and two weaponized maintenance droids shot out, racing across the lunar surface toward the main contingent of Xilinex forces closest to the shuttle hangar. They ducked and dived, weaving across the terrain, attempting to avoid enemy targeting systems.

"Everybody, buckle up. This is going to get rough!" Yuna exclaimed from the cockpit.

The hangar doors began to creak open, and as two more weaponized maintenance droids powered up their engines, lifted off from the hangar floor, and went speeding through the widening gap. Moments later, they joined the fray, engaging the Xilinex forces who were already occupied with the first wave of weaponized maintenance droids.

Inside the shuttle, Renton could feel the craft powering up and beginning to taxi out onto the concourse. Hopefully, the Xilinex forces would be fixated on the incoming drone onslaught, and too preoccupied to deal with the shuttle.

Once the shuttle had cleared the hangar entrance, Yuna increased power to the main engines. The shuttle started to ascend, slowly at first, but as more power was directed to the engines, it accelerated, its nose pointing skyward, away from Moon Base Delta. Renton felt himself pressed back into his seat as the shuttle surged into the lunar night. He opened the comms channel back to the operations room at Moon Base Delta. "How are we looking? Anything giving chase?" he asked.

They held a momentary advantage through the LunaSat constellation, allowing them to track almost everything on the lunar surface. Meanwhile, Xilinex HQ would remain in complete darkness until their comms satellite moved out from behind the lunar horizon.

"Nothing so far," replied Matteo. "Looks like you got away clean, and Alice is recalling the maintenance droids. It seems that none of them took a direct hit, which is a lot better than I thought we would do."

"That's good to hear," said Renton, sounding relieved. "Make sure they're ready to fly again once we're on the return trip."

"Will do," came the reply from Matteo.

It required a full forty minutes for the Mars ship to come into view through the front windshield of the shuttle. A truly awe-inspiring sight, with its elongated central truss adorned by a colossal rotating torus at one end and a cluster of formidable plasma engines at the aft. Several more minutes elapsed before the ship established contact with them, inquiring about identity and intentions.

"Alright, game on," Renton addressed the two former captives, who had now assumed control of the shuttle. "It's time for you guys to earn your keep."

They promptly opened a channel, transmitting that they were a support vessel for the current Xilinex delegation, acting under the direct authority of Chancellor Adarok. They also requested docking procedures. There was a discernible pause in the response, no doubt discussions were taking place on board the Mars ship. When the communication finally crackled back to life, it was a Xilinex operative this time, evidently perplexed by this unanticipated addition to the party, and seeking clarification.

Parker, one of the former Xilinex captives, then unleashed an expletive-laden response, interspersed with operational terminology that only those familiar with the Xilinex military could comprehend. A lexicon that could only have originated from someone deeply embedded within the organization. Moments later, the requested docking protocols were received.

Everyone on board breathed a sigh of relief. So far, so good.

As they approached, the docking ports came into view. Six in all, three either side of the central axis of the massive rotating torus. The three forward docking ports were all occupied, one held the previous Xilinex shuttle that had delivered the high-ranking diplomatic team, the other two ports accommodated the ship's own shuttles. The three ports aft of the central axis were all vacant; this was where they were instructed to dock.

Mackenzie entered the cockpit to observe the docking procedure and pointed out the Xilinex craft. "Once we dock, our priority is to secure that shuttle and make sure we take control of it. We need to ensure there's nobody on board that can send a message to Xilinex HQ or some other base."

Yuna maneuvered the ship into position over the free docking port with deft handling of the reaction thrusters. Once it came within capture distance, automatic systems took over, extending grab arms that pulled the shuttle onto the mount. Finally, locking bolts thumped into position, and the airlock began to equalize pressure.

They all lined up behind the airlock door, waiting for the all-clear alert to illuminate and begin entering the ship. Mackenzie was at the front, followed by Chen Jun and the rest of her crew. Renton and Selene took up the rear. Yuna, Parker, and Ash remained in their seats in the cockpit, just in case things went south and they had to leave in a hurry.

The airlock control panel pinged the all-clear, and a green illuminated strip lit up. Mackenzie swung open the inner door and floated through the short distance to the outer ship door, which she quickly opened once her team had gathered behind. They were met by two Xilinex guards and one crew member from the Mars ship. Before any of them had time to blink, the two guards were relieved of their weapons. Chen Jun and Brett Roux, another of their team, were already making a beeline for the Xilinex shuttle on the far side of the central axis.

Renton deftly exited the airlock, maneuvering through the microgravity environment and over to the bewildered Martian crew member. He lifted his visor and placed a finger to his lips, signaling for silence. "How many other Xilinex personnel are aboard?" he whispered.

Still shocked from the unexpected intrusion, the crew member took a moment to gather his wits. "Eh... who are you?"

"From Moon Base Delta," Renton explained reassuringly. "We're here to help. Now, how many others are on this ship, and where can we find them?"

By now, Selene had floated up behind Renton, her visor also open to reveal her face. "Do you recognize me?" she asked. "Selene Mene... from Moon Base Delta."

Recognition suddenly flickered across the crew member's face. "Uh... there are three more of them, high-ranking," he divulged. "They're on the flight deck."

"Okay," Renton nodded. "You're going to take us there. Try

to act casual, like we're just another group of Xilinex minions, understood?"

"Yes, sure. We can take the elevator here. It'll bring us close to the flight deck."

Chen Jun and Brett had returned from securing the Xilinex shuttle. "All clear," Chen Jun reported. "No one at home."

"Excellent," Mackenzie acknowledged. "That's good."

By now, the two Xilinex guards had been securely trussed up. Mackenzie gestured toward them. "Brett, take these guys and stash them aboard their shuttle. And make absolutely sure they can't escape."

"Understood," Brett replied, turning his attention to the immobilized guards.

"And stay with them until we return," Mackenzie ordered.

"Got it."

The rest of the group headed for the elevator.

This transitioned them from zero gee on the central truss to the half-gee environment of the torus. Renton could feel the centripetal force building up and began to realize that, because they had spent so much time in weak lunar gravity, they could not spend too long here as they would quickly become exhausted. It was another problem they would have to solve going forward. Too much time spent on the lunar surface would be debilitating, but it was not a problem to solve today; that would be for some other time. All they needed to do now was get in and get out as quickly as possible.

The elevator opened onto a wide corridor with several

people milling about. They looked over at them as they exited, curious about this new group of Xilinex interlopers. Yet, nobody interacted with them; mostly, they just moved aside as they passed.

The flight deck was wide and spacious, with a central bridge area and two operations areas on either side. Everybody on the flight deck stopped what they were doing when Renton's team entered.

"That's them over there," their escort pointed over at a wide table where several people were sitting, deep in discussions.

Mackenzie and Chen Jun raced over and leveled weapons at the Xilinex people.

Selene raised a hand. "It's okay, we're not Xilinex. We're from Moon Base Delta." She removed her helmet.

"Selene Mene? What the..." Commander Phillips stood up, looking at Selene as if she'd just been teleported onto the bridge.

"Yes, it's me. And we're here to give you some options," she continued.

"Well, thank god for that." Jack Stark stood up from the table.

"Hold up," Mackenzie shouted. "There's only two. You said there were three?" She directed her question to the crew member that had brought them up here.

"Uh, yes, but..."

"Where's the other one?" Chan Jun shoved the muzzle of his plasma weapon into the ribs of one of the Xilinex people.

"I think he said he was going to check on the new shuttle crew," said Stark.

GERALD M. KILBY

"Well, we didn't see him on the way up here," said Renton.

"He could have taken the other elevator; we've got two," offered Phillips.

"Chen Jun, go take someone with you and find him, quick. Before he starts making trouble," Mackenzie said as she moved over to the table and started shouting at the two Xilinex people. "You two, flat on the floor, hands behind your heads."

"This is an outrage, you'll not get away with this," one of them protested, before Mackenzie kicked his knees out, and he collapsed on the floor.

"What the hell are you doing up here?" Phillips gestured at them with both hands.

"Like I said, we're giving you options." Selene then turned to Stark. "You said you wanted to bring the bio-bank to Moon Base Delta, so, here we are, now's your chance."

"Wait a minute," Phillips interrupted. "I thought you were blockaded."

"We are," Selene replied, "but we're not helpless, as you can see." She swept a hand around.

"We don't have much time," Renton cautioned. "We need to go now."

Stark didn't speak for a moment; he seemed to be weighing up his options.

"I'll need my people, my team," he said, looking over at them a little uncertain.

"How many?" asked Renton.

"Seven. But they might not all want to go," he replied.

"And the bio-bank?"

"It's contained within four storage vaults stored in a cargo

148

hold just aft of the secondary docking ports, close to where your shuttle is located."

"Will it all fit in our ship?" asked Renton.

"Yes, should do. It's not that big. I'll talk to my team and see who wants to join me, and we'll start getting them loaded."

"You're not seriously going to do this?" Phillips stepped forward between them, a hand raised to Stark. "Just think about what you're doing."

"Did they get to you too?" Selene interrupted, not giving Stark a chance to answer. "Did Space Force down in Vandenberg tell you that you had to row in with Xilinex, with that madman Adarok? Have you forgotten that this is a FISA ship, that you are FISA crew? Are you just going to give in when you know what's at stake here? Goddamn it, Michael, they even tried to blow up your ship."

Commander Phillips glanced around at his crew and could sense the mood building on the flight deck. He sucked in a breath and gave a slow nod. "Okay, I take your point." He snapped around to his crew and pointed at the two Xilinex people on the ground. "Get them tied up and put them somewhere secure. The rest of you, help getting those vaults moved." He looked over at Stark, then back to Selene. "I hope to hell you guys know what you're doing."

CHAPTER 20
RETURN TRIP

They entered the elevator and were on their way toward the cargo bay located in the central truss section of the Mars ship when Chen Jun's voice broke through on comms. In the background, Renton could hear what sounded like weapons fire.

"Trouble," said Chen Jun, his voice breathless. "We found that third Xilinex guy. Only problem is, he found the two other Xilinex mercs that Brett was supposed to be guarding and now both are out, pinning us down in the docking tunnel."

"Where's Brett?" Mackenzie responded.

"No sign of him," said Chen Jun.

"Crap, we're on our way, just hold tight."

"I knew we should've brought more fighters," said Mackenzie, casting a glance at Renton. "No matter." She gave a sigh. "We'll deal with this. You go start loading that bio-bank into the shuttle; we'll keep this situation contained in the forward docking tunnel until you get everything on board."

Renton nodded, "Okay, got it." He looked over at Stark, whose face was now etched with uncertainty. Perhaps he was having second thoughts about this move over to team Delta.

"Where is this bio-bank stored?" Renton asked.

"It's just aft of the torus, past the secondary docking ports."

"Okay," said Renton, "let's get this done."

As the elevator doors slid open, the discordant sounds of a firefight echoed from somewhere off to the left. Immediately, Mackenzie and the other fighters began making their way down the tunnel toward the source of the conflict. At the same time, Renton, Stark, and a handful of his team, who had opted to join him, made their way in the opposite direction. They moved toward the secondary docking ports where the shuttle was stationed and then continued further on to the main cargo hold of the Mars ship. Renton decided to leave Stark and the others to manage the cargo loading, while he quickly ducked through the airlock, entering the shuttle.

"What's happening out there?" Yuna asked, her voice tinged with anxiety.

"Trouble," Renton succinctly replied. "You better start powering up the ship. I've got a feeling we'll need to make a fast departure."

Exiting the shuttle again, he ducked back out and surveyed the length of the docking tunnel that led toward the central axis of the ship's torus. Beyond that junction, near the primary docking ports, an intense firefight had erupted between the Xilinex mercenaries and Mackenzie's squad. While he couldn't visually discern the actual battle from his vantage point on this side of the axis, he could hear the urgent shouts through his comms unit. Bright bursts of plasma fire lit up the tunnel, their flashes reflecting off the metallic inner walls.

Turning away, Renton began to make his way back toward the main cargo hold. Where he encountered several of Stark's team floating in his direction. They were maneuvering a bulky storage container with a sleek, high-tech design. On one side of the container was a biometric scanner interface, and adjacent to that was a rugged digital screen displaying an assortment of cryptic data. He quickly directed them toward the shuttle airlock. "This way, this way," he shouted, waving his hand vigorously as he urged them to move faster. A second group appeared in the tunnel, maneuvering another one of the bio-vaults. They were closely followed by a third group, and then Stark himself finally emerged, taking up the rear.

Inside the main cabin of the shuttle, Selene, Parker, and Ash were frantically engaged in organizing storage, trying to squeeze everything in. There weren't going to be enough seats to accommodate everyone, and while this was not an immediate issue in the zero-gravity environment of space, it would become a problem once the shuttle's engines powered up. The occupants would be tossed around like rag-dolls, depending on how aggressively Yuna planned to exit the docking port. So they all concentrated on making sure that every container and each person was securely strapped down.

"Mackenzie?" Renton voiced into his comms unit. "It's time

to fall back; we're all set and ready to go." Reaching into a cargo pocket on the right leg of his EVA suit, he pulled out his plasma weapon and began to float down the tunnel toward the ongoing battle. As he drew closer, he could see that a heated firefight was in full swing. He spotted Mackenzie and the others taking cover behind a series of elongated, vertical, structural beams that spanned the length of the corridor. The Xilinex mercenaries had also taken similar cover, situated about twenty meters further down. He slid into a position beside Mackenzie. "We've got to go now; the shuttle is fully packed and ready to rock."

Mackenzie laid down a few more shots into the battle before ducking back behind cover. "It's gonna be a bit tricky; we'll have to work out a fighting retreat. These bastards don't seem to go down too easily. Also, we couldn't find Brett; looks like we've no option but to leave him behind."

She began shouting orders, and one by one, they started to retreat back down the tunnel, using the support beams for cover. As they retreated, the Xilinex fighters advanced, never giving them a chance to disengage from the firefight. They reached the central axis point of the rotating torus. This area was much more expansive and devoid of any useful cover. They would need to get across it fast, as they would be very exposed during the transition.

"Renton!" Mackenzie called over to him. "We're going to lay down some covering fire, and when we do, you get yourself across that gap as fast as you can. Don't wait for us; just go. And signal to me when you're behind cover."

Renton got a firm grip on one of the handles on the side

wall, then placed his foot on another handheld, ready to push himself off with as much force as he could muster. A barrage of plasma fire filled the tunnel as Renton set off, sailing through the wide-open central axis area, straight into the corridor on the other side. He reached out and grabbed the handhold, pulling himself in behind a support beam.

"Okay!" he shouted. "Behind cover."

A moment later, another barrage of plasma fire was followed by Chen Jun entering the corridor and finding cover. Then the others followed, leaving only Mackenzie on the far side of the central axis.

"When you're ready," Renton called back to Mackenzie, "we'll lay down some fire, and you can get out of there."

"No way," came the reply, "I won't be able to make the distance."

"Sure you can," said Chen Jun. "That exoskeleton of yours can push you off the wall at light speed."

"Yeah," said Mackenzie, "but somebody's going to have to hold these guys off so the shuttle can get away."

"No way!" said Renton, "We're not leaving you behind; you don't have to do this."

"Oh, but I do," said Mackenzie as she laid down another barrage of plasma fire. "You better get going. I don't know how long I can hold these guys off, and I'm running low on weapon charge."

Renton was about to protest, but Mackenzie cut him off. "And don't try to argue with me," she said, "just get your asses on that shuttle. Now go, go!"

Chen Jun tapped Renton on the shoulder. "Come on, let's go. You know there's no point in arguing with her."

As the others started moving down the tunnel, Renton reluctantly followed. He was the last into the airlock but hesitated before closing it, taking one last look back in vain hope that Mackenzie might have found a way out. But the tunnel was empty, save for the sound of the firefight and the flashes of light bouncing off the walls. He swung the door closed, moved through the short airlock into the shuttle, and swung the inner door shut.

Renton looked around at the sea of anxious, expectant faces, then pushed his way through to the cockpit.

"Where's Mackenzie?" Yuna swiveled her head around in the seat, anxiously looking for their former captain.

"She isn't coming; she's buying us some time. So you need to get us out of here now."

"But..."

"Just go, go. There's nothing we can do. It was her choice."

Yuna hesitated for a beat, then settled back into the pilot seat and entered the commands to disengage the shuttle from the docking port.

They drifted out from the Mars ship for a few seconds under reaction thrusters before Yuna began powering up the main engines and vectoring the craft for Moon Base Delta.

CHAPTER 21
HIGH STAKES

A subdued silence enveloped everyone on board the shuttle as it steadily powered its way through the expanse of lunar space, heading for the Sea of Tranquility and, ultimately, Moon Base Delta. Peering through the cockpit window, Renton was struck by the beauty of the Moon's silvery glow.

For the majority of his life, he had admired it from the safety and security of Earth's surface. There, he had often found himself looking up into the nighttime sky, filled with wonder about what thrilling adventures could await him if he followed in his aunt's intrepid footsteps. He fantasized about joining the Federation of International Space Agencies, FISA, and venturing into the great unknown of space. This small boy's dream gradually solidified into a young man's goal. Now, that same dream had morphed into a living, breathing nightmare. The Moon, once a symbol of adventure and possibility, had devolved into a harrowing realm of chaos, death, and untold misery. The romantic allure that once captivated his youthful imagination was now utterly shattered, replaced by the harsh, unforgiving reality of survival of the fittest, of dog-eat-dog. Base human nature, in all its brutality, was being played out on a celestial stage.

Yet Renton knew he was not just a bystander or a mere pawn in this increasingly dangerous and complex game. As the situation had continued to develop, marked by a myriad of tactical moves and counter-moves, he and everyone else stationed at Moon Base Delta had now risen to the level of key players. They had come into possession of something so vital that could potentially tip the balance of power in their favor and secure a safer, more stable future for every human being residing on the Moon. But even with this newfound advantage, their position remained tenuous, even precarious. The first, and arguably the most daunting, obstacle they faced was the task of safely making it back to Moon Base Delta in one piece. And that, given the current situation, was far from guaranteed.

The comms abruptly crackled to life, jolting everyone in the cockpit; it was DOA's voice. "Two shuttles have lifted off from a base in Lubbock Crater and are on a trajectory that will intercept you very close to Moon Base Delta."

"Xilinex?" Renton quickly asked, apprehension in his voice.

"Yes. I can't provide the exact onboard inventory at the moment, but both shuttles are equipped with exterior-mounted plasma cannons," DOA added.

"Damn it," Yuna muttered under her breath. "We're too late. Those fighters back on the Mars ship must've somehow managed to establish contact with Xilinex HQ."

"Just keep it steady and maintain our current course. We're not out of options yet," Renton assured her, attempting to instill some sense of confidence.

Yuna gave him a skeptical look, clearly not entirely convinced.

"Matteo, Alice?" Renton urgently called over the comm system.

"We are aware of the situation," Alice replied immediately. "It's not looking good; they'll arrive before you get here. We're just in the process of getting of the weaponized maintenance drones ready to engage them."

"Oaky," said Renton. Just make sure that the hangar door is wide open and ready for our arrival,"

Selene floated into the cockpit. "Trouble coming our way?"

"Xilinex HQ has been alerted somehow; they're dispatching two shuttles, presumably intending to intercept us before we manage to land," Yuna said, her voice edged with tension.

Selene took a moment to process this, then cautiously asked. "They wouldn't actually shoot at us and risk damaging the bio-bank, would they?"

"We'll soon find out," Renton replied, pointing at the navigation display that now highlighted the fast-approaching shuttles.

Outside, visible through the cockpit window, the silhouette of Moon Base Delta began to emerge on the horizon. Yuna was piloting them in low, so close that the pockmarked lunar surface seemed to race by just beneath them.

"There, look!" Yuna pointed excitedly.

Two metallic, silvery objects could be seen streaking across the sky to the East from the direction of the base. The drones closed the gap to the approaching Xilinex shuttles, ducking and weaving as they initiated a campaign to harass the oncoming craft. In response, the shuttles seemed to momentarily slow down, noticeably altering their vector to focus on neutralizing the attack drones.

For a brief, fleeting moment, Renton felt a glimmer of hope. If these drones could effectively keep Xilinex busy for enough time, then they might just have a chance of landing their own shuttle without needing to directly engage. However, this hope was abruptly shattered when a burst of plasma fire scored a direct hit. One of the drones disintegrated instantly, turning into a rapidly expanding cloud of metallic dust. A few seconds later, the second drone met a similar fate. With the immediate threat of the drones now effectively dealt with, the Xilinex shuttles resumed their primary intercept mission.

"We've lost both drones," Alice's voice broke in, interrupting the silence that hung over the cockpit. "We've two more drones deployed, currently covering the blockading forces on the ground; we're in the process of redirecting them your way. Try stay out of trouble until they can arrive."

"Wait," said Renton firmly, "There's no point in sending more drones. Xilinex will just tear those to shreds as well, just like they did with the last pair."

"We have to take some sort of action; they're almost on top of you," Alice exclaimed.

"I have another idea. DOA, is it possible for you to initiate a comms connection directly through to the Xilinex HQ orbital?"

"Yes, I can certainly facilitate that specific request," DOA responded.

"What! Are you out of your mind? Are you actually planning to surrender to them?" Selene shouted incredulously.

"No, I'm not contemplating surrender. I'm just... negotiating," Renton clarified.

Selene took a moment considering this crazy strategy. "Then maybe I should be the one doing the talking."

Renton raised a hand. "Not a good idea. We're connecting directly to their HQ, which means there's a high likelihood that Pompodur Adarok is also there. And let's be brutally honest here, the man absolutely hates you with a passion. You engaging in conversation might just provoke him, escalating the situation. We need to keep this rational, and I come with considerably less baggage."

"Connection successfully established," DOA announced.

Taking a breath to compose himself, Renton glanced over at Selene and Yuna for a moment. Both women looked back at him, their expressions tinged with a mix of concern and disbelief, as if they were witnessing the last desperate gambit of a drowning man.

"This is Renton Hicks, aboard the shuttle that's on course for Moon Base Delta," he started, briefly pausing to gather his thoughts. "Also on board are Jack Stark, his research team, and the entirety of the bio-bank that they have developed. I assume I don't need to emphasize how invaluable that cargo is. Losing it would spell nothing short of a total catastrophe for the future viability of the lunar population. And any hope you might have of breaking free from Earth's extortion will die along with it, leaving you forever a slave to Earth's demands." He paused a second time, casting a quick glance over at Selene and Yuna, both of whom now seemed to grasp his intent.

"Chancellor Adarok." He ventured a guess that the Chancellor would be listening in. "I know that living under Earth's thumb is not the outcome you desire, so let's not jeopardize our mutual interests. Order your people to stand down and refrain from attacking this shuttle. We're on our final approach for landing. Make certain that we make it down intact, or we all stand to pay an exorbitantly high price." With that, he closed the comms link.

By now, they were just a few short minutes away from the base. The two Xilinex shuttles had strategically positioned themselves to be directly in their flight path, creating a high-stakes game of chicken.

"So, what's the next move? What do we do now?" Yuna queried.

"Hold steady; bring it in to land as if nothing is amiss," Renton answered, promptly opening a comms link to the base. "Matteo, can you confirm that the hangar door is fully open?"

"It's open as wide as it can possibly go. We're all standing by, ready to slam the doors shut the instant you manage to taxi inside."

"Okay, let's all keep our fingers crossed for a smooth landing," Renton said, feeling a rising apprehension building up in the cockpit.

For the next agonizing minute, Renton was consumed by the thought that it might very well be his last. The two Xilinex shuttles maintained their positions as their own shuttle hurtled toward them.

CHAPTER 22
DECISIVE ACTION

"How would you like us to proceed, Sir?" inquired Clara Dixon, the individual selected to head up the agricultural sector within Shackleton Crater. She had spent the better part of an hour giving Chancellor Adarok an in-depth tour of the expansive facilities. More importantly, she had been detailing the meticulous preparations that her team had been undertaking for the anticipated arrival of the mysterious bio-bank, as well as the enigmatic Jack Stark and his scientific team. Her own team had been assigned the urgent task of initiating the cultivation of this new, genetically unaltered seed stock at the earliest possible opportunity.

Yet, it appeared that there were now some... complications. Pompodur's tour was abruptly interrupted by a high-priority alert coming from HQ about an incident that had just transpired on board the Mars evacuation vessel. As soon as he received this news, Pompodur promptly excused himself, retreating to a private area accompanied by a handful of his closest aides. There, he initiated a secure comms channel with General Wagner—who was stationed on board the Xilinex HQ orbital—and was stunned by what he heard.

Those arrogant little bastards at Moon Base Delta had actually instigated a raid on the Mars ship. Not only that, but they were now en route back to their base with Stark and the bio-bank. Pompodur seethed. They had humiliated him again. He should have listened to Wagner, who advocated sending a squad of mercenaries to take over the Mars ship. But no, Pompodur, for once, wanted to play nice. Instead he sent a diplomatic delegation—two high-ranking officials along with a few guards. Had he listened to the General, then maybe things would have been different.

As it stood now, both Anton Levrosky and Victor Dupont, along with all guards, were now incarcerated by the crew on the Mars ship, who had seemingly decided to take a stand after some shootout or other. Apparently, the crew of ship, seeing that their vessel was being slowly shot-up by Xilinex and the last remnants of the Moon Base Delta rearguard, decided to take action. They broke open the armory, distributed weapons to trained crew, and put a stop to the chaos. The warring factions were disarmed and incarcerated, along with Levrosky and Dupont.

Pompodur had no intention of bartering for their release, even if Wagner wanted his people back. The last time he'd agreed to that, it didn't work out so well. He would not be doing that again. As for the bio-bank, it was now in the hands of those bastards from Moon Base Delta.

What Pompodur desperately wanted now was for the General to utilize every weapon available to them and blow that Delta shuttle into smithereens, then pulverize those smithereens into atoms. He wanted to vaporize them into nothing more than the background hum of space. This was more than just a reckless heist; this was an affront, yet another that he could not let stand. It needed to be crushed without prejudice.

But as he listened to the comms message from that smug little shit, Renton Hicks, he hesitated. If they were to destroy that shuttle and everyone in it, then the consequences of such action could be catastrophic for Pompodur's vision of complete, unhindered lunar control.

He glanced up at Clara Dixon, who was still hovering over him, waiting for a reply. "Go away, far away. Get the hell out of here. I never want to see you again."

Dixon stepped back in fright. "Oh, eh... yes, sir, of course, right away." She beat a hasty exit.

"No, no, not you, General. Just some annoying minion," he explained over the comms channel that was still open, relaying everything to his location. "Options, General, I want options. Can we disable that shuttle with a low-intensity plasma blast and board it?"

"Theoretically, yes. However, I've been reliably informed that the specialized vaults containing the bio-bank are also providing critical environmental control to the sensitive biological matter within. Any sudden disruption to their dedicated power source could immediately render the contents unviable," the General elaborated.

It was precisely at that very moment that Pompodur came to the realization that he had just been checkmated.

"What's your decision, Chancellor?" General Wagner prompted, deftly shifting the weight of the responsibility for any consequential actions squarely onto Pompodur's shoulders.

Rubbing a weary hand across his forehead, Pompodur struggled to master the intense surge of anger that was rapidly welling up within him. He understood the critical need to regain control of his emotions, so as not to let the boiling rage cloud his judgment. Carefully weighing the risks of causing potentially irreversible damage to the bio-bank—arguably the singular asset that could provide him with the means to realize his ultimate objectives—he came to the reluctant conclusion that the gamble was simply too much to take. Faced with this dilemma, he chose the lesser of two evils. Reluctantly, he backed down.

"Let them proceed," he finally said, in a low, defeated, voice.

"Sorry, what was that, Chancellor,' Wagner replied. "I didn't quite hear you."

"LET THEM LAND!" he shouted into the comm. "Allow them through, unhindered," he added, slumping back in his seat as he listened to Wagner issuing the orders for the two intercepting shuttles to abort their mission and stand down.

Pompodur then directed his attention to one of his nearby aides. "Prepare my ship; we're heading back to the HQ, immediately."

"Yes, sir," the aide promptly acknowledged, springing up and scurrying off to execute his master's bidding.

· · ·

While he waited, Pompodur tried to take stock of this new, unforeseen situation. How could this have happened? How was it even conceivable for such a hodgepodge, eclectic collection of people—comprising groups as diverse as those currently residing within Moon Base Delta—to so comprehensively outplay and outmaneuver him? Throughout his extensive career, he had amassed a considerable amount of experience and skills in dealing with various rebel factions, especially in the early formative days of his rise within the Xilinex Corporation. Yet, these individuals were operating on a level that seemed to defy what was generally possible by the known laws of human society. They were alarmingly cohesive, surprisingly opportunistic, and exceedingly strategic in their actions. They had already managed to successfully fend off multiple attempts to bring them to heel. But this latest development was different, a new variable in the equation; now they were becoming increasingly bold, conspicuously stepping up their game. They were no longer content to merely sit back in a defensive posture, merely attempting to survive under a blockade. Now, they were proactively taking decisive action.

Then, like a bolt of lightning, it dawned on him. It was the AI that was orchestrating this unified effort. Under normal circumstances, such a diverse amalgamation of groups would be bickering, undercutting, and backstabbing each other, particularly as resources grew scarce and tensions mounted. But this collection of rebels was different; they were being shaped and molded into a cohesive, unified group by that artificial intelligence. Turning into a formidable force that had exhibited capabilities far beyond what anyone would reasonably expect of them. His glaring oversight had been in not factoring their AI into the equation from the start. This was the secret weapon providing them with the strategic edge.

And now, control over the bio-bank had elusively slipped through his fingers. The insurrectionists within Moon Base Delta would undoubtedly move quickly to initiate food production, undermining the effectiveness of the Xilinex blockade. Yet, the more he thought over the situation, the more he arrived at the conclusion that it didn't necessarily alter the fundamental dynamics; it merely postponed the inevitable outcome. There was now only one transparently clear option remaining, one he should have emphatically pursued much earlier—a large-scale, full-blown, no-holes-barred, military assault aimed directly at Moon Base Delta. There would be no more tiptoeing around the periphery with small, elite assault teams, or setting up blockades, or attempting Trojan Horse–like subterfuge. Every conceivable military asset that Xilinex had at its disposal would now be marshaled and directed toward the complete subjugation of the rebellious base.

The current occupants would all pay dearly for this affront to his power and ambition. No one would be spared, save for Stark and his team—they were vital for their collective future. If they rebels didn't die in the battle then he would make sure the survivors would die slow deaths in a Xilinex prison by... he thought about this for a moment... forced starvation? There was a delightful irony to this. It was poetic justice. The price they would all pay for their arrogance.

CHAPTER 23
WOOLLY MAMMOTH

The tense silence permeating the cockpit of the Delta shuttle was abruptly broken by DOA's voice breaking through over comms. "I am detecting the weapons systems on both Xilinex craft powering down. Their engines have also engaged and are moving away."

"Look," Yuna said, pointing ahead at the two craft. They were adjusting their altitude, rising higher into the lunar sky, effectively clearing a path for landing.

"Alright," Renton said, exhaling as his face broke into a cautious smile. "Take us in."

He had taken a bet on rationality, and his calculated risk had paid off. The potential loss of the bio-bank was simply too high a price for Adarok to pay.

The shuttle executed a sweeping turn and came in at a low angle over the Moon's rocky surface, zeroing in on the navigation lights for the open hangar. Yuna pulled the craft into a hovering position over the landing pad and set it down in one fluid movement. Before the shuttle even had a chance to settle onto the pad, she was already maneuvering it into the protective enclosure of the open hangar. The Xilinex forces made no attempt to halt their progress. Even so, Renton couldn't shake the feeling that this might only be a Pyrrhic victory. Yes, they had successfully retrieved the bio-bank, along with Stark and his team, but the looming question remained: For how long could they realistically hope to safeguard it?

As soon as the shuttle was safely ensconced inside, and the hangar repressurized, Jack Stark stepped out, seemingly unconcerned by just how close they had come to total annihilation—unlike his team, who were ready to kiss the ground when they disembarked.

He instantly sprang into action, wanting to get to the bio-lab, establish what resources were available, how to interface with DOA, and generally shouting instructions to his still-traumatized team to unload the bio-vaults and check for cryogenic integrity. All this was happening as many of the colonists were now rushing into the hangar. Renton spied Alice and Matteo as they came in. He raised a hand and waved as they approached.

"That was one hell of a stunt you pulled," Alice said as she threw her arms around him in a tight embrace.

As they pulled apart, he gave her a boyish grin. "It wasn't as crazy as you think. DOA ran the numbers, and worked out the probability of Pompodur risking the bio-bank. Granted, it wasn't a non-zero figure, so there was always a chance that he might pull the trigger."

Matteo began distributing comms units to Stark and all the newcomers as it was easier to just let them talk to DOA rather than constantly asking questions and wandering about getting lost. Stark seemed to take to his new comms unit instantly. He paced around the hangar, one hand over his ear, engrossed in conversation with the AI. At times, he grew increasingly animated, gesticulating wildly with his other hand and occasionally slapping his forehead at some revelation that DOA was imparting.

It took some time to get organized, but a few hours later, Renton and several others found themselves gathered around a series of high-tech crates that constituted Jack Stark's bio-bank. They had relocated to the one semi-functioning bio-lab within Moon Base Delta, only a small section of which was currently in use. Most of the equipment in the lab was beyond the comprehension of the amateur horticulturalists who were working there—growing food and managing the bioreactors. However, Stark's team was already inspecting the equipment, taking notes, and conferring with each other. Their faces alternated between approval and disapproval as they examined each item.

"It's not what I had imagined," said Matteo, looking over the crates now resting on a long lab bench. "I thought it would be much bigger, like one of those old vaults they have in the Arctic."

"Yeah," Alice agreed, "it doesn't look like these could hold much, considering they're supposed to contain the entirety of life on Earth."

These slightly derogatory comments caught Jack Stark's attention. Clearly, he didn't appreciate his creation being belittled.

"That's because it doesn't," he stated, pointing at the crates, "contain the entirety of all life on Earth. Creating such a collection of viable biological samples would be an infinite task. Just like painting the Brooklyn Bridge: by the time you're done, you'd have to start again because new life would have evolved."

"Seriously?" Kimura asked.

Stark looked at her, then threw his head back and laughed. "No, of course not. I wasn't being literal. I'm just emphasizing the enormity of the task. In reality, it's not necessary to have viable samples of everything. All that's needed is a biologically viable root stock from which many other evolutionary variants can be created, including those that are now deemed extinct. So, you see, it's more than just the sum of all life on Earth. It's the sum of all life that has ever been, and ever could be."

Stark delivered this last line with relish, as if pitching to a room full of venture capitalists. Then his expression shifted, becoming more grounded. "But that's just a dream. It's what I set out to achieve. What you see before you is only the beginning of the journey. We have a long way to go."

"But... we can grow food from this," Alice asked, a little hesitantly, "food that isn't genetically engineered to die after just one season?"

"Of course," Stark replied, sounding almost insulted. "The very starting point for any bio-bank is the preservation of our food supply. Flora is much easier to work with than the more complex biology of fauna. So that was our starting point." He moved over to a specific crate and patted the lid. "This contains the biological root stock, along with the genomic database, to create approximately eighty percent of Earth's human-edible plant life."

"Wow," Matteo exclaimed. "That's incredible. How is that even possible?"

"Evolution," Stark announced. "All life on Earth is derived from a single common ancestor, known as the Last Universal Common Ancestor, LUCA. Theoretically, given that source, one could recreate all life that currently exists, and even life that could exist in the future. Wheat varieties, for example, are simply versions of the same plant with slightly different DNA. They may have been created through natural selection or through cross-pollination or other horticultural techniques. But now we have more sophisticated methods. In here, we have several biologically viable samples of early grasses, from which we can create almost an infinite number of grain varieties." There was a stunned silence among the group of colonists who had gathered around, listening to Stark explain the deep magic of his bio-bank.

"So what about animals, then?" Alice prompted.

"Oh, that's a much more difficult process, several orders of magnitude more complicated, one we've been laboring over for many years trying to perfect. We've made some headway, but there's a lot more to do." Stark was almost apologetic.

"Essentially, it's the same process as for flora: having a biologically viable root stock coupled with a DNA database of all derivative species," he continued. "But the challenge is that DNA is just a blueprint; it's the expression of those genes within the genome that defines the physical characteristics of a cell, and by extension, a multicellular organism. For example, a skin cell is very different from a brain cell, even though both have the same DNA. So, managing gene expression is the tricky part." He then gestured at his comms unit. "But I'm confident we can make some breakthroughs with DOA's help."

He then moved on to another crate, running his hand along its edge. "This one contains biological samples of many of Earth's mammal species, all cryogenically frozen and waiting to be revived—either as their original species or as any number of variants, depending on which DNA sample we choose to implement. For instance, in here we have the DNA of the common African elephant, but we also have DNA from the ancient, long-extinct woolly mammoth. We could, in theory, create a living woolly mammoth herd to roam around this moon base." This drew laughter from the colonists, more of whom had gathered around to listen to Stark's fascinating explanation.

"Of course," he said with a smile, "it might be better to start with something smaller, something we could eat. And we don't need to create the actual animal for that purpose. We can simply create the bio-matter, and the bioreactors here can produce a very tasty protein supply in any flavor you could imagine—including woolly mammoth."

He suddenly raised a hand. "But enough of this idle chatter;

we have work to do." His mood changed instantly, from Stark the raconteur to Stark the workaholic. He looked over at his team and clapped his hands together twice in quick succession. "Let's get a move on," he announced.

Renton noticed that his team seemed to almost jump to attention at this sonic alert. They had experienced it many times before and knew what it meant. Stark was now entering power mode.

Stark glanced back at the audience of colonists he had gathered and waved a hand at them, as if to shoo them away. "Everybody out, out, no time to waste."

They drifted out of his space, leaving him and his team to get on with it.

"Well, that was... weird," said Matteo as they all headed back to the elevator.

"Did you see the way his team nearly crapped themselves when he clapped?" Yuna observed.

"Yeah, and here's us thinking Mackenzie was a pain in the ass to work with," said Renton. "He makes her look all warm and fuzzy."

CHAPTER 24
THE WAY FORWARD

They had gathered in the operations room on the upper level to discuss their preparations for the defense of the base. Pompodur might have allowed them to take control of the bio-bank rather than risk its destruction, but that didn't mean he would let them keep it. An assault was coming; of that they were all certain.

Even so, there was a palpable air of optimism in the operations room as they assembled. This was further ramped up by news that Mackenzie would indeed live to fight another day. The crew of the Mars ship, not wanting their home from home shot to bits, had taken control of the situation, successfully neutralizing the remaining Xilinex fighters. Mackenzie was currently receiving medical attention for minor injuries. However, the news was bittersweet; they had suffered a loss of Brett, who had succumbed to injuries he'd sustained while trying to prevent the two Xilinex captives he'd been guarding from making their escape.

"What are they going to do with her?" Chen Jun asked DOA.

"They're keeping her in the medical bay for observation," replied DOA. "I have been informed that her injuries are minor; however, it's unlikely she will be returning to Moon Base Delta anytime soon. Xilinex will be targeting anything that approaches the base from now on."

"I can't believe that she's still alive," said Chen Jun, shaking his head. "It's like she has nine lives. She should be dead several times over by now."

With Mackenzie out of commission, it would be up to Chen Jun to take command. Mackenzie had become the de facto leader of their ragtag defense group, organizing the fighters and developing strategy. Now, those responsibilities would fall onto Chen Jun's shoulders. There was a certain irony to this, in Renton's mind. Here was an ex-SINO contractor, someone who had worked for the very organization that tried to take control of the base at the onset of the current conflict. But their power had waned considerably now, after Xilinex had ramped up their military takeover. They were being blockaded and starved. Renton wondered how long they could hold out for.

He had been giving SINO some considerable thought recently. For pretty much all of lunar colonization history, other organizations and agencies that operated here had always considered SINO ideologically incompatible with any form of cooperation. They were seen as secretive, isolationist, with a thick layer of paranoia permeating their communications. They did their own thing, their own way, and had never seen any reason to cooperate with anyone else. In short, they trusted no one, and no one trusted them.

Yet, Chen Jun and the rebel group that had followed Mackenzie out of the old mining outpost at DaVinci Crater were not the isolationist ideologues that Renton and his crew had encountered while they were incarcerated there. These were just ordinary contract workers trying to make a living, trying to make enough money to give them a life back on Earth. And now, like everybody else here at Moon Base Delta, they were just trying to survive. Renton began to wonder if there were many more like them trapped up in the SINO base at Mare Crisium.

It was becoming ever-more clear to him that if they were all going to survive up here on the Moon, isolated from Earth for the foreseeable future, they would all have to cooperate, pool their resources, and forge some mutually beneficial agreements between all parties.

Doing so would stop ideological conflicts, or simple power grabs from destroying them all. But if there was any hope of that happening, they would need to build trust with SINO and, maybe, get their help. The reality in Renton's mind was simple: divided, they fall; united, they stand. Of course, another way to look at this would simply be, my enemy's enemy is my friend— which might suffice in the battle against the Xilinex Corporation, but was it a secure basis for moving forward? Would mistrust start to build again and lead to further conflict?

Nevertheless, having spent a great deal of time with Chen Jun and his group, Renton began to sense that there might be a way forward if they could somehow communicate the right message to the right people within the last SINO enclave.

"We need to contact SINO," Renton threw this out to the group, knowing what the initial reaction would be.

"Are you mad?" Selene was the first to react. "After what they've tried to do to you all?" She swept her hand around, gesturing at Matteo, Alice, and Yuna. "They tried to kill you; have you forgotten that?"

"No, I haven't," Renton replied, "but that was then, and this is now. And let's face it, we all know what's coming. If we go down, SINO will too. Like it or not, it's in both our interests to ensure that doesn't happen."

"You don't seem to understand," Selene countered. "They're ideologically opposed to any cooperation with any other agency or group. Even if they were to agree to help us, it would be purely as a double-cross. They're the same as Xilinex; they want complete power."

"Except," said Renton, "that we already have a group of SINO people fighting on our side. He gestured toward Chen Jun. "And we're very glad to have them. We wouldn't have managed to hold off this long without their help. Also, and correct me if I'm wrong here, Chen, but I don't get the impression your mission is total lunar domination."

Chen Jun gave a snort. "Ha, all we want to do is survive, just like everyone else." He paused for a moment, thinking. "However, Selene has a point. You see, we're all just contract workers, just trying to get by. None of us gives a toss what the SINO leaders think, never did. But there is a strong group in there that would rather die than compromise their ideology.

Which seems totally crazy to me, considering the situation we all find ourselves in." He gave a shrug.

"But there must be a lot of other contract workers just like you guys trapped up there," Renton continued.

"Oh, for sure, there's a whole bunch of us, probably starving to death at this very moment."

"Can we reach them? Can we talk to them? Could we get them to help us?" asked Matteo, who was beginning to see what Renton was driving at.

Chen Jun thought about this for a moment, tipping his head this way and that. "Maybe," he said finally.

"We have the bio-bank now; we can feed ourselves and everybody else into the future. Surely this is something they would be willing to work toward," Renton urged. "Considering the alternative is that Xilinex get their hands on it, and that would mean the end for both us and SINO."

"We should try," said Alice. "We all know that starvation is a powerful motivator. There must be quite a few people up there now, eating through their dwindling resources and wondering how they're going to get out of this."

"It might be possible," said Chen Jun eventually. "But we would need to contact the right people; we would need to get the contract workers on board first and let them see that there is a possible future, a way out. But, be warned, if the SINO hierarchy—the leaders—get wind of this, then they will do everything in their power to quash it. However, that becomes a much more difficult task for them if the general population knows that there's a way to put food on the table."

"I suppose there's no harm in trying," said Selene with a sigh, finally conceding to the inevitable. "But we would need to be really careful that we're not setting ourselves up to get shafted, where we're out of the frying pan, but straight back into the fire."

"So how do we contact them without alerting the SINO leaders?" Renton asked.

"If I may be of assistance," DOA interjected, "from my observations of the SINO enclave at Mare Crisium, I can conclude that there are a wide variety of groups from various regions of the former SINO strongholds that have coalesced in that area. The majority are comprised of contract laborers, specifically those employed by Xiang Zu Exploration and Yulong Extraction."

"Xiang Zu is the same corporation that we were contracted to," said Chen Jun.

DOA continued. "I have also ascertained that there are multiple, semi-private, communication channels in use, which I've taken the liberty of monitoring. My analysis of the chatter is that the situation in Mare Crisium is becoming critical; while they haven't run out of food just yet, their supplies are running very low, and there have already been growing signs of discontentment within the enclave. This discontentment is primarily being instigated by the ex-employees of the Xiang Zu Corporation. They would seem like the obvious cohort to try and make contact with. I can establish a secure, encrypted communication channel, but there's no guarantee that it won't be deciphered by agencies opposed to any form of cooperation."

This was met with several nods of approval from Chen Jun and his fellow fighters.

"Okay then," said Renton. "That sounds like the place to start, but we need to do it soon, and the message needs to be clear: that we have the bio-bank, a way of securing everyone's food supply for the future. And we are willing to distribute this to everyone so we all have security. But to do that, we need help."

"What sort of help are we asking for?" said Chen Jun. "Remember, they're in the same situation we are in. There's a blockade and they can't get out, so there's no way they're going to arrive down here with a force to help us fight off an assault."

"We don't need them to do that," said Renton. "Here's my thinking. Xilinex will try to pull together as large a force as possible to assault our base here, considering their last efforts with smaller forces were complete failures. This means they've got to pull people from everywhere, including the blockade on the SINO enclave. So we need them to start causing trouble up there, start taking potshots at Xilinex, make it look like they're planning a breakout so that Xilinex is forced to maintain numbers up there. That means there's less available for an assault on Moon Base Delta."

"Then we should start agitating elsewhere," offered Selene. "Ramp up the propaganda, so to speak. Get the message out there that we have a way out of this mess. All people need to do is start engaging with XIlinex security, keep them busy trying to maintain control. If we can get enough people causing trouble and holding down Xilinex forces, then we may just have a chance to fend off this assault."

"For the time being, at least," said Renton. "But in reality, Xilinex needs to be defeated completely and irrevocably. That's the only way the rest of us can have any peace on this godforsaken rock."

"Whoa, that's a tall order," said Matteo. "How do you propose we do that? Let's face it, they hold all the cards; they have the military force."

"I honestly don't know." said Renton, shaking his head. "But it's the only way; we all know this. Unless they're defeated, the future for all of us remains bleak. Yet, we have to try to find a way, and we have to succeed."

CHAPTER 25
CRASHING

For five days straight, VTOL aircraft had been coming and going at the Strawstack Mountain Astronomical Facility, disgorging enough men and material to take over a small country. It was clear that the top brass had no intention of letting this facility fall into the hands of some local warlord. Nevertheless, its days as a scientific research center were over. The all-pervading chaos and societal breakdown that had followed in the wake of the devastating solar storm were now gradually giving way to a phase of consolidation and stabilization. Han thought about this development and supposed that, all things considered, it was likely a good sign. It signified that some measure of control had been finally achieved, enough stability to start earnestly considering the best possible routes for moving forward. Perhaps, just perhaps, the absolute worst of the societal chaos and disorder was behind them, and from this point on, the situation would begin to progressively improve.

Han, Sheneese, and twenty-five other people that constituted the bulk of the analysis team, all piled into an awaiting VTOL aircraft, which, being military-issue, was short on comfort but long on utility. They arranged themselves on rudimentary seating along either side of the cargo hold. Han, being a former board member of Strawstack, was afforded more comfortable seating—akin to standard aircraft passenger seats —along with Sheneese, in the forward cabin. This had a window on his right-hand side, where he could watch the world pass by beneath him.

The aircraft gently spun around on its axis while it ascended, orienting itself methodically toward its intended direction of travel. Han gazed down at the facility observing the buildup of military personnel and firepower. Adjusting its rotors for horizontal flight, the craft began to gradually move away from the facility, steadily building up speed as it did so. Before long, Han lost sight of the compound, and instead, the broader, sprawling countryside unfurled beneath him. Bright morning sunshine bathed the landscape, making it appear pleasantly idyllic, with nothing in this serene view to indicate the ongoing day-to-day struggles for survival.

The craft veered westward and started to parallel the course of a major interstate highway. For the next hour or so, as Han peered down upon this once bustling artery of human civilization, he did not see a single vehicle in motion; all traffic had simply ceased to exist. Yet, every so often along the way, he caught sight of clusters of abandoned vehicles. These forsaken cars and trucks bore various scars of past altercations—overturned, burnt out, or mangled after experiencing a particularly violent crash. Here and there, in close proximity to these grim sites, he could see the lifeless bodies of the vehicles' former occupants, lying motionless precisely where they had fallen.

After some time, they deviated away from the interstate and began to traverse across country, maintaining a relatively low altitude as they flew. They passed directly over a variety of towns and small villages, all eerily abandoned, with absolutely no signs of life or activity anywhere—except for one significant enclave. Han was not entirely sure what this particular town was called, as he was unfamiliar with this region of the country. However, it was abundantly clear that the town had served as a refuge during the early, tumultuous days of the societal chaos and had somehow managed to survive relatively intact.

As they flew over, Han noticed a massive fortified barricade that had been erected using an assortment of shipping containers on the main road leading into this enclave. A rampart had been welded to the top of the barricade, along which he could distinctly see a considerable number of armed townspeople manning various gun emplacements. Situated in front of this imposing barricade, the road was strewn with crudely crafted obstacles, constructed from welded sections of old railway tracks. These were strategically positioned to effectively prevent any direct path toward the steel gates that marked the fortified entrance to the town. Situated further back from these elaborate obstacles lay the twisted remains of several shattered and broken vehicles—likely the unfortunate outcome of some failed, desperate attempt to breach the enclave's defenses.

Inside the fortified town, all was neat and tidy, and well-ordered with every square inch of open space having been allocated for growing food or animal husbandry. Every rooftop that Han could see had either a rainwater collection system or a bank of solar panels to generate electricity, complemented by a towering wind turbine that dominated the edge of the enclave. All in all, Han estimated there could be as many as ten thousand people in this small island of civilization. It gave him hope. If ordinary folk like this could find a way, then maybe it was possible that humanity could find a way back from the brink of the abyss.

Around forty minutes later, they finally touched down on a military airbase on the western side of the heavily fortified sanctuary city of Yorktown. which was situated on the confluence of two broad rivers. These provided a formidable barrier making it relatively easy to protect, and no doubt it was chosen for that very reason. It was now bolstered by the might of the military-industrial system. For the first time, he actually saw traffic on the streets; and if he hadn't known better, it looked like any city anywhere, with people going about their business as they always had.

The airbase was a vast, sprawling concrete apron peppered with military aircraft and support machinery, along with rows of hangars and warehouses, all bursting with supplies. There seemed to be a constant stream of people and machines ferrying goods and supplies onto waiting aircraft, presumably

GERALD M. KILBY

to be shipped or airdropped to other cities and enclaves that still held out against encroaching anarchy.

They were transferred directly into a much larger passenger craft, which took off almost as soon as boarding had been completed. This was considerably more comfortable and quieter than the previous transport, and within a few minutes, Han had fallen asleep, not waking until a few hours later when the aircraft began to descend in preparation for its landing at Vandenberg Space Port—their new home for the foreseeable future.

Originally the main base for the Space Force, Vandenberg was now slowly but surely turning into the epicenter of the nation's efforts to regain some foothold in space beyond Earth's atmosphere. With the entire country now almost completely governed by the military and its closely integrated state apparatus, Vandenberg had taken on all the hallmarks of a strategic command center. Here, all available resources to counter the debris cloud that now shrouded Earth were gathered together and consolidated into one location.

For Han, though, this meant a drop in rank. Where he had once been one of the directors on the board of Strawstack, with unparalleled access to information, he was now just another data analyst, and cut off from all the external information sources the he had relied on. He had no doubt that this was intentional, not just for him but for many others. The consolidation of resources was in progress, and with it came restricted access to information concerning the outside world and developments on the Moon—limited now to only those at the very top of the military command.

What he had lost in terms of rank was somewhat compensated for by gains in creature comforts. The new accommodation consisted of an entire apartment, not that dissimilar to the one they had left behind when they made the fateful decision to abandon the city and head for the observatory. Not only that, but the base had a comprehensive entertainment sector replete with a cinema, restaurants, and even a few stores selling a wide variety of goods. These could be purchased using the new monetary exchange system that had been gaining traction over the last couple of months. Unsurprisingly, to instill confidence in this fledgling exchange system, citizens could, if they so wished, walk into any of the banks that now functioned within the system and literally exchange their digital money for physical gold or silver.

Han considered it quite extraordinary that instead of moving forward as a society, they were, in effect, moving backward in time, utilizing systems first developed centuries before. The idea of exchanging money for precious metals had all but disappeared shortly after the end of World War II. But here it was again, making a comeback now that trust needed to be rebuilt. Even the concept of sanctuary cities seemed almost medieval. When marauding hordes threatened the hinterlands, everyone moved their families and livestock into the safety of fortified towns, where the invaders could be held at bay. Even knowledge of the outside world was now as it must have been back in the late eighteenth and early nineteenth centuries, prior to the advent of the telegraph—a time when news from afar took weeks to arrive by ship or train.

However, his newfound comfort was short lived. On the

third day after their arrival at Vandenberg Space Port, after he had settled in and begun to familiarize himself with the new working regime, a knock came on the door of his new apartment. When he opened it, he was confronted by two officious-looking bureaucrats, flanked by three well-armed security guards.

"Dr. Han Sundar?" one of the officials asked, his tone clipped.

"Yes, that's me," Han replied, slightly unnerved by the vibe he was getting from these people.

"Can you come with us, please." His tone left no room for argument.

"Eh... what's this about?" Han asked, feeling his heart race, and wondering if this may have something to do with his clandestine communications to Moon Base Delta.

"All will be explained," the official replied brusquely. "It's important that you come with us." He stepped to one side and gestured for Han to comply.

Han glanced back at Sheneese, who had been observing the exchange, concern growing on her face.

"It's okay, Sheneese, just some bureaucratic nonsense," he said, trying to sound casual before turning back to the officials. "Okay, let's go."

As Han walked away from the sanctuary of his new home, he couldn't shake a gnawing feeling in the pit of his stomach. Did they know? Had they somehow found out that he was the one passing classified information to Moon Base Delta? Was this the moment when his and Sheneese's life of safety and security came crashing to the ground?

CHAPTER 26
DESPERATE ALLIANCES

"I have fantastic news for all of us who find ourselves marooned on this rocky life raft orbiting the Earth," Jack Stark spoke directly to the camera. On either side of him sat various members of Moon Base Delta, carefully chosen to represent as many of the different groups now struggling to survive the new reality of lunar isolation. The message they were in the process of recording would be disseminated as widely as possible through all the networks open to them. This included the last SINO enclave, even though the message would most likely be blocked by the officials. However, it was hoped that Chen Jun would be able to convince his contacts within the enclave to disseminate it internally.

There had been some debate as to who would be best placed to face the camera and deliver this message. Selene, of course, considered herself the obvious choice, citing her expertise in persuasion through the craft of carefully chosen words. Yet, if their objective was to break down all the old alliances, associations, rivalries, and enmities that had existed from the very start of lunar exploration, they needed someone without the baggage Selene carried as a former director of FISA. What they needed was a fresh face, an outsider, and there was no one who fit that bill better than the eccentric trillionaire, Jack Stark. After all, it was his bio-bank that was giving them all a future.

Placed strategically on the table in front of Stark were two individual trays containing several rows of small sprouting plants. He pointed to one tray. "This is a species of plant called Chantenay, otherwise known as a variety of carrot." He then lifted one of the samples out of the tray and held it up to the camera. "This however, is a genetically modified version of that species, one designed to produce a single crop that doesn't produce seeds, so new seed stock must be acquired from the predatory corporation that developed this product." This was said with no attempt to hide his distain as he held the sample up and glared directly at the camera. "This represents slavery—slavery to the corporation that engineered it, but more importantly, slavery to the powers on Earth upon whom we now must rely on to send us supplies; otherwise, we will all die of starvation."

He carefully replaced the sample back in its tray and picked up one of the plants from the second tray. "This, on the other hand, is an almost identical variety of plant but this one will reproduce like any other plant in nature. It is, in every respect, the real deal. It has no such genetic restrictions or patents belonging to any corporation." He paused for dramatic effect, rotating the plant in his hand, showing it from different angles.

"This is from the bio-bank that myself and my scientific team have been developing in our facilities on Mars. We have brought this vault with us when we had to evacuated. It is now here at Moon Base Delta and we have already started to propagate new food crops. But it's not just for the people that seek sanctuary in this base, it is for everyone who now finds themselves marooned on this godforsaken rock and struggling for survival—and I mean for everyone. We cannot allow our food source, our future, to be controlled by any group that simply sees it as a way to enslave us all."

He put the sample back in its tray and gestured to Renton, who was seated beside him. It was now Renton's turn to speak directly to the camera. He began by introducing himself as a simple maintenance engineer who found refuge in this base. He then proceeded to introduce the others seated around the table. "This is Chan Jun, a former contractor with the Xiang Zu Corporation at DaVinci Crater, and Kimura and Tanaka Aoi from the Hamamatsu Corporation over at Secchi." He continued around the table, finally ending with, "and Ted Parker, pilot and former Xilinex Mercenary."

Renton looked back to the camera. "We are all just the same as you," he said, as he swept a hand around. "We're all just trying to survive, trying to find our way to a better future. And now we have that possibility, with the arrival of the Mars evacuation ship and the bio-bank that Mr. Stark had the foresight to create." He paused for a moment before continuing. "Yet, as I speak, Xilinex Corporation forces are building up outside our base, preparing for an assault so that they can take control of this vital resource. Their leader, Pompodur Adarok, is hell-bent on acquiring this resource so he can put us all back into slavery in the service of his ego. We must not let that happen. If we are to survive and prosper up here on the Moon, then we must leave all the old rivalries behind and truly come together as one group with a common purpose. We cannot let Earth, or the Xilinex Corporation, or SINO, or any other faction that sees only power and control as their objective, takeover this resource." He swept an arm around again at the others seated at the table. "All these people you see before you are all from different groups, different agencies, different places on Earth. But realize this." He focused all his attention on the camera. "All those old associations are long gone; they mean nothing anymore. They were completely destroyed by the solar storm, just as it destroyed the satellite constellations orbiting Earth. If we are to survive, we must put the old allegiances behind us, we must forge a new one, we must come together and fight for our collective future—and that means taking on the Xilinex Corporation. If Moon Base Delta falls to Xilinex, then they will control the food supply, your food supply." He jabbed a finger at the camera. "And with it, they will control all the people on this moon." Again, he paused to let this sink in. "But we believe they can be defeated. They do not have the resources to assault this base and also maintain the blockade on SINO in Mare Crisium, not to mention quelling all the protests that are increasing at Shackleton and Amundsen. We need everyone to not just maintain this pressure, but to dramatically increase it. Keep Xilinex forces busy, keep them tied down. If that happens, then we have a chance at defeating them. We have a chance at... freedom." Renton stopped talking; the camera ceased recording.

Almost immediately, Stark rose from his seat at the table and walked out of the operations room without another word. His entourage silently followed in his wake.

"That guy is seriously weird," Yuna observed as her eyes followed Stark out.

"Yes, but he's our weirdo," Matteo replied with a laugh.

"You'd need to have a screw loose to agree to come down here because, let's face it, we're about to be the center of a major shit-storm," Selene said as she began gathering up her notes. "It's arguably the worst place to be on the Moon right now,"

"Do you think this will work?" Kimura gestured at the monitor where the recording they had just made was beginning to be replayed.

"We'll get it out to as many places as possible," Selene replied with a shrug. "Those that still have access to outside broadcasts. Our secret weapon is Stark and his bio-bank. Remember, most of these people are under food rationing, so they're hungry, even desperate."

"Any word from your SINO contacts?" Renton asked Chen Jun.

"Nothing so far. We've put the word out through some back channels. But I'm still hopeful that they'll try and make direct contact. As Selene said, they're hungry and desperate."

"I do not wish to alarm you," said DOA, apologetically, "but two Xilinex shuttles have touched down just outside the base."

The main wall monitor flickered to life, showing a camera feed from the perimeter surface. It showed more Xilinex forces disembarking from the shuttles and hauling a lot of equipment.

As he watched, Renton wondered if their own desperate attempts at fomenting rebellion and striking alliances were too late. Had time finally run out for Moon Base Delta?

CHAPTER 27
GOING DOWN

Han found himself being shepherded out of his apartment building and bundled into a ground transport, along with two officials and three security guards. They drove for a while across the vast Vandenberg Space Port to an out-of-the-way area that accommodated a number of nondescript office buildings. They came to a halt outside a low, three-story office block that had seen better days and, from what he could see, looked completely empty. As they approached the glass-fronted entrance, Han found no sign or plaque indicating what purpose this building served. The transport came to a halt, everyone got out, and Han was ushered through the entrance doors into a spacious, dusty, and eerily deserted lobby—again, there was nothing to indicate what went on in this building. Han wasn't sure what to make of this. He imagined he would be brought to some high-tech center to be presented with a fait accompli from the security apparatus in Vandenberg. He had been found out, and now he would be charged. But a semi-derelict office building? Was this a good or a bad omen?

They made their way across the barren lobby to a very old-fashioned elevator, which, much to Han's surprise, still worked. The doors creaked open, and he was directed inside, accompanied by the two officials. The three guards were left outside. He wondered if the reason for this might be that the elevator was dangerous, not capable of carrying more than three people?

They stepped out again into a drab third-floor corridor that led them to a set of double doors. These were opened, and Han was led into what looked to be an old boardroom with a long, chipped and stained, oval table. Five people sat around one end, all civilians. Han recognized Alan E. Dyson, who acknowledged him with a nod and then gestured at a seat at the opposite end of the table.

"Please, have a seat." Dyson seemed uncomfortable, not surprising since he was now party to the formal interrogation of a friend and colleague.

Han sat down. The two officials retreated out of the room.

"Dr. Han Sundar," said a tall, well-groomed, middle-aged man sitting in a central position, directly opposite Han. "Thank you for joining us today."

"Do I have an option?"

"Eh... yes, well... indeed." He too seemed uncomfortable, giving furtive glances at his colleagues as if looking for moral support.

"So what's all this about?" Han braved a question.

The central figure rested his arms on the table and clasped his hands together, looking down at them, thinking for a moment. "You are aware, no doubt, of our situation here on Earth, our dependence on Helium-3 from the lunar surface, the fuel that drives our fusion society, and how critical this is for our future survival?"

"Of course," Han replied.

"And that we have been at pains to exert any influence we can over the Xilinex Corporation up on Luna to ensure that this vital fuel supply is secured."

Han remained silent, simply nodding his understanding.

"Yet, it seems as if all our plans are already known by other factions on the Moon, most notably Moon Base Delta, all despite our best efforts to keep them secret."

Again, Han remained mute as the five men eyed him as if he were a specimen.

"We've been wondering about this," began another of the men. "We thought it might be due to intercepted communications or possibly that powerful general AI they possess. Yet, certain recent events, where no communication was involved, were still known to third parties. This led us to consider that the leak was coming from within. We began investigating all communications traffic out of Strawstack Mountain. And do you know what we found, Dr. Sundar?"

Han shook his head, bracing himself for what was coming.

"Someone had been sending hidden, encrypted attachments to elements within Moon Base Delta. They knew everything that we were planning."

The room fell silent, allowing the weight of this revelation to sink in.

"Look, we know it was you, Han." said another of the interrogators, a block of a man with a distinct military bearing, yet dressed in civilian clothes. "We know that you were sending messages to Professor Hendrickson, and that your wife, Sheneese, might have been aiding you."

"Leave her out of this!" Han exclaimed, jumping up from his chair.

Dyson gestured with a hand for him to sit back down. "Take it easy, Han. Take it easy. This is not what you think it is. Please, sit down."

Han hesitated for a beat, then sat back down.

Furtive glances were exchanged among the men, as if they were somehow communicating telepathically. Finally, it was Dyson who spoke again.

"Some of us, eh... have not been comfortable with the direction our leadership have been taking regarding the Xilinex Corporation. We feel it's leading us into morally questionable territory."

Han arched an eyebrow. This was new to him. Were there others who shared his own views on the tactics of Space Division and the newly formed Alliance?

"While we fully understand, and support, the necessity to make hard choices in the pursuit of achieving energy security— some of which require us to turn a blind eye, no matter how uncomfortable that may be—the situation has now changed due to your involvement."

Han sat up in his seat. "Changed?" he probed.

"The arrival of the wild card in the form of one Jack Stark and his Ark on the Mars evacuation ship, was seen by our leadership as an existential threat... as you yourself anticipated." Dyson looked down at his clasped hands for a second and gave a sigh. "However, as a consequence, an attempt was made by Space Division and the Alliance to remove this element from the equation in the form of a... small, tactical nuclear device." He gave Han a hard look. "Yet somehow, they figured it out and managed to avoid the catastrophe that would otherwise have occurred. I might add, that this... preemptive action... was not fully endorsed by all of the current leadership. There were many dissenters. Many of us are very glad that it failed."

"My god, that's insane, all those people." Han had by now given up the pretense of perplexed innocence. They knew he had sent the messages and he got the impression they were very happy he did.

"But there's more. After you alerted Moon Base Delta to the existence of this Ark, this bio-bank, they conducted an insanely daring raid and managed to persuade Stark to bring it down to the base. Needless to say, there was a standoff with Xilinex, but, for once, good sense prevailed, and now Stark, his team, and the bio-bank are safely tucked away in Moon Base Delta."

Han smiled. "Good for them. And, in my humble opinion, we never should have abandoned them in the first place."

This elicited a few mumblings from the group. "Yes, well, be that as it may, they now hold all the cards," said Dyson.

"Look, the situation is like this." The military-looking guy placed a fist on the table. "Had Xilinex and that madman

Adarok gotten hold of that Ark, they would have extracted a very high price from us for any Helium-3 supplies. Heck, they could even start a resource war down here. But..." he paused for a second, "with Moon Base Delta, well, they're a much more reasonable bunch of folks, mostly ex-FISA. So, in many ways, your clandestine transmissions may have saved all our asses."

Han let out a sigh, no longer able to hide his relief at this admission from the group. He slumped back in his seat. "So, what now?"

"I'm afraid, you're not out of the woods just yet, Dr. Sundar." The central figure now took over. "On the one hand, there are many of us in leadership who believe, as you do, that our original strategy to control Xilinex was doomed to failure and that FISA, our own people, should never have been abandoned. But on the other hand, there are those still firmly wedded to the Xilinex strategy. And whoever manages to gain the upper hand in formulating policy going forward will very much depend on the outcome of the battle for Moon Base Delta that is now brewing. Should the base prevail, then your misdemeanors will be seen as just that—misdemeanors, subject to some minor admonishments. However, should the battle go the other way and Xilinex emerges victorious, then your actions will probably be seen as treason and subject to much harsher punishment."

"Treason?" Han was shocked; this was his worst fear.

"Yes. By alerting Moon Base Delta, they were able to reason out the supply capsule's true purpose; they alerted the Mars ship, and ultimately that could have allowed the bio-bank to fall into Xilinex hands—the one thing few people on Earth want to see happen. You could have plunged us all into an even worse global crisis. Fortunately, for the moment, it did not turn out that way. But it's not over yet. Should Moon Base Delta fall and Xilinex secure the bio-bank, freeing them from our control, then the hardliners in the leadership will have been vindicated —and you will also take the fall."

Han's sense of relief quickly vanished. Should Moon Base Delta go down, then he and Sheneese would go down with it. All he could hope for now was that, somehow, Moon Base Delta could win this battle.

CHAPTER 28
CHEN GONGBO

The former head of internal security for SINO, Chen Gongbo, sat in the living room of his run-down accommodation module in an overcrowded sector of Mare Crisium, the last SINO stronghold, contemplating his steady fall from grace. His perceived incompetence in allowing the FISA maintenance crew to escape captivity in DaVinci Crater and his subsequent failure to secure the reboot codes for Moon Base Delta had allowed his enemies within the SINO hierarchy to target him as a liability. Possibly, he could have weathered that particular storm. But in reality, his downfall was self-inflicted. He had the temerity to question the ideology of the leadership that, in his mind, was clearly leading them to a humiliating defeat against the superior military might of the Xilinex Corporation. This was the hearsay that became his undoing.

It had been clear to him, from the very outset of the conflict, that existing SINO security teams were no match for the well-trained and well-armed Xilinex mercenary machine. And no amount of patriotic zeal or self-sacrifice could compensate for a lack of skill and weapons. The rout at Scott Crater had been a disaster; they'd lost over a third of their security force there, much of which was completely unnecessary. But the loss of the Mass Accelerator was the final nail in the coffin. After that, he had openly voiced his criticisms of the leadership, arguing that their rigid adherence to an outdated ideology was leading to defeat after defeat. They needed to change, or SINO would cease to exist. Needless to say, this did not go down well and, for his efforts, he was rewarded with a demotion and banished to this dilapidated sector. His job now was to oversee the defense of this area, an enclave populated by refugee contractors from the various mining and industrial outposts that SINO once controlled across the lunar surface. This was his lot now, representing the party in an area that had nothing but disdain for their former paymasters.

He waited the requisite three minutes for the Lapsang Souchong tea leaves to fully brew within the teapot before pouring it into a delicate china cup. It was a family heirloom, an antique, an item of luxury in this world of despair and decay. He held it up to his nostrils and inhaled the delicate aroma before taking a sip and savoring the last of his carefully husbanded stash of authentic Chinese tea. By the second sip, he had begun to relax. He sat back into his seat and began to review the figures from the quartermaster's office for this sector.

It made for grim reading. Every time he read one of these reports, it only highlighted the speed at which their resources were dwindling. The leadership had spun the narrative that they were completely self-sufficient and could survive here indefinitely. But the truth was very different; with a Xilinex blockade in full swing, nothing was getting in or out. Sooner or later, the population trapped within this stronghold would start to become desperate. This was inevitable; it was written in the figures in the report. There would be no escaping this reality, no matter how hard the leadership tried to say otherwise. He sighed, took another sip of the aromatic tea, and tried to enjoy this moment of peace and tranquility while it lasted.

Which, as it turned out, was not very long. His moment of peace was interrupted by a knock on his door. He looked at the time; it was late, well past midnight. Normally, he could just check the intercom to get a visual on this late-night caller, but that hadn't worked for a very long time, hence the need to physically knock. He considered ignoring it, but it came again, a little more insistent this time. He put down the teacup, reached under the low table, and pulled out a small plasma pistol, then made his way to the door.

Since the intercom no longer functioned, he would have to open it to find out who was on the other side. And simply shouting from the inside wouldn't work either, as the door was heavy, forming an airtight seal when closed. He checked the weapon, braced a foot on the inside of the door, and opened it a crack.

He was relieved to see it was only Wang Wei, leader of a ragtag group of refugee contractors, a friend, and colleague.

"Wang, what are you doing here? Trouble?" Chen Gongbo's immediate reaction was to assume the worst.

Wang shook his head. "No, but there have been some... developments." He flicked a glance up along the corridor, clearly uncomfortable about being seen standing in front of Chen Gongbo's front door. To many of the refugee contractors, Chen Gongbo was viewed as the enemy. Gongbo swung the door open, flicking his head to indicate for Wang to come inside, then gestured for him to take a seat. Wang complied, as Gongbo poured him a cup of the aromatic tea.

"So," he said, sitting down and taking another sip, "what are these... developments... that have you knocking on my door in the dead of night?"

Wang extracted a comms slate out from inside his jacket, powered it up, and gave a flicking gesture to initiate a 3D projection. A broadcast from Moon Base Delta began to play, showing a group of people gathered around a table facing the camera. The central figure, Jack Stark, began to speak.

Gongbo watched in stunned amazement as the broadcast played out. When it had finished, he turned to Wang. "You know, possession of that broadcast or even exposure to this filthy propaganda is a direct violation of SINO directives. This could land you in prison or even have you banished to some godforsaken corner of Luna." He paused for a moment, casting his arms around his dilapidated accommodation module. "Such as this place."

"Ha." Wang gave a laugh. "Well, we don't have anything to worry about then, do we?"

Gongbo had, over time, grown to regard Wang's complete

disregard for SINO ideology as a breath of fresh air. He had a way of cutting through the bull and breaking everything down to the fundamentals. When he had first found himself banished to this sector, it was Wang who had begun to change his mind about so many things he had once believed in. Initially, he had no option but to engage with Wang. He led a significant group responsible for the security and defense of this sector. SINO now relied on people like Wang, ever since their own resources had been decimated by various battles with Xilinex mercenaries. Yet, Gongbo was still a party official and had to toe the party line. Still, SINO needed Wang, so his vocal disdain for the leadership had to be ignored; otherwise, SINO would have no one. Gongbo had no choice but to turn a blind eye to Wang's heresy and, over time, he began to see the sense in some of what Wang believed. This was partly because he himself could see the fruitlessness of SINO doctrine. It had now become a running joke between them that he, being an official, would always have to remind Wang of his ideological transgressions.

Gongbo looked again at the projection, now displaying a still image of this Jack Stark person. "Is this for real?" he asked.

"It was broadcast less than half an hour ago; we picked it up through our... eh... channels."

Gongbo sighed. "So, what you're saying is that everybody in the enclave knows about it, while the graybeards in the SINO leadership will be denying its existence."

"Yes, but that's not really what's important here." He pointed at the screen. "If these guys really do have a magical lunchbox, then this is seismic, no matter what the graybeards think."

"Be careful, Wang," Gongbo admonished. "Don't underestimate the power of a regime under threat. This would constitute an existential crisis for them."

"Like we don't have our pick of those already. They could add one more onto the pile."

"Maybe so. But this is dangerous to them."

Wang's face turned grave. "You need to realize, Chen my friend, that the rules are becoming less important to the people with each passing day. What's occupying their minds now is hunger. Everybody knows that it's unsustainable here, regardless of the propaganda. We're sitting on a powder keg, and this," he pointed at the screen again, "could be the spark that ignites the fuse."

Gongbo spent a long moment just staring at the screen. He raised a hand and pointed slowly at one of the figures sitting to the side of Jack Stark. "You see that guy there?" he said. "The young guy, the engineer?"

"Yeah, what about him?"

"He is partly the reason I am sitting here talking to you." Gongbo looked over at his colleague. "His name is Renton Hicks, a maintenance engineer. Their ship crashed during the solar storm, landed in SINO territory. We arrested him and his crew, locked them up, and made plans to release them once we got some concessions out of Earth. It turns out his aunt was a FISA director, leading the negotiations for the new Lunar Accord."

"Interesting," said Wang, arching his eyebrows. "That must've got our glorious leaders salivating."

"It certainly did," Gongbo said. "However, they escaped and made a dash for Moon Base Delta. Hicks managed to secure the boot-up codes for the AI, something that most people considered nonexistent. So now our glorious leaders, as you call them, were jumping up and down with excitement at the prospect of getting ahold of those codes. I was the one tasked with recapturing them and taking control of the codes."

"Am I correct in assuming," said Wang with a hint of a smile, "that since this Hicks guy is sitting there making this broadcast, you failed in that task?"

"Correct. And that was the beginning of my demise. I was disciplined, demoted, and eventually, I ended up here, hanging out with the dregs of humanity and cavorting with lowlifes such as your good self." He raised his delicate china teacup in a mock salute and took a sip.

"You mean it was the beginning of your transition into being a decent human being," said Wang with a laugh.

"They don't have a chance, you know," Gongbo said, his tone somber. "Xilinex will blast that base apart rather than let them have control of this... bio-bank."

"They might have a chance, if we help them."

Gongbo looked at his friend for a beat before bursting out laughing. "SINO help Moon Base Delta? No offense, Wang, but you really are naive if you think that would ever happen. The graybeards would rather die an agonizing death in the black void of space, wrapped in the SINO flag, than help their enemy."

"Then maybe it's time for them to move aside?"

Gongbo suddenly turned serious and gave Wang a long, hard look. "What exactly are you suggesting?"

"Oh, I think you know."

Gongbo was silent for a moment as he contemplated this before giving a long slow sigh. "There was a time when I would have had you executed for such treasonous utterances."

"Indeed, there was a time," Wang repeated. "But that was then and this is now, and we're all starving to death, in case you haven't noticed. The only thing that could potentially allow us to live past the next six months is in that base."

Again, Gongbo was silent for a moment, looking at the screen, thinking. He rose from his seat and went to the small kitchen, where he began boiling more water for the teapot.

"How many people are left up here, on the Moon?" Wang asked, calling over from his seat. "Three, maybe four thousand," he continued. "That's way too small a population for SINO to think they can continue to live in splendid isolation. Earth may as well be on the far side of the galaxy. The old ways are dead; they make no sense up here. SINO, Xilinex —they will drag us all into the abyss if we don't rise up and do something."

"Oh, and you and your crew of refugee contractors are going to take them all on? Considering we've not even been able to break out of this blockade." Gongbo lifted the lid of the teapot and poured in some more hot water. He would get a second round out of it; not as fragrant and aromatic as freshly brewed tea leaves, but still, needs must, and if he was going to discuss insurrection, then he needed a cup of tea. He stirred the pot and poured two fresh cups.

"We can't break out of this blockade because SINO has too few fighters," Wang finally replied as he took the cup being offered by Gongbo. "You wasted them all on useless suicide battles. Now you rely on us. But we're just industrial contractors, not fighters. We'll fight for survival, but not for the regime."

Gongbo sat down again and took a sip of tea. It had that slightly bitter taste of a second brew, not unlike his current mood. Here he was, openly discussing a coup against his current masters, people he had dedicated his life to but now had nothing but disdain for. Wang, of course, was right; the regime offered nothing that could give them a future. Their old mantras had lost their power, if they ever really had any. The real power now lay in people like Wang.

"What you say is true; I won't deny it." His tone was resigned. "But let's be clear, what you're talking about is a coup, insurrection, a revolution to overthrow the leadership and take power." He turned to Wang and gave him a cold, hard look. "Would that not just give Xilinex the opportunity they need? They launch an attack while we tear ourselves apart?"

"They can't," Wang replied emphatically, then jerked a finger at the frozen image on the screen. "That's the reason why. They'll be pulling out everything they can to take on Moon Base Delta. That gives us an opportunity."

Gongbo shook his head. "I can't believe that I'm even discussing this."

"You know it's the only way. That's why I came to you. You're one of the few officials who see where the regime is taking us. You know the score."

He was silent again, contemplating the action he knew he was inevitably going to take. "There are others," he said eventually. "You don't know them, but there are more officials higher up than me who think the same way."

Wang reacted with a broad grin. "I knew you'd see the sense in it."

"Be that as it may, this would need to be planned very, very carefully, with people we can trust implicitly. I will talk to some of the disaffected within official circles, but you need to put together an armed force, one that can be relied on to dig in if things get dirty."

"You can be sure of that. My people are becoming desperate; all we need to do is channel that desperation." He nodded at the screen, "Once this gets out, then they'll be itching to do something. Now is our moment."

"And what about those people on Moon Base Delta? They want us to engage Xilinex, but if we're going to pull this off, then we need to back off, make it look like we're already beaten. That's not going to help them."

Wang pursed his lips and rubbed a hand over his long, scraggy hair. "I've given that some thought. If we can eliminate the SINO leadership, then the people will be high on victory; that's the moment to take on the remains of the Xilinex blockade. Once they have been defeated, then we can send help to Moon Base Delta."

"That's a lot of things that need to go our way. And even if they do, who's to say that Moon Base Delta can hold out that long?"

"It's the only way. We need to think of ourselves first, then Moon Base Delta."

CHAPTER 29

PREPARATIONS

D espite Moon Base Delta's exterior existing in the deadly vacuum of space, the facility had the added defensive advantage of being predominantly underground. However, it was an expansive and complex facility with multiple airlocks and hangar bays dotted around its surface exterior. Defending all these multiple vulnerable access points would have been more feasible with a substantially larger force, perhaps numbering in the thousands. The current population of Moon Base Delta, however, stood at just over one hundred residents, including only a limited handful of capable fighters. To attempt and bolster their somewhat limited defenses, this modest fighting force was augmented by a small but versatile army of robots and drones, as well as a multitude of hastily fabricated, ad hoc weapons systems.

Having learned several invaluable lessons from previous incursion attempts by Xilinex mercenaries, the defenders had long since abandoned the notion of safeguarding the perimeter of the base. The complex was simply too expansive and sprawling to effectively defend its multiple entry points. Instead, they meticulously choreographed a set of calculated counterattack points situated within the base's interior, all strategically aimed at funneling the invading forces into well-defined kill zones. Their tactical approach involved leveraging the intricate, labyrinthine structure of the base to their advantage, guiding the attackers along carefully predetermined routes that would distinctly favor their own smaller numbers. In the end, the ultimate outcome of the battle would pivot on just how effective they were at systematically attriting the Xilinex force.

With the recent landing of Xilinex shuttles depositing even more fighters and essential equipment just outside the facility, a palpable sense of heightened anxiety was permeating throughout the entire population in the base. It was a shared sense that the long-imagined, and much-feared, assault was about to descend upon them imminently. As an inevitable consequence, there was a significant ramping up of defensive preparations all around. This heightened state of readiness was most evident in the maintenance hangar, which served as the epicenter of their ongoing weapons development efforts.

The air inside the hangar was thick with the cacophonous sounds of last-minute preparations—the spark and clang of frantic fabrication, the distinctive click-clack of railgun ammunition magazines sliding into their slots, and the persistent hum of charging energy packs.

Renton tightened the final bolt securely on the refurbished

plasma rifle that he had been diligently working on. It was the last one among the many Xilinex weapons that had been zapped by the EMP during their previous ill-fated incursion attempt. He flicked the switch to initiate the power-up sequence and heard the deeply satisfying high-pitched squeal of the ultra-capacitors as they began charging up. He glanced up from his work to see Chen Jun and a few members of his crew making their way into the hangar. Catching Renton's eye, Chen Jun flicked his head subtly in the direction of the makeshift break area, signaling that he wanted to have a talk—clearly, he had news to share.

Renton was joined by Matteo, Alice, Yuna, and a handful more of the people who were feverishly striving to complete as many weapons and defensive systems as humanly possible before the inevitable onslaught commenced. As Chen Jun made his way toward the break area, the expression on his face looked grim.

"So, any news?" asked Renton.

Chen Jun scratched his chin. "DOA managed to establish comms with the enclave, and I talked to Wang Wei, an old contractor friend of mine. He told me that the situation is pretty desperate up there. They have very little food left; the people are growing more and more despondent by the day. SINO has also lost most of their professional fighters and is relying on contract workers to secure the enclave. These guys are people like us." He gestured to his crew. "Industrial workers with no training in fighting."

"Sounds pretty bad," said Alice.

"It is, but the upshot is, they can't engage the Xilinex blockade... just yet."

"Goddamnit, don't they see? We can supply all the food they want if they help us defeat Xilinex. Why are they just sitting there, doing nothing?" Matteo shook his head in frustration.

Chen Jun shrugged. "Look, I'm just talking to the workers, not the regime. But—and I'm just speculating here—there may be more going on up there than meets the eye."

"What do you mean?" Renton asked.

"Wang Wei wasn't saying it outright, but he was dropping hints. He said our broadcast is making the rounds in the enclave; a lot of people are talking about it. The regime is trying to stomp it out, but they don't have the hold over the workers like they used to."

"They're using us," Renton observed. "Using our situation as an opportunity to make their own moves. At least, it seems that way to me."

"You mean like a takeover?" asked Yuna.

"Maybe. What do you think, Chen? Did you get that feeling talking to this Wang Wei guy?"

Chen Jun nodded. "He was very cagey, not revealing much. But reading between the lines, something's going on up there; something is in the works. So, yeah, it's possible they might be making a move. Remember, SINO employed vast numbers of contractors, most of whom never bought into the ideology; they just wanted to make some decent money. If they're the majority of the remaining population up there, then there will come a point when they get really pissed off."

"So Xilinex moving out forces gives them that

opportunity," Renton said, almost to himself. Then he looked around at the others, who were clearly very subdued by this news. "Okay, so they can't help us now," Renton continued. "It was a long shot anyway. But if they do manage a regime change up in the SINO enclave, and we're still standing, then maybe they will come to our aid. Remember, we have the only sustainable food source. And we all know how much hunger can motivate." While Renton's observations didn't do much to fundamentally change the mood, they at least offered some hope. "We all know what we need to do, so best we get on with it."

The group broke up and drifted back to their various tasks, leaving Renton and Alice still finishing their coffee. It wasn't real coffee; it was a synthetic concoction manufactured by Stark and his team in one of the new bioreactors they had gotten up and running. "Damn, this tastes good," he said, raising his mug to Alice.

"I know. It's hard to believe that it's not real." She looked into her mug. "Just some... chemical formula." She glanced back at Renton. "Do you think Stark is crazy? I mean, he seems completely unfazed by the fact that this place might soon be consumed by violence."

"I'm not sure I'd exactly call him crazy. He probably feels that this battle is not going to affect him or his work. Xilinex will make sure to protect him and his team. When the dust settles, he'll continue on as if nothing happened."

"Then why is he here then?"

"DOA, the AI. He needs it to progress his work. As long as he has access to DOA, he's happy."

Alice was silent, looking into her mug again. Renton reached out and put an arm around her shoulder. "We'll get through this; we'll get to the other side."

"Sometimes I wonder if we will... see the other side."

"You've got to believe that we will. This place is a hard nut to crack. They've tried several times already and each time they failed. This time will be no different, you'll see."

Alice sighed and gave a slight nod in reply.

"And do you know what else I think?" Renton gave her his best smile.

"No, what?"

"I think when this is all over, it will be the start of something bigger. A new Lunar Accord, if you will. It will be the beginning of a bright new future."

Their moment was suddenly interrupted by DOA's voice over the PA.

Attention, movement of Xilinex forces has been detected toward the base. Multiple directions.

Renton glanced at Alice. "Well, it's begun. The battle that will define the future of the Moon."

CHAPTER 30
THE BATTLE BEGINS

This was the critical moment they had all known would inevitably come. They had planned for it, repeatedly rehearsing and fine-tuning their strategy within the limited time frame they had been granted. Now that the moment was finally upon them, everyone knew precisely what to do, and so they all hurried off to their designated stations with renewed purpose. For Renton and Alice, this meant making their way to the operations room, at least for the moment. They downed the last remnants of the synthetic coffee and began their trek to the upper levels of the base complex.

The large, panoramic wall monitor in the room displayed multiple real-time camera feeds from the exterior of the base, each one picking out various elements of the Xilinex forces as they moved into position. Several distinct groups of slowly advancing rovers were closely followed by squads of mercenaries on foot.

"What... is that?" Renton inquired, pointing toward a sizable, quadruped robot that was keeping pace with the advancing enemy.

"That is a battle droid," DOA responded. "Developed by the Rallion Corporation specifically for engaging enemy forces in highly hostile environments. It is constructed primarily from titanium, is equipped with several formidable weapons systems, and possesses the capability to operate autonomously under certain circumstances. Also, I have identified at least four such machines in the field, so far."

"I've actually heard of those before, back in the days when I worked on specialized control software," Alice revealed. "They're said to be virtually indestructible."

"Jesus," Matteo exclaimed with clear concern. "How do we even begin to counter those things?"

"EMP, same as before," Renton quickly responded.

"Eh... I think they might be hardened against EMP attacks," Alice cautioned.

"It doesn't matter, we'll find a way, perhaps we can lure them into one of the tunnels and effectively trap them there," Renton suggested, a little too optimistically.

"Do we know specifically which entrances they're targeting?" he then asked DOA.

"My calculations indicate they are targeting four separate access points," DOA answered, as the holo-table suddenly blossomed into life to display a detailed 3D schematic of the entire base. Four areas were illuminated with pulsing red markers, situated at approximately each cardinal point of the sprawling base. "This estimate comes with a ninety-eight percent probability," the AI further confirmed.

"Okay then, let's get going."

As soon as the potential ingress points had been definitively established, several groups immediately sprang into action, rushing to these designated areas, eager to implement some unexpected surprises for the advancing Xilinex mercenaries. Given their limited resources and manpower, it was simply not feasible to protect and defend every possible route into Moon Base Delta. As a tactical workaround, they had set up agile mobile units that would stand ready to move to any location once they had gained sufficient clarity on the Xilinex plan of attack.

Much has been written and debated about the crucial element of surprise in the art of war. For the vastly outnumbered group of defenders at Moon Base Delta, employing this age-old tactic to its fullest extent was perhaps their only hope—doing precisely what the opponent least expects. And the first of these surprises was now unfolding.

The initial test of Matteo's rapid-fire railgun had been very impressive. The team had taken the prototype down into one of the numerous underground tunnels that crisscrossed beneath the base—tunnels formed from old lava tubes—and had established a makeshift firing range. The weapon had easily decimated the robust metal targets they had set up further down the length of the tunnel. Encouraged by this, they decided to put more energy and resources into fabricating a few more of these potent machines.

These newly constructed railguns were now being

transported, piece by intricate piece, to the various points that DOA had indicated the Xilinex forces were planning to use for gaining access to the base. The weapons were then carefully reassembled, loaded with as much of the specialized metal barb ammunition as they had in their stockpile, and then set to autonomous mode, primed and ready to unleash hell fire.

Already, one group of mercenaries had reached the southern rover access gate and were diligently trying to get through using high-powered plasma cutters. A second group had just arrived at one of the main hangars and was busily getting themselves set up. The third and fourth groups were making their way toward smaller maintenance access points and were nearly in position to commence work on breaching the secured doors. Renton, along with everyone else in the operations room, waited with bated breath for the pivotal moment when all four enemy groups would be actively engaged in their attempts to force their way into the base.

"Okay," said Chen Jun, breaking the tense silence, "looks like they're all engaged now. So, are we actually going to do this?"

There was a brief moment of hesitation as Renton mentally grappled with the gravity of what they were about to attempt. The Xilinex forces were expecting that they would either need to cut through the outer doors laboriously or else hack the sophisticated locking mechanisms to gain entry through the various airlocks they were targeting. They had strategically amassed their forces behind their specialized cutting crews, all poised and waiting for the moment the heavy doors would finally be breached, and then they planned to surge through en masse. What they certainly weren't expecting was for the fortified doors to willingly open for them. And yet, that is precisely what was now happening.

On the wall monitor, they could clearly see the Xilinex forces momentarily step back, visibly surprised as the outer airlock doors began opening. There was a brief moment of uncertainty, as they wondered whether this development was the result of their own engineers' hacking efforts or something else entirely. However, this hesitation was short-lived. As the gap in the doors continued to widen, they quickly bunched up again, ready to flood into the base.

That's when the railguns activated.

The first wave of mercenaries, those who were already entering the airlocks, were mowed down, not even getting the fleeting opportunity to squeeze off a single retaliatory shot. Those who were further behind frantically ran back out onto the lunar surface and dove for whatever cover they could find. Yet, the railguns persisted in their relentless firing, their muzzles aimed out through the still-open doors, sweeping back and forth across a narrow angle. They struck down anyone and anything that had been too sluggish to remove themselves from the line of fire.

The first of the guns ran out of ammunition after only thirty seconds of sustained fire; the second one lasted about thirty-five. The third and fourth railguns were still firing when they were abruptly silenced, struck by blasts from plasma cannons.

"Shut the doors, shut all the damn doors!" Matteo shouted frantically. The heavy airlock doors began to close once more.

Those Xilinex mercenaries who remained standing inside

the airlocks were seized by a sudden wave of panic, making frantic attempts to scramble back out before the doors could complete their closing sequence. When they did finally seal shut again, the only occupants left within the airlocks were either lifeless or grievously wounded. Teams from Moon Base Delta were promptly dispatched to clean up the aftermath and to commandeer any weapons left behind by the enemy.

Outside, on the lunar surface, Xilinex forces regrouped, gathering their injured and initiating a tactical retreat. Round one had decisively gone to Moon Base Delta, and a dent had been made in the operational capabilities of the Xilinex forces. However, everyone in the base, Renton included, understood this wouldn't be enough to stop the enemy's relentless advance. Already, they could discern several battle droids methodically approaching the entrance points. They all knew that Xilinex would employ a more cautious strategy for the next wave, likely using these robots to spearhead their entry efforts rather than risking human lives.

There was very little that the defenders could do to counter this new threat. The railguns were either completely out of ammunition or had been destroyed.

The real battle was about to begin in earnest.

CHAPTER 31
THE FULL MIGHT

Pompodur Rossen Adarok felt a profound sense of trepidation rising up within him as he observed the turbulent events unfolding around the perimeter of Moon Base Delta. Sitting in the war room aboard the Xilinex HQ orbital, he watched as General Wagner and his aides, who were in a state of near frenzy, barked commands and instructions at the commanders on the ground. However, it was the moment when Pompodur distinctly heard the words "regroup, regroup" echo through the room that he fully grasped the extent of the disaster unfolding from the initial assault.

A clear pattern was emerging in his mind: General Wagner and his commanding officers had consistently underestimated the resilience and tactical acumen of Moon Base Delta's defenders. Perhaps they had been lured into a false sense of security by their earlier overwhelming triumphs over SINO forces, not to mention the minor pockets of resistance and micro-uprisings that had sporadically occurred in the Shackleton and Amundsen Craters.

As much as Pompodur felt a compelling urge to seize control of the deteriorating situation, he held back, hesitant to fall into a perilous trap that had ensnared many a greater man than himself—namely, the presumption that they were better military strategists than seasoned, battle-hardened generals. The unfortunate outcomes that had befallen those overconfident individuals should serve as a cautionary tale for all aspiring despots. And so, with this lesson in mind, he resisted the impulse to intervene.

"Status," Wagner called out.

A flurry of anxious situation reports from field commanders was being continually relayed back to the command center at Xilinex HQ. These firsthand accounts were swiftly consolidated, tabulated, and presented as data sets on the primary visual display, complemented by real-time positional information that appeared on a 3D topographical map, projecting out from the central holo-table. Pompodur did not have to be a military genius to figure out that the initial Xilinex assault had experienced a severe setback. A good portion of the first wave of assault groups had already been incapacitate in some way—far from an auspicious beginning. It was abundantly clear to him that additional forces were desperately needed to bolster their offensive capabilities.

For some time now, Adarok had been advocating for assembling the most formidable force they could possibly muster. Unlike General Wagner, he had never underestimated the cunning trickery and inventive resourcefulness demonstrated by Moon Base Delta's defenders. The majority of their leaders were highly skilled engineers with the capability to craft an array of sophisticated weaponry. Add to this the fact that they had at their disposal what many considered to be the most powerful artificial intelligence in the known universe advising them on tactical strategies. And now Xilinex was already in disarray. The full-scale assault had barely commenced, and Pompodur's deepest fears were already becoming a reality.

But the General, at least, had changed tactics; they were now deploying battle droids and drones at the forefront of the assault, serving as the vanguard. These machines were being remotely piloted by techs situated in the war room aboard the Xilinex orbital. Already, plasma bombardments had blown the doors off two of the targeted access points. The General was evidently growing increasingly frustrated with being second-guessed and questioned; now, the metaphorical gloves were coming off, and the literal big guns were being deployed with intent.

Sensing that the tide was finally beginning to turn in their favor, Pompodur slowly walked over to stand beside General Wagner, who was assuming a posture of control with his arms folded behind his back, intently watching the live video feeds displayed on the central monitor.

"Much as I'm hesitant to utter the words 'I told you so,' it's becoming increasingly evident to me that we're going to need additional resources committed to this battle," Pompodur remarked, casting his eyes toward a feed that showed a battle droid making its way through a charred, gaping hole in one of the hangar doors.

Taking a deep breath, Wagner replied, "I won't argue that more resources would be advantageous, but we must also consider the ramifications of reallocating such assets. Lowering the blockade around the last remaining SINO enclave could compromise our position, potentially exposing us to a new axis of attack."

"That assumes that the regime operating that enclave suddenly finds the courage to grow a pair, and quite frankly, there's no evidence to suggest that will ever happen," Pompodur argued back. "They've been decisively defeated and have retreated to Mare Crisium to lick their wounds. Meanwhile, we require more resources for the task at hand. Because one thing is absolutely certain, General: the inside of Moon Base Delta will be a literal minefield of defensive trickery."

For a brief moment, the General fell silent as he weighed the available options in his mind. Ultimately, he agreed to the proposed withdrawal of some forces from the perimeter of the SINO enclave. This reluctant acquiescence from the General occurred just after a tech announced that two of their scout drones, which had finally managed to penetrate into the inner sanctum of the base, were promptly neutralized by an EMP detonation.

To sweeten the deal for the General, Pompodur volunteered his own personal security detail. "They would be far more effectively utilized on the lunar surface, supplementing the existing forces," he suggested. "Which leaves us with the forces we have stationed at Shackleton and Amundsen. These also need to be redeployed to the battle," Pompodur urged.

But Wagner seemed hesitant to pull these groups into the fray. "These aren't seasoned mercenaries; they're just fighters committed to the Xilinex cause. Also, they're locals who have an intricate knowledge of the landscape within these enclaves. Removing them from their current security responsibilities could be perceived as an opening for dissidents to stir up more trouble."

"So what?" Pompodur retorted. "If they do decide to cause trouble, then let them. We can tackle that issue later; after all, they are lightly armed and have minimal support."

Finally, Wagner relented.

By now, the four initial access points to Moon Base Delta had been successfully compromised; scout drones and battle droids were advancing into the base. Following them were an elite squad of highly trained mercenaries. In addition to this, fresh reinforcements were now en route from the beleaguered SINO enclave. Pompodur's own security detail was also on the way; they were slated to assume command of the additional security guards that were being sent from both Shackleton and Amundsen. All things considered, virtually the full might of the Xilinex military apparatus was now being mobilized for the subjugation of Moon Base Delta.

CHAPTER 32
BATTLE DROID

An elated cheer erupted in the operations room of Moon Base Delta when the first EMP detonation successfully disabled two of the scout drones that Xilinex had dispatched to probe the way ahead. Although it was only a minor victory, it was a victory nonetheless, and it lifted spirits. Their defense squads were now actively working to funnel the advancing enemy assaults into several prearranged kill zones. These zones had been strategically positioned deep within the labyrinthine subterranean tunnels. At this very moment, four distinct groups of defenders, aided by a small army of maintenance robots, were busy sealing off bulkheads, locking down airlocks, and hastily erecting barricades. As they did so, they were also evacuating the atmosphere from these targeted sectors to make them even more inhospitable.

However, one specific group of Xilinex fighters had split off from their main assault force and were now navigating their way toward the upper levels of the base. From there, they would have a clear path to the operations room, where they could have full control of the facility. The only thing standing between them and their objective was a heavy bulkhead door, which was currently being slowly but steadily cut open.

"We really need to get down there and do something," said Matteo. "That bulkhead isn't going to hold them off for much longer."

"DOA, what are our available options for rerouting them down to the lower levels?" Renton asked, his eyes intently fixed on the live camera feed that was now displaying a battle droid employing a high-energy laser to slice through the formidable steel bulkhead door.

"Projecting optimal pathways onto the holo-table for you now," the AI responded. Almost instantaneously, new pathways illuminated on the intricate three-dimensional schematic displayed on the table.

"What's that structure right over there?" Matteo pointed toward a broad shaft situated near one of the newly highlighted routes.

"That's an old ventilation shaft. It dates back to the early days. It was used during the initial construction of the base," DOA clarified.

"And how deep does it go?" Renton inquired, leaning closer over the table to get a more detailed view.

"It extends for approximately fifty meters," DOA revealed. "It also has no atmosphere as it's exposed to the vacuum of space via a network of connecting vents," DOA added.

"Are you thinking what I'm thinking?" Matteo looked at Renton with a sly grin.

"If by that you mean the idea of dropping that battle droid down that shaft and blasting out into space, then absolutely," Renton affirmed.

"Nice idea, but how exactly are we going to do that?" Alice questioned, her gesture causing the projection on the holo-table to zoom in on the location of the old ventilation shaft.

"Do we have any old maintenance hatches to that particular shaft on that level?" Renton asked the AI.

A newly highlighted area appeared on the 3D schematic. "There's an old maintenance airlock located along the JAXA-KARI sector," DOA began. "It's been covered over and sealed for a number of years as a safety precaution due to the shaft becoming structurally unsound."

Matteo leaned closer and focused his attention on the highlighted access point. "If we could isolate this sector here, and also this one..." He moved his finger around the projection, indicating specific airlock bulkheads that could be employed to seal off various sectors of Moon Base Delta. "We could then load that old maintenance airlock with a load of high-grade explosives. We lure the Xilinex force down this particular corridor, securely lock down the area behind them, and then— boom!—detonate the airlock. The explosion would create a rapid pressure differential, and everything and everyone in that confined space would be forcibly sucked down into the ventilation shaft." He looked up, seeking some feedback from Renton, Alice, and the rest of the team that gathered around the holo-table.

"That could work," Renton said, nodding.

"We could get the maintenance robots to handle the high explosives," Alice suggested. "Can that airlock hatch be opened remotely? I mean, can you do it from here, DOA?"

"Yes and no," came the cryptic reply from the AI. "I can open the outer airlock hatch, but the inner door has been covered over with a false wall. This will have to be removed physically."

"No matter, the robots can handle that. But whatever we're going to do, we need to do it quickly," Alice said, glancing up at the main monitor where live camera feeds showed a second group of Xilinex mercenaries breaking through one of the barriers. Already, Kimura and the Secchi squad were engaging in a raging firefight, attempting to lure the attackers into a sector that would lead them into the tunnel network in the lower levels.

Less than thirty seconds later, both Alice and Yuna were remotely controlling separate maintenance robots, each loaded with a generous supply of high explosives concocted in one of Moon Base Delta's labs as a part of their ongoing weapons program. The explosives had been crafted according to a specialized recipe provided by DOA, which assured them that one kilogram of the substance would suffice for the task at hand. However, just to err on the side of caution, they decided to use nearly three times that amount.

Meanwhile, Renton and Matteo had quickly assembled a small contingent of reserve fighters. Their mission was to head down and engage the Xilinex squad and lure them into the specific sector of the base where the ancient airlock was located. It didn't take long for the engagement to begin. The first to spot them was a scout drone, which was promptly destroyed by a concentrated barrage of plasma fire.

"Alice." Renton called over his comms. "Got a status update on those maintenance robots?"

"Almost there. We've torn apart the wall and just managed to expose the old maintenance hatch. DOA is in the process of activating it as we speak," Alice responded quickly. Just as she did, Renton felt an elbow prodding his ribs. Matteo, was trying to draw his attention to the battle droid that had just come into their line of sight, appearing at the far end of the corridor. "Best get ready to fall back," Matteo cautioned.

They unleashed a concentrated burst of plasma fire at the droid, which seemed to do little more than irritate it. However, it did take the bait. The droid's head swiveled to perform a quick scan in their direction before retaliating with several short bursts from its mounted railgun. By the time the railgun's metal barbs found their final resting places—in the floor, walls, and ceiling of the corridor—Renton and his squad had already vacated their positions, retreating further down a side corridor. Renton then hastily fired off a few more rounds without aiming, simply shooting around the corner in an effort to continue luring the droid in their direction.

"It's working," Matteo confirmed, his hand cupped over his earpiece as he received live updates from the AI on the battle droid's movements. "It's heading our way."

Over the course of the next few frantic minutes, they engaged in a calculated game of shoot-and-scoot, making sure to stay just far enough ahead of the advancing battle droid to ensure their own safety, but also close enough to keep it hot on their heels. Finally, the battle droid lumbered into the corridor with the rigged maintenance airlock hatch. Close behind it, a squad of Xilinex mercenaries advanced, using the formidable machine as cover.

The explosives had been carefully concealed inside the airlock hatch and securely attached to its outer door, while the inner door that faced the corridor was left slightly ajar. Renton and the squad took cover behind a thick steel bulkhead door situated at one of the exits leading out of this sector. They waited for the Xilinex force to enter the corridor and position themselves alongside the rigged airlock. Once that happened, they would close this bulkhead door, effectively sealing off the sector.

Xilinex advanced cautiously, their eyes continually darting around as they no doubt referenced their own internal schematics overlaid on their augmented reality displays. The battle droid, leading the way, paused for a brief moment; the squad leader raised his fist, signaling for the group to halt. Then the droid rotated its head to perform a full scan of the surrounding area, searching for any potential threats. Its behavior was reminiscent of a large cat encountering an unfamiliar opening at the edge of its territorial range, moving with extreme caution lest it trespass into a rival's domain. After its momentary hesitation, however, the droid resumed its advance, and the squad fell in behind it.

"What are they doing now?" Matteo's voice betrayed a hint of impatience as he spoke.

"They're moving again, still heading in the direction we want," came Alice's response over the comms. "Get ready. I'm closing the perimeter bulkhead doors in three... two... one."

The Xilinex squad stopped dead in their tracks, instantly alert to the sudden hum of servos activating from multiple directions. They swiftly assumed defensive positions and promptly deployed a small scout drone to reconnoiter the path that lay ahead of them.

"Scout drone," said Renton. "We'd best get out of here."

They broke cover and ran past the only remaining open bulkhead door in the sector, entering an intersection. Renton glanced back to see the scout drone trailing far behind and moving slowly. He fired a few potshots at it before taking cover.

"Everybody's out," he announced into his comms.

"Okay, isolating the sector," Alice replied as the bulkhead door began to close.

Renton sat down on the floor and pulled out a comms slate. He flicked it on and began viewing live camera feeds from inside the now-sealed-off sector, visuals that were being relayed from the operations room. Matteo crouched beside him, along with some of the others from the team.

The Xilinex squad inside the corridor continued to advance, seemingly unperturbed that all exit routes were now blocked. No doubt they had ways to blow open any of these doors, regardless of their apparent strength. They reached the area where the maintenance airlock for the ventilation shaft was located. Renton shot a glance at Matteo. "Here we go."

The airlock hatch exploded, violently slamming the battle droid against adjacent wall. The entire area filled with billowing clouds of dust and debris—for a split second. But almost as suddenly as the dust cloud was created, it began to rapidly retreat, sucked back into the ventilation shaft and ultimately expelled into the vacuum of space. The smoke and dust evacuated, followed by several of the mercenaries. The battle droid was frantically scrambled to find purchase on the bare floor and walls as it too was being drawn into the void created by the explosion. Despite its tumbling, twisting, and clawing, it was inexorably pulled into the shaft. The last they saw of it was one limb clinging to the edge of the hole before it disappeared from sight.

"Yes!" Matteo shouted, jumping up and punching the air.

"Don't get too excited; we've still got major problems," Alice's voice came through urgently. "Xilinex have broken through our defense in Chen Jun's sector. His team are taking a beating. We're sending most of the reserve robots to help; you'd better get down there."

"Damnit," Renton said, sitting up and getting himself orientated. He checked the schematic on his AR display trying to find the safest route to Chen's Jun sector.

"Hey, you'd better see this," Yuna chimed in on comms. "Relaying to you now."

Renton lifted the comms slate and saw a live feed from the perimeter. Outside, several Xilinex troop transports were landing, some already offloading more fighters and equipment.

"Where the heck are they coming from?" Matteo asked, not believing what he was seeing.

"DOA says the blockade of the SINO enclave has been lifted; almost all resources are being transported here," Alice informed.

Renton shook his head in disbelief. "There must be at least fifty of them."

"More," Alice corrected. "Shackleton and Amundsen Craters have also been cleared out. They're all heading here."

"They're not making this easy, are they? said Matteo, with a shake of his head.

Renton pulled out his plasma weapon again and checked its charge. "Well, they're not inside yet. In the meantime, Chen's crew are in trouble, we'd better go help him."

Matteo sighed, then pulled out his own weapon. "Lead the way."

As the team moved away from the devastation of the now-isolated sector, far down inside the old ventilation shaft, the battle droid clung on to a metal strut. One of its limbs had been ripped off, and several of its systems were malfunctioning, but somehow it began clambering back up. Now that all atmosphere had been evacuated, it didn't have to battle against a raging tempest of evacuating air and debris. All was quiet. Soon it reached the edge of the shaft, crawled over the gaping hole created by the explosion, and dropped silently onto the floor. It was back in the fight.

CHAPTER 33
DEEPER

As Renton and the team hurried to assist Chen Jun's group, more updates were streaming in over comms. The situation was beginning to deteriorate rapidly. While they had initially found some success in slowing down the Xilinex incursion by channeling the mercenaries into carefully prepared ambush zones, their defenses were now becoming overwhelmed by sheer numbers.

Chen Jun's group had been actively engaging Xilinex forces in the level housing most of the old research labs. However, now faced with the addition of Xilinex reinforcements coming in from other areas, they had no choice but to enact a tactical retreat. This unfortunate development meant that Xilinex forces would soon breach the agri-sector, where Stark and his team were currently holed up.

"Chen? We need to get to Stark before you guys fall back,"

Renton shouted into his comms, urgency filling his voice. "We have to get them out of there."

"Seriously? You're kidding, right? I thought they didn't care," Chen Jun's reply was barely audible, almost drowned out by the sound of a fierce firefight going on in the background.

"I'm sure Stark couldn't care less, but the others on his team might have a different opinion. We have to give them the option. It took a lot of effort to get them here; I don't want to just hand over the bio-bank to Xilinex without a fight."

There was a pause from Chen Jun, a second or two longer than Renton was willing to wait. "Are you still there?"

"Yeah, yeah, damn it. Fine, you've got ten minutes, no more. Then we're falling back," Chen Jun conceded.

"Ten minutes? Hell, that's hardly enough time to do anything," Matteo said, with frustration.

"Well, it's all the time we've got," Renton pivoted around to the others. "Come on, let's move."

By the time they reached the agri-sector, five minutes had already passed, and yet another Xilinex squad had managed to break through, compelling another one of the defense teams to fall back. The persistent problem with their defense remained the near-indestructibility of the battle droids. They would have to come up with some solution to these machines, and soon.

They rushed into the bio-lab where Stark and his team were still diligently working away, eliciting startled reactions from the techs.

"You've got to move to the fallback location right now; we have no time to waste. Soon this place will be swarming with Xilinex mercenaries," Renton urgently announced.

The scientists and techs began to cease their work and started to move toward the exit. That is, until Stark raised a hand and declared, "We're not going anywhere."

This pronouncement elicited a moment of stunned silence from everyone present. The scientists and techs were uncertain what to do, frozen in time, paralyzed by indecision.

"We're perfectly safe here," Stark asserted. "Even if Xilinex forces do manage to infiltrate the agri-sector, we have nothing to fear. Remember, they need us."

"You can't be sure of that," said Renton, clearly skeptical.

"Actually, I can be," Stark retorted. "We've had assurances given to us already."

"By Xilinex? You've been communicating with them?" Renton questioned.

Stark seemed a bit embarrassed by this admission. "Yes, in the interests of resuming our work here, I've sought various assurances from the Xilinex Corporation. We have been told we're in no danger and that we can remain here at Moon Base Delta and continue our work. Even your AI, DOA, has calculated that the threat to our continued work here from Xilinex is minimal."

For a moment, Renton felt a sense of betrayal; how could DOA do this to them? Then again, it was merely a machine, an AI calculating the probabilities and providing an honest answer. It was true that Stark and his team, along with the bio-bank, were essentially what this entire battle was about. They would likely be safe either way, and this was a fact that Renton and the others at Moon Base Delta would have to come to terms with.

Renton threw his hands up in the air. "Fine," he said finally, exasperated. "Good luck with that." He turned and signaled to the others that it was time to leave and head back to the operations room.

"That smug bastard," said Matteo as they rushed toward the elevators that would take them up to the next level. "He thinks he's so high and mighty, like some kind of god, sitting above the petty squabbles of us mere mortals."

"Yeah, he does give off that impression, for sure," Renton agreed. "But he's right... in a way. No matter what happens here today, he's still going to be fine."

"And did you see the look on those scientists' faces when he raised his hand?" added Matteo. "It's like they were all afraid of him."

"I wouldn't mind so much, but he's not even a scientist. As far as I know, he was just the guy bankrolling this entire project," said Bale, the former tech from the Axial. "Maybe Xilinex will see right through his façade, and take him for a long walk out a short airlock," he speculated.

"Yeah," said Matteo with a laugh, "I'd really like to see him talk his way out of that."

The mood in the operations room was grim as Renton and the others made their return. They might have slowed down one incursion, but more of the newly arrived Xilinex mercenaries had begun entering into the base, reinforcing the initial vanguard and making advances on multiple fronts. For a fleeting moment, Renton contemplated the unthinkable: he wondered if surrender might actually be the best option. They had fought the good fight, made a commendable stand, but was it worth shedding more blood to try to fend off what was beginning to seem like the inevitable?

The assault groups that they had initially tried to corral in the tunnels on the lower levels were now regrouping and breaking out. Their own fighters were falling back more and more, retreating into the central structure of the base, and even there, they were finding it nearly impossible to hold the line.

They had already lost most of the army of industrial robots and drones that Alice, Yuna, and a number of other operators had been controlling. Most of whom now stood around the operations room, with nothing to do, anxiously fretting about each retreat and how they were now powerless to help prevent further losses—their machines having been destroyed in battle.

On the other hand, the battle droids that Xilinex had brought to the fight seemed impervious to all their attempts to take them down—except for the one they had successfully blasted out through the old ventilation shaft. Still, try as they might to find other opportunities within the Moon Base Delta complex to perform the same trick, they simply didn't exist once Xilinex had broken out of the lower levels and began advancing on the central structure. Even DOA, normally highly resourceful, had seemed to run out of ideas.

In the midst of the desperation and panic filling the operations room, Renton took himself off to a quiet corner. Taking a deep breath, he asked DOA to give it to him straight.

"What are our chances, DOA?" he whispered, cautious not to let the others overhear the conversation.

"I assume you are referring to the ongoing battle and the prospects for achieving a successful outcome?"

"Yes, absolutely. Do we have any chance of defeating them?"

"My current estimates indicate a five to seven percent chance of a favorable conclusion to the hostilities."

Renton exhaled deeply, "So, basically no chance, then?"

"That's not exactly what I said," replied DOA. "There's a chance that the conflict could go in your favor; it's just a slim one."

"It's those damn battle droids. They're almost impossible to kill."

"Indeed, they are a significant factor," DOA concurred.

There was a sudden burst of activity in the operations room, and Renton glanced up at the main wall screen to see a real-time feed of a battle droid breaking through yet another one of their defensive lines. Immediately, two industrial robots rushed forward in an attempt to contain the droid and buy the fighters enough time to fall back once more. One of the robots took a direct hit and began to shake and judder as the plasma blast fried its electronics. Yuna ripped off her VR headset and flung it down on the desk in a fit of frustration.

"Goddamnit, there goes another one."

However, it did allow the fighters to retreat to an upper level, leaving the single operational robot to close the bulkhead doors, cordoning off that particular sector. It would buy them just a little more time until the Xilinex forces managed to break through again.

"There has to be something we can do to disable those battle droids?" Yuna stood up and walked over to where Alice was still diligently operating.

"We could try to target their operators, but I think they are located out on the surface somewhere," Matteo replied.

"My analysis of the signal data indicates that they are being operated from the Xilinex orbital HQ and relayed through several ground stations," said DOA.

"So even if we hit one of the ground stations, we still wouldn't stop them." Yuna shook her head in frustration.

Renton could now sense it—the moment had arrived. He glanced over to where his aunt sat in silence, transfixed by the images of the battles being relayed on the big monitor. *Is it time?* he wondered. Time to throw in the towel, admit defeat, and save the people, his people, from further bloodshed?

"I am detecting several military transport shuttles heading toward this location," DOA announced. All eyes shifted to the monitor. A blurry satellite feed displayed a fleet of around seven shuttles flying low over the lunar surface at high speed.

"I don't believe it, not more Xilinex," said Matteo, vocalizing what everyone else was thinking.

"These are not from the Xilinex Corporation," DOA clarified. "These ships have lifted off from the SINO enclave in Mare Crisium."

"SINO?" Renton couldn't believe what he was hearing. "Is that possible?"

"It appears that a change of regime has taken place, facilitated by the withdrawal of Xilinex forces from the blockade."

In that instant, Renton and the beleaguered defenders of Moon Base Delta began to feel hope rise again. And with that, he put all thoughts of surrender aside.

CHAPTER 34
INTERTWINED

Han now found himself in a kind of limbo. They were not yet ready to officially charge him with a crime, yet neither was he free to go home. Dyson, along with those who supported him, had negotiated a deal with the leadership: Han would be held under house arrest until the current developments on Luna had run their course. However, he would not return to the same apartment given to him and Sheneese upon their arrival at Vandenberg Space Port. Instead, they took Han to a rundown apartment that had been specifically set up for him in the very same building as the interrogation had taken place. He was now effectively under a form of house arrest. This particular apartment would be his makeshift home for the foreseeable future. He was not allowed any visitors; not even Sheneese was permitted to call in and see him, at least not just yet. This, Dyson had assured him, was for the best if he truly wanted to keep her out of the precarious situation that he now found himself ensnared in.

The deal they had negotiated on his behalf was tenuous at best. Others were actively seeking to reverse it, wanting him to be made an example of. But for the moment, the deal held. Maybe in a few days, when the animosity within the leadership settled down somewhat, she might be allowed to visit. This was Dyson's way of doing him a solid, an earnest attempt to minimize the inevitable fallout. The authorities had no hard evidence that she had any prior knowledge of what Han was secretly up to, so Dyson and the others had argued that she be kept entirely out of this predicament—for the moment, at least.

Reading between the lines of the semi-official interrogation he had just been through, it became abundantly clear to him that a power struggle was unfolding at the highest levels. Dyson and the others were in one distinct camp, the one that was actively and diligently working to shield Han from the dire repercussions of his recent actions. The other camp, of course, was still in power and vehemently wanted Han to suffer the full, unmitigated force of the law and to be formally charged with treason. If this latter group were to ultimately prevail, then Dyson's faction could do absolutely nothing to protect either him or indeed Sheneese. At best, they would be unceremoniously ejected from the safety and relative security of the Vandenberg Space Port and left to fend for themselves in an unforgiving, hostile environment. At worst, they would both be incarcerated. So, for the time being, he was placed into a sort of deepfreeze while the larger events continued to play out around him.

The apartment itself was spacious but decidedly Spartan, outfitted with plain, utilitarian furnishings that offered minimal comfort. There was no comms system, no data link, absolutely no means for him to contact the world that existed beyond his four walls. The kitchen was stocked with essentials, so at least he would not go hungry. Outside the front door to the apartment, two security guards had been posted to make absolutely certain he did not make any attempts to escape. All the windows had been fitted with thick, imposing metal bars; at some point in the past, these were installed to keep unwanted people out. Now, however, their primary function was to keep him in.

He sat down beside one of these barred windows and gazed out across the expansive concrete lot situated in front of the building toward a row of low-rise offices on the far side. He spotted a few people entering—ordinary people, office workers, maintenance staff. He found himself envying them; they were free and blissfully unburdened by the troubles and complications that he had so carelessly brought down upon himself.

His fate, and likewise that of Sheneese, was now being ultimately decided by a battle that was raging almost four hundred thousand kilometers away from here, in a long-abandoned base, over the control of that most basic and essential of human needs—food. Both his immediate future and that of Moon Base Delta were now inexorably intertwined. If they went down, then inevitably, so would he.

CHAPTER 35
NOT A GOOD IDEA

Renton raised Chen Jun on comms; he and his team were still holding the line one level below the agri-sector.

"We've still got them tied down in the storage areas," said Chen Jun, his voice labored and filled with urgency. "But that won't last for very long. They've already cut through one door and are now starting on the second."

"Well, I have some good news. I think some serious help might be on the way," said Renton.

There was a momentary pause in the conversation before Chen Jun came back with, "Help? From where?"

"Several military shuttles have departed from the SINO enclave, and they're making their way down toward us. It appears there's been a coup of some sort up there, so it looks like your friend might have come through after all. We're going to need you in the operations room; DOA is attempting to make contact with their lead ship. If it is your friend Wang Wei and they're here to help, then we're going to need you to help in coordinating it."

"Well, I'll be damned," said Chen Jun. "He actually did it. And here I was thinking he had abandoned us." He paused for a moment, and in the background, Renton could hear him shouting instructions to various fighters. Before long, he came back on comms.

"Okay, I'll head up there. Fingers crossed it really is Wang Wei."

By the time Chen Jun arrived in the operations room, the video feed from the lead SINO ship was flickering to life on the main screen. All activity in the room ceased, and everyone fell silent as an image of the interior cockpit came into view. Two men stood behind the pilot and co-pilot seats, one of whom was instantly recognizable to Renton, Alice, Yuna, and Matteo. It was none other than Chen Gongbo, their former SINO captor from DaVinci. Renton was taken aback by this revelation, and for a fleeting moment, a worrying fear rose up inside him that maybe this was not the help that he and the others had been hoping for.

But his fears were quickly put aside when Chen Jun shouted out, "Hey, Wang, you crazy bastard! Last time we talked, you were trying to convince me you and you crew were just a bunch of useless wimps."

"Ha, sorry about that, Chen. We had to make it look like we were beaten down, with no fight left in us. I wanted to make

Xilinex think we were no threat. And it worked," Wang responded.

"Yeah," said Renton, "except they're all down here at Moon Base Delta." He paused for a moment and then continued, "I see you brought a friend with you, Chen Gongbo. We've met before, haven't we?"

"We have indeed," said Gongbo, "but that was a different time, in a different place. This is not the same moon that we all once lived on. Now, we all have new priorities. For the last few months, the Xilinex Corporation has been trying to starve us into submission, just like you at Moon Base Delta. So, it would seem that we now find ourselves fighting on the same side."

"What my good friend Gongbo is trying to articulate," Wang chimed in, "is that the era of the old SINO ideology is over. If we're going to survive, then we need to pull together. The old regime had to go; there's no place for them here anymore."

"Well, you have no idea how relieved we all are to hear that," said Renton. "But I'll be honest, we're under extreme pressure here; time is critical for us now. There are simply too many Xilinex forces here for us to effectively handle."

"Not to mention those damn battle droids they brought into the fight," Alice added.

"Battle droids?" asked Wang Wei.

"Yes, a sort of hardened industrial robot," Alice explained. "They can take a significant amount of punishment and seem almost impervious to EMP detonation. We've thrown everything we have at them, but nothing seems to be effective, except the one we managed to blow one out through an old ventilation shaft."

254

"They're going to be a tough nut to crack," concluded Matteo.

Over the next few minutes, Chen Jun, Renton, and some of the others coordinated a tactical plan of attack. The newly arrived SINO fighters would land at multiple points around Moon Base Delta and engage the small contingent of Xilinex support technicians who were still stationed out on the lunar surface. The hope was that by demolishing their surface infrastructure, they would interrupt the control signal emanating from the corporation's HQ that was directing the battle droids. Then, they would begin to enter base through the access points already compromised by the initial Xilinex forces and commence attacking from the rear. This maneuver would relieve some of the defensive pressure, and Xilinex would find themselves caught in a pincer movement.

There was already a discernible shift in movement by the mercenaries inside the base. Clearly, they had received word that there had been a coup in the SINO enclave, and that the blockade had collapsed. Now, all those workers and civilians whom they had attempted to starve into submission were coming to exact revenge. A small contingent of the rearguard started to reinforce the intrusion points into the base, sending additional fighters and weapons back to the entrances. Meanwhile, outside on the lunar surface, the small Xilinex support garrison had begun reoriented their weapons to aim at the incoming shuttles. But before they even had a chance to fire a shot, all three of their plasma cannon emplacements were obliterated by a volley of incoming fire. With this threat neutralized, the SINO craft began landing.

It didn't take much time for the remaining Xilinex fighters positioned on the lunar surface to be eliminated. Soon, their entire infrastructure—including shuttles, habitation modules, supply dumps, and command centers—were systematically taken out, one by one. Yet, for the squads of fighters inside Moon Base Delta who were still trying to fend off attacks from multiple directions, their hope that the seemingly indestructible battle droids would finally deactivate was crushed. The droids just continued their relentless assault.

As Renton and the others looked on from the operations room, monitoring the intense battles that were unfolding both inside the base and now out on the surface, their optimism for a quick victory evaporated. The battle droids had failed to deactivate. Worse, some of these droids now shifted their focus from the internal attack and began to move back toward the entrance points, back to engage the newly arrived SINO fighters. There was no doubt in Renton's mind that it was going to be a brutal bloodbath. And worst of all, there appeared to be absolutely nothing they could do to halt these unstoppable machines.

And the Xilinex forces within the base still kept exerting immense pressure on their defensive positions, one of which appeared to be on the brink of collapsing. If that were to happen, Xilinex could potentially break through into the central structure of Moon Base Delta. From that point, they would have a relatively unobstructed path leading directly to the operations room. Kimura and Tanaka, who had been leading this defensive squad, were already beginning to fall back, reporting their losses, and urgently requesting reinforcements with a sense of growing desperation.

Renton was in the midst of organizing a crew to go down and help in the fight, when suddenly a new communications channel flickered to life on the wall monitor. It displayed a familiar head and shoulders—it was none other than Mackenzie, in a full EVA suit, and piloting a shuttle.

"Mackenzie?" Alice exclaimed, visibly shocked. "I heard that you were injured, what are you doing piloting a shuttle?"

"I heard my man Chen Jun and his buddies were leading the charge against Xilinex. There's absolutely no way I'm going to be left out of this battle. But the Martians wanted no part of it, so I had to take matters into my own hands and 'borrow' one of their shuttles. I'm en route to you right now."

"Not a good idea," warned Renton. "There's an intense battle unfolding on the surface, and they're deploying battle droids—killing machines that are nearly impossible to neutralize. We've tried everything from EMPs to standard high explosives, but they just keep on coming. There are a few of them on the surface, so if you attempt to land, you're very likely going to get yourself killed."

Mackenzie paused to consider this for a brief moment. "Are they autonomous, or is someone actively controlling them?"

"They're remotely controlled directly from the Xilinex HQ in orbit. There's absolutely no way for us to interfere with that," Alice chimed in.

A broad smile broke across Mackenzie's face. "Oh yeah? Well, maybe I can do something about it."

"Like what?" Matteo questioned, intrigued.

"Leave that to me. I'll catch up with you guys later," Mackenzie said, and with that, the comms link disconnected.

"What the hell is she planning?" Yuna exclaimed. "If she's seriously contemplating taking on that Xilinex orbital station, then she must've had one too many plasma blasts to the head."

"Whatever it is," added Matteo, "you know Mackenzie; she's going to do whatever she wants, and there's absolutely no stopping her. In the meantime, we've got more pressing issues to deal with." He pointed at the live feed on the monitor, which displayed Xilinex forces trying to breakthrough.

"Come on, let's move. Kimura urgently needs our help down there."

CHAPTER 36
TRAPPED

"Can you believe Mackenzie?" said Matteo as they took the elevator down to the lower levels of the central structure, the core of Moon Base Delta.

"Yeah, she never ceases to amaze, that's for sure. Still, I have no idea what she thinks she's actually going to achieve up there," Renton responded, his eyes focused on the rapidly descending numbers above the elevator control panel.

The doors slid open, bringing them out on a level just above where Kimura and her crew were fighting a desperate rearguard action. Xilinex forces were almost breaking through. Renton's plan was to set up new defensive positions in this sector, by shutting down all access routes including this elevator shaft. Kimura and the others could fall back via the emergency stairwell, which they would blow up after them. They stepped out into a vast open space that had originally been designed as a communal gathering area. On one side, there was tiered seating facing what once had been a stage. A space which might have been used for community events in a more peaceful, saner past.

Other, smaller sectors, branching off from this main area were also originally designed for entertainment and recreation. Somewhere in this complex layout, there was even a swimming pool, now long since drained and lying dormant. Renton contacted Alice, who was still in the operations room, and asked her to deactivate the elevators. These elevators had shafts that ran vertically through multiple levels, equipped with numerous bulkhead doors designed to isolate various sectors in the event of an emergency. All of those situated below their current position were already securely closed off.

If Xilinex forces were to advance into this sector, they would have to do so through a stairwell on the far side of the area. That's exactly where Renton and his team now made their way. Their plan was to establish, as effectively as they could, a defensive position that would allow Kimura, Tanaka, and the rest of their crew to fall back. Once that was achieved, they would then seal off all remaining bulkhead doors and blow the stairwell. Implementing this strategy would, at least, slow down the advancing assault.

The team was cautiously navigating through an old, long-disused gym area when Matteo suddenly grabbed Renton's arm and pointed a finger toward a dimly lit corner. "I think there's something moving over there," he said, his voice filled with urgency. They all came to a halt and crouched down, their eyes scanning the shadowy area Matteo was indicating, looking for any signs of movement.

"You think Xilinex has broken through already?" Renton questioned. But before anyone could offer a reply, he noticed the movement himself. A metallic flash caught his eye—a reflection from their helmet-mounted lights. It was a machine of some sort.

"A battle droid?" Matteo looked at Renton, his face awash with incredulity as he noticed the movement too.

"No way, can't be. I thought they're all outside, engaging Wang Wei's forces?" Renton countered.

But at that very same moment, the machine on the far side of the gym seemed to become aware of their presence and it rose up on its hind legs. Even from a distance, there was no longer any room for doubt; they could clearly see it was a battle droid.

"Where the hell did that come from? Has one of them come back inside?" Renton was genuinely puzzled.

His answer came immediately from Alice, who was still stationed in the operations room. "No way it could have come from outside. I'm actively tracking all three of them on the lunar surface right now."

"It can't be," Renton said, as it began to dawn on him. "Is that the same droid that we blasted out of the ventilation shaft?"

The droid now arranged itself onto its remaining legs, they could clearly see that one of its front limbs was missing. It began to advance toward them, albeit slowly, as one of its rear limbs also seemed to be malfunctioning.

"I don't believe it," Renton exclaimed, "that's got to be the same droid. It's taken a lot of damage, but how in God's name did it manage to survive that explosion?"

"I wonder if it still has a functioning weapon system?" Matteo mused. His answer was promptly delivered in the form of a burst of railgun fire that whizzed over their heads and slammed into the rear wall.

"I think the answer is a definite yes," said Matteo, as he and the rest of the team unleashed a heavy barrage of plasma fire at the machine. Under normal circumstances, such an onslaught would have stopped even a space freighter dead in its tracks. But as the smoke cleared, the dust settled, and the crackling of electrical energy fizzled out, they could see the battle droid arranging itself up again. It might be damaged, but it was still very much operational.

Kimura's voice broke in over Renton's comms, and in the background, he could hear the unmistakable sounds of intense fighting—yelling, shouting, and the distinctive *whoomp whoomp* of plasma weapons firing. "Be alert, DOA says there's a droid somewhere in your location," she cautioned.

"Yeah, it's the same one we blew out of the ventilation shaft; it must've found its way back in somehow. It's badly damaged but still very much a threat," Renton replied.

"Can we fall back yet? Say yes, because we're getting absolutely hammered here." Renton could hear the palpable desperation in Kimura's voice.

"Not yet," said Renton, "we still need to set the explosives to take out the stairwell. And that droid is right in our way. If we move now, we'll run straight into it. We're going to try and direct it away from the access door. Once we manage to do that, we can set the charges. I'll give you the all-clear signal, and then you can fall back."

"Okay, but make it quick," Kimura urged. "We're already moving back, heading for the stairwell. We won't be more than a few minutes, I think."

Renton turned to the others, who were all huddled together behind a thick concrete dividing wall. "I'll try to lead this droid away from here. Once it's gone, you guys can then set the explosives on the stairwell, okay?"

"Yeah, except I'm not letting you go do this on your own," Matteo countered. "Jason, can you set the explosives? You know how to do it, right?"

Jason, a veteran of the old Axial Luxor security team, nodded. "No problem, I can handle it."

"Are you sure you want to do this?" Renton asked Matteo.

Matteo grinned. "I'm as sure as you are, my friend."

"Okay then. But first, we need to figure out a route. DOA? Any suggestions?"

"There is an old industrial elevator shaft at the southern end of this level," DOA replied. "It's derelict, so I can't reactivate it; however, you can use the maintenance ladder inside the shaft to move up."

"Won't we be leading this thing back up toward the operations level?" Renton questioned.

"No, this elevator shaft terminates in a decommissioned warehouse sector," DOA clarified.

"Is there any way out of there?" Renton inquired further.

"The main access route is no longer operable due to a tunnel collapse, which is why the sector was decommissioned in the first place. The only way in or out is via the maintenance ladder inside the elevator shaft," DOA confirmed.

"That could be both a good and a bad thing. We could end up being trapped in there," Matteo observed.

"We'll figure it out," Renton assured him as they readied themselves to move out.

He felt a tug on his sleeve and looked up to see Jason pointing ahead. "It's on the move, getting closer."

Peering cautiously around the edge of the dividing wall, Renton strained his eyes in the dim light. Sure enough, he caught the glint from the system lights of the advancing battle droid.

He hefted his weapon and glanced over at Matteo. "You still up for this?"

"No," Matteo grinned, as he readied his own weapon. "Come on, lead the way."

As soon as they stepped out from their cover, the droid immediately reacted. They could hear the skittering sound as the machine tried to find traction on the hard floor. With only two of its limbs functioning properly and a third one partially operational, the droid struggled to move quickly, which was fortunate for them. Yet, despite its compromised mobility, it remained a deadly; a reminder of this came when a plasma blast whizzed over their heads, mangling a stack of gym equipment further ahead.

"Damnit, looks like its plasma weapon is still functioning too," Renton said as he ran.

"At least its aim is way off," offered Matteo.

They managed to keep a reasonable distance between them

and the droid, making themselves difficult targets. Yet, the droid was taking the bait, following them. After a few heart-pounding moments, Renton received a message from Jason indicating that the team had reached the stairwell and explosives had been primed. Now, Kimura and her crew could begin their retreat. They planned to detonate the explosives along the stairwell behind them, once they got through, effectively sealing it off. They would then ascend to the upper levels through the same elevator shaft that Renton and his group had initially descended in and disable it. As Renton processed this situation, he came to a sobering realization that with their planned route back to the operations level shortly to be cut off, he and Matteo were venturing into what could potentially become a dead-end trap.

Up ahead, Renton could see the doors to the elevator shaft highlighted on his AR display. They had now entered an area on this level that seemed the most derelict. Even the doors leading to the elevator shaft were battered and misaligned, making it abundantly clear that this area had not been maintained for a very long time.

They both grasped the edges of the battered sliding doors and tried to wrench them open. But only the door on Matteo's side seemed willing to budge, so Renton adjusted his position to assist. Together, they managed to slide it open just wide enough for them to squeeze through. They stepped into the elevator carriage, its final resting place after what must have been its last journey a great many years ago. Renton looked up to locate the escape hatch, leapt up to grab its edge, and forcefully bashed it out of the way. He clambered up through the hole in the roof and then stood on the edge of the carriage to make room for Matteo to follow him. Casting his light around the dark elevator shaft that towered above them, he estimated that it was not far to its endpoint—perhaps about thirty meters. He located the maintenance ladder, placed a foot on it to test its stability, and when it held firm against his weight, he began his ascent, with Matteo trailing a little behind.

As he climbed, he started to realize that the shaft was blocked. The original pulley motor mounts had collapsed, and the entire assembly had plummeting down the shaft, and bringing with it a tangled mess of metal beams, motors, and cabling, effectively blocking their way.

"We've got a problem," he called down to Matteo. "The shaft is blocked. The motor housing has collapsed and created a tangled mess up here."

"Is there any way through?" No sooner had Matteo spoken these words than they heard a grating, scraping sound emanating from the bottom of the shaft. The droid was forcing its way through. In a frantic rush, Renton scanned the jumbled wreckage above him, desperately seeking a gap or a loose beam he could yank free to clear a path. His hands latched onto a truss that had wedged itself tightly into the surrounding wall, and began pulling with all his might, but it wouldn't budge, not an inch.

"Renton, we need to move, hurry!" Matteo's voice was tinged with urgency.

"It's wedged in tight. There's no way through this mess," Renton responded, his eyes darting back just in time to see the droid commence its slow and awkward climb up the maintenance ladder. It was an ungainly ascent but relentless. Matteo unleashed several rounds of plasma fire at it, but the blasts were wholly ineffective. The droid twisted its head to lock its gaze directly on them. Then, as if sensing that it had finally trapped its prey, a plasma cannon elevated from its shoulder mount and took aim.

And at that very moment, Renton came to a grim realization: it was game over.

CHAPTER 37

KEEP FIRING

Pompodur Rossen Adarok surveyed the unfolding battle for Moon Base Delta through the multitude of live video feeds displayed on the expansive wall monitor in the war room of Xilinex HQ's orbital station. He felt a sense of deep satisfaction wash over him. Finally, after enduring countless setbacks, the future of the Moon was being decisively settled, and all indications were looking good.

There had been a brief moment of apprehension when news broke that a coup had erupted in the SINO enclave, followed by the lift-off of several military shuttles aimed directly at Moon Base Delta. General Wagner had been livid, asserting that the decision to divert Xilinex resources from the blockade and reallocate them to the battle at Moon Base Delta had been ill-advised. However, Pompodur had painstakingly persuaded him that, inevitably, Xilinex forces would have to engage with the same SINO rebels at some point. And that the inevitable confrontation might as well happen now, rather than later.

Yet, as events unfolded, the new SINO involvement hadn't significantly swayed the course of the battle. True, Xilinex would incur a higher rate of casualties than originally desired, but as things stood at this particular moment, it appeared that the momentum of the battle was decidedly with them. Neither the faltering forces of Moon Base Delta nor the late-arriving reinforcements from the SINO enclave seemed capable of turning the tide.

The pivotal component in the Xilinex assault was the deployment of the experimental battle droids that had been included in the initial wave of reinforcements from Earth, before the travel window between them had been irrevocably closed. General Wagner had been reluctant to utilize these droids, as they had not yet been proven in combat. Despite his role as commander of a cadre of spacefaring mercenaries, he harbored a notable distrust of untested technology. Yet, it was these very same battle droids that were now decisively tilting the balance of power in their favor. These machines were virtually indestructible, easily withstanding the feeble counterattacks that the defenders of Moon Base Delta could muster. Only in one isolated incident had one of these lethal machines been damaged, but even that particular droid was still actively engaged in the fight, having cornered two unfortunate defenders in an abandoned elevator shaft.

Pompodur was currently watching the video feed from this

particular droid, among the myriad of other feeds streaming in from various locations across the battlefield. Each feed narrated a different chapter of the same overarching story: defeat for Moon Base Delta and the SINO rebels, and an unmitigated victory for Xilinex—and, by extension, for Pompodur Rossen Adarok himself.

"Sir, we've detected a shuttle departing from the Mars ship, and it's heading in our direction," a technician called out from one of the workstations.

"Establish contact," General Wagner issued a gruff command. "Find out what its intentions are."

"We've attempted to contact them multiple times, sir. No response."

"Get in touch with the Mars ship then; perhaps they have some information."

"Understood, sir."

A moment later, the technician spoke up again. "Sir, it appears the shuttle has been stolen by someone from Moon Base Delta they were holding captive. The individual is identified as... Mackenzie."

"Broadcast a warning. Inform them that they're entering a military exclusion zone and that they'll be shot at and destroyed if they persist on this course."

Pompodur's focus now shifted away from the unfolding drama in the old, derelict recreational sector of Moon Base Delta—where the damaged droid was closing in on two ill-fated defenders. His attention was now directed toward a somewhat blurry image of a shuttle on what appeared to be a direct intercept course with their orbital station. While the shuttle itself was not a major concern, the fact that it was being piloted by one Mackenzie Arnold caught his attention. Mackenzie was the very captain of the maintenance ship Aurora, which had formerly employed the key members of the current leadership team of Moon Base Delta. This development prompted him to sit up and take notice.

"Sir, it appears the shuttle is decelerating—yes, it's slowing down quite dramatically and has now come to a complete standstill relative to our own vector."

This development caught General Wagner's attention, prompting him to turn and scrutinize the video feed displayed on the monitor. "It looks like our warning was enough to give them pause for thought."

However, as they watched the screen, they saw that the shuttle had opened its rear cargo door and begun jettisoning everything from inside into the vacuum of space.

"What in the hell is it doing?" asked Pompodur, puzzled. "Taking out the garbage?"

On the monitor they could see a drifting stream of crates, bundles, and machinery floating away from the shuttle. Then it started to gradually accelerate once more.

"Sir, it's moving again and continuing to head in our direction."

"Wait until they're well within our range, and then obliterate them."

"Aye, aye, sir."

Pompodur considered this unfolding situation and preemptively opened a comms channel to his assistant, inquiring about the readiness of his personal shuttle. Maybe he was displaying an overabundance of caution, but such vigilance had served him well in the past and would likely continue to do so in the future.

The initial salvo of plasma fire missed the approaching shuttle entirely. Its small profile and the considerable distance from the orbital made it a challenging target to hit.

"What the hell are you doing?" General Wagner barked at the technician operating the lone plasma cannon that constituted the orbital's defenses. Initially, the space station had served as the headquarters for the civilian Xilinex corporation's mining operations on the lunar surface. During its initial construction, no one had ever thought it would need defenses more robust than good security. Back then, the notion that the station might ever need to fend off a shuttle attack was unthinkable. Consequently, a single plasma cannon was all they had for defense. The shuttle continued its approach, its speed and momentum increasing with each passing second.

By now, Pompodur was growing increasingly concerned by this audacious action taken by the former FISA maintenance crew captain. Up to this point, the shuttle had not fired on the space station. It was highly likely that it did not possess any such weapons, considering it was part of the Mars ship's inventory. So, what could her game plan possibly be? Was she seriously contemplating ramming the space station? A second burst of plasma fire erupted from the orbital's lone defensive cannon. This time, the shuttle took a direct hit on its starboard bow. Yet, it still continued to accelerate, the impact seemingly having little-to-no effect on its course or trajectory. These Mars shuttles were clearly built of stronger stuff than those rated for lunar activities.

Pompodur wondered if he should take this moment as his cue to vacate the war room and make his way to the shuttle dock. Yet, he steeled his nerve and convinced himself that this was nothing more than a minor inconvenience, simply another inconsequential skirmish in a battle that was, for all intents and purposes, already won. It would be his greatest achievement, his crowning glory. It would be the pivotal moment when he would gain control over not just the entire lunar population but also exert influence over the faltering governments and major corporations back on Earth. He relished the thought of making them squirm, forcing them to beg for the Helium-3 supplies they so desperately needed, savoring the spectacle of watching the world descend into chaos.

He scanned the multitude of live feeds, each one showing various individual battles taking place throughout Moon Base Delta. A laugh escaped his lips when he saw that the two hapless defenders had now found themselves trapped in the elevator shaft. The battle droid was zeroing in on them; their end was near.

But his attention was abruptly pulled back to the immediate situation as the noise level in the war room suddenly ramped up several notches. The General was on his feet, barking frantic commands, while the techs called out a cacophony of warnings and alerts.

Visibly agitated, the General was waving his arms wildly, gesturing emphatically at the feed of the approaching shuttle displayed on the screen. The craft was close enough now that the scars on its hull from multiple plasma hits were visible, yet it appeared there was no halting its advance. It was now perilously close to the orbital space station.

"Keep firing, keep firing! You have to destroy it, don't let it get any closer, Goddammit!" The General was becoming increasingly apoplectic.

"Can't, sir," one of the techs shouted back, the panic in his voice unmistakable. "The shuttle is below the firing elevation of our cannon; there's simply... no way to stop it now." His eyes met those of the General, and his face showed a mixture of shock and disbelief. It was at that exact moment that Pompodur knew he had to get out—immediately—while a fleeting chance for escape still existed. Jumping to his feet, he gave a quick signal to his assistants and made a dash for the exit.

A few tense seconds later, he was already in the elevator, which began transporting him and his entourage from the artificial gravity conditions of the outer rotating torus to the shuttle dock situated at the central hub.

"Come on, come on," he muttered to himself under his breath, his impatience intensifying as the elevator moved with what felt like agonizing slowness. Gradually, he started to feel lighter, almost as if being lifted by an invisible force, until at last the elevator doors opened, releasing them into the zero-gravity environment of the central hub.

He was just about to float into the short airlock tunnel that would lead them onto his personal shuttle when a rumble reverberated throughout the station. Almost instantly, a decompression klaxon blared out, and the entire area was bathed in the harsh glow of an orange strobe light.

"Quickly, sir," one of his assistants urged, hurriedly guiding him down the airlock tunnel. "The station's been hit; we're losing atmosphere."

They all piled into the shuttle, and Pompodur quickly tethered himself into a seat. Up front, the pilot fired up the ship's engines, sealed the outer airlock door, and disengaged from the station's docking clamps. As they began to pull away, Pompodur glanced out of the window. He could see that a massive chunk had been torn out of the rotating torus, as if someone had taken an enormous bite out of a donut. Debris was already spewing out from the impact site, and one by one, the lights on the station began to flicker and fade—it was clearly losing power. The shuttle must have hit something critically important.

Pompodur kept his eyes riveted to the station as they powered away toward the Axial Luxor. He could now see a section of the torus detaching itself from one of the central spokes of the orbital. It peeled away, driven by the centripetal force, broke free, and then spiraled off into the void of space. With the structural integrity of the space station now critically compromised, the very rotation that had once provided them with artificial gravity was acting as a destructive force, tearing the station apart. Another central spoke suddenly splintered, initiating a cascading wave of destruction. Eventually, the stresses and strains to which the compromised structure was being subjected became too much to bear. The remaining outer ring began to peel away, bit by bit, and he could see debris erupting from its interior, including the bodies of many of its occupants.

CHAPTER 38
ANYTIME

With the droid poised to unload a barrage of plasma fire, Renton frantically yanked on the jumbled, twisted mass of debris that hung precariously above his head. A desperate act, yet, what else could he do. He exerted all his adrenaline-fueled strength to pull on a heavy, crumpled metal panel. It suddenly shifted. A shower of dust and debris rained down around him, peppering his face and shoulders. He almost lost his grip on the shaky ladder, as the stubborn metal panel finally dislodged itself and went tumbling down into depths of the shaft below.

"Watch out!" he shouted as Matteo instinctively pulled his body flush against the wall, narrowly missing being hit by the sharp edges of free-falling panel. The droid also made a frantic attempt to retract its plasma weapon and pull itself in against the wall of the shaft. However, the panel hit an obstruction as it plummeted, causing it to spin erratically and violently. The droid miscalculated the trajectory and the panel slammed into it, sending it falling back down the shaft and through the hatch in the roof of the elevator carriage.

Renton, sensing that they might just live for a few more minutes, decided to use this time wisely. "DOA, we're trapped," Renton shouted into his comms. "We're stuck in this elevator shaft, it's blocked up. Is there another way out? A side hatch, a maintenance door, anything?"

"There should be a maintenance hatch located at the fifteen-meter mark from the base of the shaft," DOA responded.

Renton took a second to assess the distance they had managed to ascend so far within the elevator shaft. "Eh... it seems like that would be above our current position. Hold on, no, wait a minute. I see it."

Through the chaotic tangle of metal and debris above him, Renton zeroed in on the maintenance hatch, located about a meter above where they currently were. But the elevator's motor housing had jammed into the hatch, completely obstructing access. This was what had arrested the motor housing's free fall toward the bottom of the shaft. A support truss had collided with the hatch and had become lodged in place. There was absolutely no way he could access that hatch now.

"Renton, it's Alice" her voice tinged with concern. "You need to get out of there!"

"There's no way out, Alice. It's a total mess up here, the maintenance hatch is completely blocked." Renton responded, his voice heavy with grim acceptance.

"Xilinex forces have moved up to that level, Renton. We

can't send anyone down to help you." Alice's desperate voice crackled through his comms.

"It's okay, Alice," Renton tried to reassure her. "We're not going down without a fight."

"Damn right," Matteo added.

"Renton, no... There has to be another way, some way to—" But her plea was cut off.

At that very moment, the battle droid clambered out through the elevator hatch, scanning intently to regain a lock on its human targets. Renton pulled out his plasma weapon and got ready.

"Got to go, things are really hotting up here. I love you." Renton closed the comms link and, without wasting another second, unloaded the entire charge of his plasma weapon into the oncoming battle droid.

Matteo did likewise, shouting at the top of his lungs, "Die, you metal bastard, die!"

But despite the torrent of plasma they unleashed, the droid was still operational. As the smoke cleared and electric discharge fizzled out, they could see the machine renew its ascent up the ladder. It paused momentarily, its head pivoting to scan for targets. Renton clenched his teeth as the droid's plasma cannon unfolded from a hatch on its shoulder. It took aim. He closed his eyes, tensing every muscle in his body as he waited for the inevitable.

Nothing happened. After what felt like an endless stretch of time, Renton cautiously opened one eye, then the other. To his astonishment, he saw that the droid seemed to collapse inward, retracting its limbs. It then lost its grip on the ladder altogether and plummeted, clanging noisily as it hit the roof of the elevator carriage.

"What the heck?" Matteo exclaimed. "Maybe our weapons did inflict some damage after all."

Renton's heart was racing, adrenaline coursing through his veins, he found it difficult to form words. "I think... I think it deactivated itself."

Both of them remained suspended in uncertainty for a moment, half-expecting the droid to reanimate and resume its climb. But it didn't. It just lay there, inert and completely inactive.

"Renton, Renton, are you still there?" It was Alice's voice, breaking the tension.

"Yes, we're still here, still alive. The droid, it just... died," Renton stammered out.

"They all did," Alice replied, her voice a blend of relief and excitement. "All Xilinex systems that were being controlled from the orbital station have gone dead. It appears that Mackenzie's shuttle rammed into the space station; it's destroyed, breaking up in orbit."

"What? Are you serious?"

"Yes, yes, it's true. All the battle droids have stopped functioning; all the drones, even many of the Xilinex forces have become inactive. No one knows exactly what's happened. There's a whole lot of confusion down here, but Chen Jun and the others are starting to capitalize on it and push back. I really think... we may have actually won this."

In the background, Renton could hear jubilant whoops and ecstatic cheers erupting from the operations room. "Did you hear that, Matteo? Did you hear it? That insane Mackenzie just took on the Xilinex orbital station and totally obliterated it."

He looked down to where Matteo was intently listening to the live updates coming in from the operations room. When he looked up at Renton, his face was plastered with a huge, ear-to-ear grin.

"I'm glad she's on our side," Matteo said, chuckling heartily before turning more somber. "I wonder if she survived?"

"Eh... doesn't sound like it." Renton replied, shaking his head.

"Trust her to go out in a blaze of glory," said Matteo. "Come on, let's find our way out of here and head back."

"Hold on, wait," Alice's voice interrupted them again. "Stay where you are. There are still plenty of Xilinex forces roaming around on that level. Kimura and her squad are pushing them back. So just hold tight, we're coming to get you."

"Okay," said Renton, "I think we can manage that."

They began their descent back down the elevator shaft, finally reaching its base where they examined the now-deactivated battle droid. Just to make sure it was truly out of commission, Renton gave it a kick.

"Whoa," Matteo jumped back. "Don't do that," he exclaimed.

Renton chuckled. "I'm just making certain it really is dead. The last thing I want is for this thing to wake up on us."

Matteo grinned and shrugged. "Okay, but just don't... kick it again."

They sat down together, their backs leaning against the elevator shaft's cold walls, tuning into the distant sounds of combat echoing from outside. After what seemed like half an hour or so, the cacophony of battle started to wane. Then they heard a scraping noise at one of the elevator doors, which was suddenly pushed aside. Kimura's face appeared.

"Hey," she said. "All's clear out here. You can come out now. Oh, and by the way, major thanks for leading that battle droid away from us."

Renton waved and grinning back at her. "No problem, anytime."

CHAPTER 39
AFTERMATH

As confusion mounted within the Xilinex ranks, the battle for Moon Base Delta had devolved into a chaotic, uncoordinated rout. The original defensive game plan aimed to lure the attackers into a labyrinthine series of traps and ambushes, systematically whittling down their numbers while retreating to progressively fortified positions. However, with the sudden incapacitation of Xilinex's most formidable asset—the battle droids—a rapid shift in tactics was needed. If Moon Base Delta was to quickly and decisively end this battle once and for all, their game plan had to be altered, and fast, before Xilinex had a change to regroup and reorganize. Renton and Matteo rushed back to the operations room to help bring some semblance of order to the chaos.

When they arrived, Renton was enveloped in a deeply emotional hug from Alice, who was visibly shaken by his

GERALD M. KILBY

harrowing encounter with the battle droid in the elevator shaft. Even Yuna, not typically one to display her emotions, couldn't help but wrap her arms tightly around a very surprised Matteo, and holding on as if she never intended to let go.

"I genuinely thought you were... gone," Alice said, finally pulling back and wiping away a solitary tear from her eye.

"Trust me, for a moment there, so did I," Renton grinned. "But it seems we all owe Mackenzie a big thank you for pulling off that kamikaze stunt."

"That crazy woman, she just... she flew her shuttle directly into the orbital station," Alice said, her voice steadying as she regained some emotional control.

Yuna continued to hold onto Matteo as he gently rubbed her shoulder and whispered into her ear—something that neither Renton nor Alice could hear.

Alice glanced over at the couple then back at Renton with raised an eyebrow. "Who would've thought?" she whispered.

"Yeah, who knew?" Renton responded, grinning.

By this time, the sounds of the ongoing combat, broadcasted live into the operations room, began to seep into Renton's consciousness. He glanced toward the massive wall-mounted screen. "What's the current situation?"

"It's chaotic," Alice answered, her eyes flicking back to the operations room for a moment. "But it's the kind of chaos that's working in our favor."

With Xilinex losing their command and control structure, their forces became increasingly disorganized, some retreating, some

284

trying to hold ground. Sensing the shift in momentum, their own fighters within the base grew bolder, advancing more quickly, risking exposure. Pressing in from the outside, the SINO fighters threatened to squeeze the Xilinex troops into a pincer between them and the defenders inside the base. It was a complex dynamic, unfolding on multiple fronts, highlighting the urgent need for a coordinated strategy to bring an expedient end to the combat.

With DOA's help the fighters coordinated and combined their attacks in an effort to herd the floundering Xilinex forces into a single designated sector of the base. Once they were isolated in this area, DOA issued an unambiguous ultimatum: surrender or face elimination. Given the circumstances they now found themselves in—unable to retreat, unable to move forward—it didn't take long for what was left of Xilinex mercenary command to acquiesce. Within less than five minutes of surrendering, the process of disarming was underway. All weapons and equipment were being systematically collected. Meanwhile, the mercenaries were being divided into smaller, more manageable groups and placed in hastily arranged, makeshift detention areas. It was over. The battle for Moon Base Delta had ended. What had seemed impossible just an hour or so earlier, was now reality. They had defeated the Xilinex Corporation, completely destroying its ability to wage war.

Yet, the celebrations were noticeably subdued. The protracted battle for Moon Base Delta had drained its populace both physically and emotionally. The medbay was swamped, overflowing with casualties, from all sides. In response, Dr. Maria Jensen issued an urgent broadcast for anyone with medical know-how to come to the medbay and lend a hand. This triggered a minor revolt among Jack Stark's cadre of scientists and technicians, some of whom were trained medical professionals. Upon hearing the call, they abandoned their workstations in the bio-labs, much to the angry objections of Stark himself, and headed straight for the overwhelmed medbay to offer their expertise and assistance.

Stark, clearly furious at this abandonment, followed them to the medical facility and continued to berate them for their perceived lack of dedication to his life's work. His tirade reached a boiling point when one of his head scientists, having had enough of Stark and his attitude, spun around and landed a solid punch on Stark's face. A wave of spontaneous cheering erupted from all the Moon Base Delta people in the medbay.

Yet this small moment of revolutionary zeal was not confined just to Stark's team, it now appeared to be engulfing the entire Moon. Reports were trickling in from places like Shackleton and Amundsen Craters where the meager security details that Xilinex had stationed there were being swiftly overwhelmed by local populations, clamoring for a new chapter. Renton found himself once again in the operations room this time grappling with the challenge of understanding and coordinating this burgeoning revolution that was sweeping through the Moon's various communities like a wildfire, as the news of the victory at Moon Base Delta began to spread.

DOA , almost immediately, presented them with a comprehensive dossier on all the factions operating in both

Shackleton and Amundsen Craters, including in-depth profiles of each faction's leaders, outlining their fears, motivations, and most crucially, what incentives would be needed to foster a spirit of unity and cooperation.

This was when Renton came to understand that the true strength of Moon Base Delta didn't solely lie in their access to a stable food supply. Rather, it was also their access to a powerful AI that afforded them the advantage in comprehending any situation they encountered. Equipped with this in-depth analytical insight into the complex political landscapes of various lunar population centers, Selene could execute her diplomatic initiatives with unparalleled efficacy.

But there was one remaining unresolved issue: Pompodur Rossen Adarok and the last remnants of Xilinex power still holed up on the Axial Luxor Orbital. He needed to be confronted and brought to heel. Renton viewed this as a personal mission. However now was not the time for this final showdown. It had been a mere four hours since the cataclysmic obliteration of the Xilinex Orbital, and it felt to Renton like an eternity had elapsed. So many pivotal events had unfolded in that short span of time. He's thoughts inevitably drifted to Mackenzie and the monumental sacrifice she had made for their collective future; he felt profoundly humbled.

"I can't believe that she actually went through with that," he remarked to Alice as they watched a replay of the space station's destruction. The footage had been captured by DOA through one of the satellites in the LunaSat constellation.

"Really?" Yuna interjected, "It doesn't surprise me in the slightest. It's precisely the kind of crazy thing she would do, almost as if she wanted to give us all a lesson in courage and determination."

"What confuses me," Matteo chimed in, "is why she slowed the shuttle down just to eject some garbage?"

"Garbage?" Renton perked up, suddenly intrigued by this new tidbit of information.

"Yeah, she dumped a load of cargo just before her final death run," Matteo confirmed.

"DOA, could you replay that specific segment?" Alice requested.

On the big wall monitor, they saw a somewhat pixelated image of the shuttle, its rear cargo bay door wide open, exposed to the vacuum of space. A flurry of objects seemed to be gradually drifting out from the hold.

"Strange," Renton mused aloud. "That makes absolutely no sense... unless..." Energized by a sudden realization, he leapt up from his seat. "DOA, is there a higher-resolution image of that drifting debris?"

"I apologize, but this is the best quality image I have," DOA replied.

"And where is that cloud of debris currently located?" Renton pressed further.

"It's still in lunar orbit, more or less tracing the same trajectory as the one followed by the now-destroyed Xilinex Orbital HQ," DOA informed.

"We need to dispatch a shuttle up there to investigate immediately," Renton announced.

"Why, what for?" said Yuna, intrigued by his sudden enthusiasm.

"Because I have a strong suspicion that Mackenzie was not on that shuttle when it collided with the orbital. I think she might be out there, floating among that scattered cargo."

CHAPTER 40
LEGEND

R enton felt utterly drained. It was as if he had been running purely on adrenaline for the last thirty-six hours, but the opportunity for rest still eluded him. Yet, if there was even the faintest chance that Mackenzie was out there, adrift among the detritus of her shuttle, they had to find her— even if that meant bringing back a lifeless body.

But now, more than four hours had passed since the destruction of the Xilinex orbital, and by the time they could reach the cloud of discarded remnants that Mackenzie had jettisoned from her shuttle, it would likely be another thirty minutes at least. If she was indeed out there, how much oxygen remained in her EVA suit? How much power was left in the fuel cells? There was no time to lose.

They commandeered one of the SINO shuttles that had previously transported Wang Wei, Chen Gongbo, and a cohort of rebels from Mare Crisium. Renton, Alice, Matteo, and Yuna hastily climbed aboard, setting their coordinates for the search area. With so much time having elapsed since the cargo was ejected, it had now spread out to cover a significantly large area, each item having originally been imparted with a slightly different momentum and slightly different vector. It would be like looking for a neutrino in radiation blast. Add to this the danger of the debris cloud that the disintegrating Xilinex orbital had created. They would need to be very careful not to get hit by anything that could damage their ship. The more Renton thought about it, the more he realized they may be embarking on a fool's errand.

After lifting off from the lunar surface and transitioning into a weightless state, Renton had dozed off, only to be jolted awake some time later by a sharp elbow to his ribs from Alice.

"Renton! We're coming up on the first object in the debris trail," she announced, pointing toward a bright, oblong object that was slowly rotating on its own axis about a kilometer ahead of their position.

"It's just a crate," Yuna confirmed, as she consulted a combined lidar-radar data screen. "It's Martian in origin, so we have no detailed information on its contents."

"At least we know we're on the right track," Matteo commented, craning his neck to get a better view through the cockpit window.

"We're approaching more objects," Yuna updated the team. "So far, there's nothing to indicate any life-forms."

They proceeded cautiously through the debris field,

focusing their attention on any object that triggered a blip on their radar screen.

"I feel obliged to inform you," came DOA's voice, resonating from the cockpit communication system. "You'll soon be reaching the outer edges of the Xilinex orbital debris cloud, in approximately ten minutes."

"Thanks, noted," Yuna responded, her eyes glued to the navigation screen. "Wait a sec," she added. "I'm detecting a human-shaped object, an EVA suit. It's got a very low energy signature, which means it's active."

"Which means there might be someone inside it," Alice clarified.

All eyes were riveted to the screen as the lidar system started to generate a 3D model of the object it was scanning. Gradually, the outline of a human figure began to take form.

"It's three point five kilometers ahead, directly in our path," Yuna updated the team. "I'll bring us in closer for a better look."

Renton felt a slight jolt from the reverse thrusters as Yuna began to decelerate the shuttle.

"I see it!" Matteo exclaimed, pointing excitedly. "Right there, look!" He gestured toward an unfamiliar looking EVA suit—definitely not a standard lunar model, likely Martian in origin.

"I just hope the suit isn't empty," Renton mused.

"You mean, not something that Mackenzie jettisoned as a decoy," Matteo suggested.

"I'll suit up and go check it out," Renton declared, already moving back into the shuttle's cabin to get ready.

"Be quick out there," Alice cautioned. "That debris cloud is nearly upon us."

Renton swiftly ran through the check routine for the EVA suit as he stepped into the side airlock. "Ready," he declared, closing his helmet visor.

"Coming alongside now," Yuna chimed. "Alright, the EVA suit should be floating approximately twenty meters directly ahead of you as you make your exit."

The airlock cycled through its decompression procedure. The outer door finally opened, and Renton could see the lifeless EVA suit slowly rotating in the vacuum of space. He clipped a tether to a rail inside the airlock and gently tapped on his thruster controls to propel him forward. A few seconds later, he coasted in beside the floating body and quickly fastened a tether onto it to prevent it from drifting away from him.

"Is it Mackenzie?" Alice inquired over the communications channel.

"Checking," Renton replied as he maneuvered the body to get a clearer view. He peered through the frosted helmet visor. There was no question; it was his former captain.

"Well, I'll be damned. It's actually Mackenzie; we've found her." In the background, he could hear a spontaneous cheer erupt from the others.

"Is she still alive?" Alice asked, focusing on the crucial question at hand.

Frost fingering out from the inside edges of the helmet visor was never a good sign. Renton already knew what this indicated. The suit was operating at a dangerously low power level and had deactivated all but the most essential systems, mainly those for air recycling and internal temperature control. Ordinarily, with full exposure to the sun's rays, the suit would be working strenuously to keep the body cool. However, they were effectively operating in the Moon's shadow, with little or no ambient radiation to warm any object drifting in space. Therefore, Mackenzie's suit had the critical job of keeping her body warm. With the power dwindling, the suit had resorted to lowering its energy consumption to the bare minimum required to sustain life. This wasn't a conscious state, but rather a form of suspended animation designed to eke out the last remnants of available power. He couldn't check the suit's external bio-monitor since this had also been deactivated. Whether Mackenzie was still alive or not was something he couldn't determine until he got her back into the shuttle.

"I can't say for sure; the suit is extremely low on power and has lost a lot of thermal energy. I'm bringing her in, get ready," Renton replied. With that, he gently tapped on the thruster controls to maneuver himself and his tethered cargo back into the airlock. Once inside, they immediately connected Mackenzie's EVA suit to an auxiliary power supply. In her current condition, it was best to let the suit's internal systems take control. Once it regained power, the suit would initiate the slow, meticulous process of thawing her out.

The external bio-monitor came back online almost immediately.

"She's still alive," Matteo announced as he scrutinized the data display. "She's in a semi-comatose state, but there's a detectable pulse. Her core temperature is dangerously low, however."

"Nothing more we can do at this point, except to get her back to the medbay," Alice advised. "For now, it's best to let the EVA suit handle the internal environment."

Renton and Alice stayed with Mackenzie while Yuna and Matteo took to piloting the shuttle back to base. They were roughly twenty-five minutes into the flight when Renton thought he noticed a slight flicker of Mackenzie's eyelid. He quickly checked the bio-monitor.

"Her core temperature has risen, and her vitals appear stronger," he announced as he glanced back at the face of his former ship captain. Her eyes flickered once more and then slowly opened.

"Mackenzie? Can you hear me? It's Renton."

Her eyes shifted, seemingly tracking toward the sound of Renton's voice. Her pupils dilated and she made an attempt to speak. "Ren-ton," she mouthed in a barely audible whisper.

"Yes, yes, it's me, Renton," he affirmed.

"What-took you-so-long?" she managed to mouth in reply.

Alice chuckled. "Ha, she's definitely back."

"Take it easy, conserve your strength," Renton advised her. "We'll be back at the base in just a few minutes."

Slowly, Mackenzie raised an arm, evidently disregarding Renton's cautionary words, and gently placed her hand on Renton's wrist. It was a heartfelt gesture of gratitude from his former captain—one that deeply touched him. She had saved all their lives, and there was no doubt that she would become a legend, much spoken of in future tales, in hushed and reverent tones.

CHAPTER 41

THE AXIAL

P ompodur Rossen Adarok sat watching a live feed of three shuttles rapidly closing in on the Axial Luxor Orbital. Two of these craft were repurposed SINO vessels, while the third was a former Xilinex military ship. Yet now, all of them had effectively become part of what was increasingly being referred to as the Moon Base Delta fleet.

He found himself contemplating how his circumstances had changed so dramatically. A mere forty-eight hours earlier, he had been on the verge of becoming the de facto ruler of Luna, a position that would have granted him unmitigated control over its population and resources, not to mention wielding significant influence over Earth. In short, he had been tantalizingly close to becoming the most powerful ruler the universe had ever known. But that was two day ago. Now, he found himself holed up in the control room of a repurposed orbital hotel. With him were a modest Xilinex security detail and a handful of loyal allies, all anxiously observing as their inevitable endgame rapidly unfolded as the ships closed the distance.

"We're receiving an incoming communication from the lead ship, sir," announced one of the technicians, breaking the tense silence that had enveloped the room.

"Play it," Pompodur commanded, his voice edged with defiance.

"This is Selene Mene of Moon Base Delta..."

That conniving witch, he thought irritably, *they actually sent her to negotiate with me—just to try and humiliate me.*

"Please heed these demands. We request complete access to The Axial Luxor Orbital, the unconditional surrender of all Xilinex security forces and affiliates on board, and the handover of Pompodur Rossen Adarok to face charges of crimes against humanity."

Charges? Against him? Who do these insolent upstarts think they are? He scoffed to himself, then spun around to face the comms tech. "Inform them that access is unequivocally NOT granted. Make it clear that if they continue on this course, we will blast them into background radiation"

"You know full well we can't do that," interjected Lieutenant Wilson, in a tone of exasperated reason. "This facility is a repurposed hotel, not a fortified military installation. We don't have the weapons to make good on such a threat."

"It doesn't matter; they don't know that," Pompodur replied dismissively, then motioned impatiently to the tech. "Go ahead, send the message."

The lieutenant, clearly not willing to let this go any further, raised his hand to the comms tech. "Hold on, just wait a moment."

Caught in the crossfire of conflicting orders, the tech froze on the spot, like a computer system stuck in a loop, hopelessly trying to process incompatible commands.

Pompodur slowly turned to face his lieutenant, raising an eyebrow as he spoke in a deliberate, condescending tone. "Is there a problem that you'd like to share?"

Lieutenant Wilson, visibly frustrated, exhaled deeply. "We need to confront the reality of our situation. What exactly do you think is going to happen here?"

Feeling the tension rise palpably in the room, Pompodur recognized this as the moment he had always dreaded—the moment when his authority was openly being challenged. He lifted his hand dramatically, pointing decisively at the large display screen. "Let's not kid ourselves. We all know precisely what catastrophe awaits us if those rebels set foot on this orbital. It won't end well for anyone in this room." He swept his gaze around at the faces of his assembled group, hoping that each of them grasped the gravity of the unfolding situation.

"They absolutely cannot be allowed entry," he emphasized, jabbing his finger toward the screen as if to punctuate his verdict.

Wilson glanced up once more at the feed of the approaching shuttles, then shifted his eyes meaningfully toward several of his subordinates. Sensing a significant shift, Pompodur felt the weight of hands being placed firmly on either shoulder. A shiver ran down his spine as he realized that this was the very moment of his downfall.

"We're finished playing your game, Adarok. Xilinex is a thing of the past. Our headquarters is now nothing more than a cloud of orbital debris. What remains of our forces are confined in a cavern at Moon Base Delta. Shackleton is in open revolt, and even SINO has succumbed to the sweeping new revolution that's engulfing every enclave on the Moon. The world has fundamentally shifted on its axis and there's no turning back to the way things were before. The dominos have all toppled over, and you, Adarok, are the final piece to fall. In short, it's over; you are done."

With that, he stood up decisively, asserting his control. "Effective immediately, I am assuming command of this orbital." He directed his gaze to the comms technician. "Send them our reply. Tell them we will comply with all their demands."

"You treacherous bastard," Pompodur spat out, his eyes blazing with contempt. "I'll have you ejected through the nearest airlock for this insubordination."

The lieutenant calmly moved over to where Pompodur was seated, still pinned down by the firm hands on his shoulders, and leaned in close. "No, you won't." He then turned to the two security guards flanking Pompodur. "Secure his wrists and escort him to the lobby. That's where we'll conduct the handover.

Renton floated out from the shuttle and into the expansive docking area of the Axial Luxor Orbital, leading a delegation of thirty personnel from Moon Base Delta. They were greeted by

Lieutenant Wilson, Adarok's former personal bodyguard, and several former Xilinex security members, all conspicuously unarmed.

Chen Jun's crew immediately seized control of the station's security systems, and began to efficiently spread out to take control of all key areas, while Renton, along with the senior leadership team, was escorted to the grand, opulent lobby of the once-luxurious orbital hotel. Standing at the center of the lobby, flanked by two unarmed security guards, was Pompodur Rossen Adarok. He maintained a defiant stance, his face was a mask of stoicism, and the corners of his mouth curled up in a subtle smirk.

"So, Pompodur," Selene began as she confidently walked up to him, "we meet again. Circumstances are a bit different this time, wouldn't you agree?"

"Selene Mene," he responded, the smirk on his face intensifying. "How pathetic, finding you here leading your ragtag troupe of idealists."

Selene paused, taking a moment to glance back at Renton and the others from Moon Base Delta. "That's where you're mistaken, Pompodur. We were never idealists; we're simply pragmatists. That's why we've managed to outlast everyone else on this godforsaken rock."

"And what comes next?" Pompodur questioned sarcastically. "A tiresome, self-righteous monologue, followed by a sham trial, and then what? An exile to a place like St. Helena, à la Napoleon?"

"To be honest, Pompodur, we haven't given you much thought," Selene replied, moving closer to lock eyes with him.

"But here's what I can tell you: whatever happens, you're not going to like it." She then took a step back, signaled to the security team, and watched as they escorted the self-proclaimed Chancellor of Luna back to the waiting shuttle, destined for a dimly lit cave within the bowels of Moon Base Delta, where DOA and Adarok could get to know one another a little better.

CHAPTER 42
WAITING

H an Sundar sat on a hard metal chair, peering out through the small, barred window in the sparse, functional apartment where he had been put under house arrest. Outside, he could see across a large concrete lot, encircled by low-rise office buildings that constituted the main administrative hub of the Vandenberg Space Port.

He hadn't seen Sheneese in quite a while; her visits were strictly monitored and needed official approval from the authorities. Whenever she did arrive, she would be escorted by security staff, who would then wait outside for the predetermined time. After that elapsed, they would reenter the apartment to formally end the visit.

They both assumed the apartment was bugged and that their every action was being observed by some unseen operative, so their conversations had naturally become quite guarded. Yet, Han found himself counting down the days and hours until Sheneese's next scheduled visit. Unlike him, she seemed upbeat about his predicament; perhaps she was merely attempting to lift his spirits. She kept reminding him that he hadn't been formally charged or sent to prison, and the terms of his house arrest weren't extremely burdensome either. True, the authorities had provided him with a decent array of creature comforts. But he still felt very isolated, limited to sporadic, short visits from Sheneese and almost no communication with anyone else. Even the security personnel were tight-lipped, responding mostly in monosyllables whenever he attempted to engage them in conversation.

He had nothing to do all day except to ruminate on the choices and decisions that had led him to this particular crossroads in his life. He had been playing fast and loose with his future, taking unnecessary risks that put his life in jeopardy. In retrospect, he had been foolish and reckless, showing more concern for individuals who were no doubt completely unaware his current predicament, nor able to help him. But dwelling on this only plunged him into a state of deep introspection that bordered on depression.

His sole source of entertainment was peering out the small window at the comings and goings within the administrative sector of the military base. This was one of the few distractions that could divert his mind from sinking further into a state of gloom. Day after day, he would sit in the same spot, finding a small but significant respite in simply watching people go about their business.

After a week or so of this aimless observation, he had started to discern the daily patterns of the staff: the times they clocked in and out, when supplies were delivered, and the to-and-fro movements of cleaning and maintenance personnel. He even began to familiarize himself with the faces of these individuals, recognizing them as they stepped out of cars and buses, heading to work in the morning and then back home in the evening. He found himself envying the simple, uncomplicated rhythms of their lives. How he wished he could escape his current confinement, or at least receive some update on what future awaited him. The uncertainty was the worst part. Any pressure that either he or Sheneese exerted on the authorities for his release, or for any information regarding the legal process, was invariably met with the same opaque response: "There are complex developments in progress. You must wait until these play out. Best not to push it right now."

And so he waited in isolation, completely cut off from any news of the outside world. He had nothing to occupy his time aside from his introspective reflections on the consequences of his actions, and the daily rhythm of the administrative staff as observed through his small apartment window.

However, over the past week, he had started to notice a shift in this established routine. There was a clear uptick in the comings and goings of the personnel. More individuals were arriving, and their arrival was accompanied by an increased flow of traffic to and from the various administrative buildings that bordered this sector of the base. It soon dawned on him that a change of guard seemed to be in progress. Old familiar faces were vanishing, whisked away on military transports along with their office belongings, seemingly never to return. In their place, new faces began to emerge, accompanied by large trucks delivering new furnishings and equipment. He couldn't help but wonder what was transpiring; something significant was clearly unfolding.

A knock resounded on his door. Initially, he thought it might be Sheneese, but the knock's rhythm was different—this was a hard, staccato rap. The door swung open, and two officers stepped inside, triggering in him a sensation of déjà vu. He had been in this situation before, and it had not worked out well for him that time. However, behind the officers, four civilians entered the room. Two of them were familiar faces. One was his friend, Alan Dyson, and the other he recognized as the military guy from that initial, fateful interrogation when he had first been placed under house arrest.

Dyson strode briskly toward him, placing a reassuring hand on his arm. "We need to have a serious discussion, Han. There have been some substantial developments you need to be aware of."

"Developments?" Han felt a twinge of uncertainty; he couldn't determine whether this was good news or bad news.

Dyson pivoted to introduce the rest of the group. "This is General Aaron Miller; you've met before, if you recall. And this is Zachary Garcia and Theo Girard, both are integral members of the new administrative team."

Acknowledging the introduction, Han nodded. The visitors then began to seat themselves on the few utilitarian chairs that his sparsely furnished apartment had to offer. Miller took the lead in the conversation. "I'll get straight to the point. What I'm about to tell you may come as a shock. The Xilinex Lunar Corporation has ceased to exist."

"What?" Han's expression was one of stunned disbelief. "How's that even possible?"

Miller raised a hand. "It's a long story, but that's not all. SINO has also ceased to exist as it once was. All the reins of power have now shifted to Moon Base Delta."

"My God, that's astounding," he replied, shaking his head as he tried to wrap his brain around this seismic change in events.

"There's a new reality taking shape on the Moon," Dyson now took over. "And for us here on Earth, this is very good news. It means not only greater stability but also, more crucially, it means that the flow of vital mineral resources is set to resume, unrestricted."

Han found himself completely dumbfounded. How could such a monumental shift have occurred? Like many others, he had assumed that the Xilinex Lunar Corporation would ultimately win the battle for control.

"This, of course, has sparked an equally seismic reaction back here on Earth, especially among the top echelons of the Alliance." Dyson continued. "As you may have gathered from our previous conversation, there were some of us who were very uncomfortable about the trajectory we were taking. Particularly with the plan to destroy the Mars evacuation ship, a morally indefensible action that a considerable number of people found utterly appalling. Now, in the wake of the abrupt shift in power up on the Moon, those policies have been recognized as complete failures. As a result, the old regime here has been ousted, and a new leadership has been installed, more rational set of policies. In short, sanity has finally prevailed."

Han's mind was swirling with questions; this was monumental news. Yet, his primary concern was: What did all this mean for him? But before he could sift through the myriad thoughts racing around in his head and formulate even a single question, Garcia now began speaking.

"There are quite a few among us who firmly believe that these transformative events wouldn't have transpired without your crucial interventions." He cast a quick, meaningful glance at his colleagues, then turned his focus back to Han. "If you hadn't relayed that information to Moon Base Delta, we would, in all likelihood, be subjected to whatever insane retribution that madman Adarok had conjured up for us. That would been the worst imaginable scenario for everyone down here. However," he gestured toward Han, "you saved us. In fact, it could be said that the world owes you a significant debt of gratitude."

Han was feeling overwhelmed, his head spun.

"I'd say you deserve a goddamn medal," Miller added.

"However," Garcia resumed, "the reality is that you're not likely to get any official thanks or even an acknowledgment. The new leadership prefers to turn the page on past actions and simply move forward. So, to get to the point, Han. You're a free man. You'll be reinstated as the project leader of the new MASTERM project, with full benefits intact. There will be a few strings attached, though: your security clearance will be reduced, limiting your access to state secrets and imposing restrictions on your communication capabilities. But I anticipate that will only be a temporary measure, at least until the dust settles and the new structure establishes itself."

Han felt his entire body uncoil with relief. He slumped back into his chair and drew a long, deliberate breath, still struggling to fully comprehend the situation. "So... am I truly free to go?"

"Absolutely," said Dyson. "We've got a car outside all ready to transport you back to your family's apartment. Sheneese is waiting there for you, along with a group of your friends and colleagues." He leaned in closer and lowered his voice. "Though I'm not really supposed to tell you this, a surprise party is in the works." He tapped the side of his nose, winking.

Han jumped to his feet. Then opened his arms wide and declared, "Well, what are we waiting for? Get me the hell out of here."

CHAPTER 43
THE FUTURE

R enton took a leisurely, slow sip of the first beer he had savored in quite some time. The experience was sublime. The beer was cool, invigorating, and locally brewed right here on the Moon by the Apollo Brewing facility located at Shackleton Crater. He was comfortably seated on a plush sofa in one of the many observation decks aboard the Axial Luxor Orbital. Through the panoramic window, he could see the majestic curve of the lunar surface bathed in brilliant sunlight. Beside him, Alice sat curled up like a contented cat, her head gently resting on his shoulder. Quietly enjoying her own glass of sparkling water.

A profound sense of deep contentment washed over him, permeating every fiber of his being. The harrowing traumas and conflicts of the past felt well and truly behind them. A newfound peace had been declared, and the scattered remnants of what was once a thriving lunar colony were beginning to be methodically reassembled. There was now a palpable sense of shared purpose energizing the community; essential facilities were actively being repaired and systematically brought back into operation. Consolidation efforts were also underway, and once more, people found themselves on the move, drawn to those emerging population centers where a critical mass was forming. In these places, resources were becoming plentiful and a promising new future felt attainable.

They had traveled to the orbital just a few days prior, largely at Alice's insistence and with a bit of nudging from DOA. The rationale was straightforward: they needed to spend time in an Earth-like gravitational environment to counteract the physiological effects of extended periods spent on the lunar surface. Many of the other remaining orbitals were also being refurbished and brought back into service, and the Moon's population was starting to establish a regular routine of rotating their time between the lunar surface and environments with Earth-like gravity. He had initially been hesitant to make the trip, but Alice, along with many others, had insisted that everything at Moon Base Delta was well and truly under control and that he should take some time off for some much-needed rest and relaxation. Now, sitting here, he was grateful he'd heeded their advice.

He raised his glass to Alice, who reciprocated the gesture; their glasses clinked together. "To the future," he toasted.

"To the future," she echoed back.

"We've come a long way, haven't we?" he observed, his tone philosophical. "There were moments when I couldn't even imagine us sitting here like this—enjoying a drink and genuinely feeling like we have a future ahead of us."

Alice offered a warm smile. "That's true, but there is, um... more to our future than you might realize."

"Oh. What's that?"

She sat up, adjusted herself, pausing for a moment before giving him a deeply considered look. "You're going to be a father."

Renton almost choked on his beer. A torrent of emotions slammed into him as if he'd been hit by an asteroid impact: joy, elation, and a ripple of fear all at once.

"This is fantastic, absolutely fantastic." He leaned over and swept her up into his arms, holding her in a tight, joyful embrace. "I can't believe this is happening." He then pulled back a little to look into her eyes. "When did you find out?"

"Actually, it was DOA who first told me," she said.

"You're kidding me. How?"

"Well, I had my suspicions, to be honest. Then, DOA confirmed it for me one morning after I had felt sick. I then went and talked with Dr. Jensen. So yes, it's happening. Game on."

Renton's elation suddenly shifted to concern, as if a new door had swung open in his mind, revealing an array of complex emotions only reserved for soon-to-be parents— feelings ingrained in human consciousness through millennia of evolution, only to be revealed when the time is right. "But what about the conditions here? We can't get back to Earth. What about issues like gravity, and all that?"

Alice offered a reassuring smile. "Don't worry, everything is okay. Both Dr. Jensen and DOA have assured me that the environment here is fine. We have nothing to worry about."

This went some way toward allaying his immediate fears. But he knew that becoming a father ushered in a whole new phase of life filled with responsibilities. They would be bringing a child into this unique, alien lunar environment. Despite these thoughts, he chose not to voice his concerns. Alice understood the magnitude of this moment just as much as he did. Instead of dwelling on uncertainties, he simply squeezed her a bit tighter.

"So this will be the first baby born on the Moon?" he ventured.

"Actually, no," she replied. "There are three other moms-to-be, and all of them are already up here with us. Which is great because we can all support each other while helping to establish the first-ever maternity ward in space."

Renton fell silent for a moment, contemplating the enormity of it all. "I suppose it's inevitable," he finally said, glancing over at her. "Human nature being what it is, a new generation in the making."

Alice remained silent, choosing instead to snuggle in even closer.

He looked down at the brilliant lunar surface below and saw it through a new lens. This was genuinely home now. Not just for him, Alice, or their soon-to-be-born child, but also for nearly four thousand other individuals, not to mention the new generation that would inevitably follow them. According to DOA, there would be no physical travel back to Earth for many decades. Only small supply capsules would make the journey, and perhaps, at some distant point in the future, an intrepid astronaut might venture back when the debris cloud encircling the Earth was finally tamed. But large-scale travel, like what existed before the Carrington Event, was now all in the past. They were essentially on their own up here, isolated from their home planet.

Yet, he could see their future more clearly now. A new human civilization was unfolding here, one that would increasingly diverge from its roots. Already, they were preparing the Mars ship for a return flight, laden with vital supplies and bringing a new sense of hope to the few remaining colonists on the Red Planet. And he could foresee that this new society, governed by advanced AI, would go even further, pushing the boundaries out into the solar system. This emerging, space-faring human species would do more than merely survive; they would thrive, evolve, and ultimately liberating themselves from the constraints of the home planet, including all its old norms and dogmas.

Perhaps in a century from now, some of his and Alice's descendants might make that landmark journey back to Earth. What would that experience be like for them? Would they be viewed as gods, as aliens, or a lost race returning to their ancestral home?

But all of that was mere speculation. The present moment was what truly mattered. It was a time to relish this new life and the promise of the future that lay ahead.

THE END

APPENDIX: LIST OF MAIN CHARACTERS

Aurora crew:

- Renton Hicks - Young FISA engineer on the maintenance vessel Aurora.
- Alice Tyler - Fellow engineer stranded with Renton, control system expert.
- Matteo Cristoforetti - Another stranded engineer. Renton's close friend.
- Yuna Djinn - Pilot, member of the Aurora crew, skilled navigator.
- Captain Mackenzie Arnold - Former Captain of the Aurora.
- Becker De Havilland - Chief engineer.

Axial Luxor Hotel:

- Selene Mene - Renton's aunt, lead negotiator for FISA.
- Professor Lars Henriksen - Heliophysics, stranded on the Axial orbital with Selene.
- Alan E. Dyson - Former head of FISA, returns to Earth.
- Nicci Anderson - Selene's former assistant on the Axial orbital.
- Deejay Bale - Tech expert on the Axial.
- Gabriel Grando - Representative of the Non Spacefaring Nations (NSFN).
- Dr. Maria Jensen - Doctor stranded on the Axial who joins Selene's group.
- Jeff Bodega - Hotel floor manager stranded on the Axial orbital.
- Theo Girard - Former hotel employee also stranded on the Axial.

Xilinex Corporation:

- Pompodur Rossen Adarok - President of Xilinex Lunar Corporation, power-hungry.
- Anton Levrosky - Xilinex board member.
- Ossian Corbell - Xilinex board member.
- Marcus Coldiron - Xilinex board member.
- General Kurt Wagner - Xilinex military leader, focused on capturing stranded assets.
- Lieutenant Ben Wilson - Xilinex mercenary commander.

- Sergeant Wesley Zhang - Member of Wilson's squad, speaks Mandarin.
- Christophe Dubois - Pompodur's servant who he turns against.
- Lane Zeebos - President of the Xilinex Corporation on Earth.

Moon Base Delta:

- DOA - The powerful, semi-sentient AI system that runs Moon Base Delta.
- Spider/Price - Space Division agent, imbedded with SINO at DaVinci Mining Outpost
- Saito Yuuta - Escaped from Secchi. Joins the Moon Base Delta group.
- Kimura Aoi - Escaped from Secchi. Saito's associate.
- Tanaka Aoi - Also from Secchi, Kimura's father.
- Haruki Kobayashi - A miner from Secchi who betrays Saito's group.
- Kato Tsubasa - Inside contact at the Secchi mining facility.
- Rina and Ryou - Kato's wife and young son who escape with him.

Earth:

- Dr. Han Sundar - Debris cloud analyst recruited to the Strawstack facility.

- Sheneese Richmond - Physics Lecturer, communications specialist, married to Han.
- General Philip Grant - Space Division.
- Ethan - Young electronics expert recruited to the Strawstack facility.
- Zachary Garcia - Engineer working on debris cloud solutions at Strawstack.

Also by Gerald M. Kilby

BRAIN GAIN

A TECHNOTHRILLER

One brain. Two minds. No where to run...

Dawn Harrison wakes up in a research lab with no memories and an AI implanted in her brain. She escapes into a world she no longer recognizes only to quickly become the most sought-after person on the planet.

Pursued by shadowy agencies desperate to reclaim the technology in her brain, Dawn races against time to uncover both the truth of her past and secrets in her head.

But in this high-stakes thriller, even a single thought can be deadly.

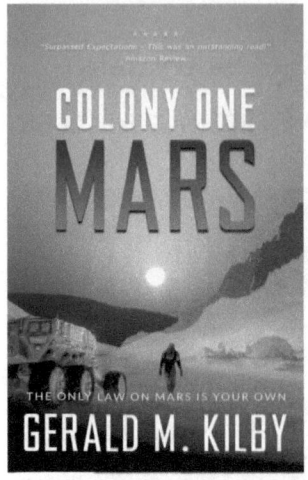

How can a colony on Mars survive when the greatest danger on the planet is humanity itself.

All contact is lost with the first human colony on Mars during a long, intense sandstorm. Satellite imagery of the aftermath shows extensive damage to the facility, and the fifty-four colonists who called it home are presumed dead. Three years later, a new mission sets down on the planet surface to investigate what remains of the derelict site.

ENTANGLEMENT : THE BELT

The discovery of game-changing quantum technology sparks an AI war between Earth's powerful dynasties and the solar system colonies.

A long-lost ship transporting an experimental quantum communications device has just been found in an uncharted region of the asteroid belt. For Commander Scott McNabb, Flight Officer Miranda Lee, and the ragtag survey crew who accidentally stumble upon this lost tech... life is about to become a whole lot more complicated.

ABOUT THE AUTHOR

Gerald M. Kilby grew up on a diet of Isaac Asimov, Arthur C. Clarke, and Frank Herbert, which developed into a taste for Iain M. Banks and everything ever written by Michael Crichton. His novels CHAIN REACTION and BRAIN GAIN are very much in the old-school techno-thriller style while his latest book series: MOON BASE DELTA, COLONY MARS, and THE BELT are all best sellers, topping Amazon charts for Hard Science Fiction and Space Exploration.

He lives in the city of Dublin, Ireland, in the same neighborhood as Bram Stoker and can be sometimes seen tapping away on a laptop in the local cafe with his dog Loki.

You can connect at: geraldmkilby.com